T0279234

WHEN
MIMI
WENT
MISSING

WHEN MIMI WENT MISSING

SUJA SUKUMAR

Content warning: death / murder, depiction of depression.

Published by Soho Teen
an imprint of Soho Press, Inc.
227 W 17th Street
New York, NY 10011

Library of Congress Cataloging-in-Publication Data
Names: Sukumar, Suja, author.
Title: When Mimi went missing / Suja Sukumar.
Description: New York : Soho Teen, 2024. | Audience: Ages 14 and up. |
Audience: Grades 10-12. | Identifiers: LCCN 2024012395

ISBN 978-1-64129-536-9
eISBN 978-1-64129-537-6

Subjects: CYAC: Bullies and bullying—Fiction. | Missing persons—Fiction. |
Memory—Fiction. | Cousins—Fiction. | East Indian Americans—Fiction. |
Mystery and detective stories. | LCGFT: Detective and mystery fiction. |
Thrillers (Fiction) | Novels.
Classification: LCC PZ7.1.S84625 Wh 2024 | DDC [Fic]—dc23
LC record available at https://lccn.loc.gov/2024012395

Interior design: Janine Agro

Printed in the United States of America

10 9 8 7 6 5 4 3 2 1

To my parents, who instilled in me a love for books and stories.
I owe you both a debt I can never repay.

WHEN
MIMI
WENT
MISSING

PROLOGUE

I AM EIGHT years old.

The bullies are waiting for me outside the girls' bathroom.

I race down the school hall as fast as my young legs can carry me, but the bullies are faster. They pounce, pushing me down, and I hit the floor hard, the air slamming out of my lungs.

You're a killer, a boy yells. *Like your mom.*

Killer, killer.

I tell myself not to look at them. That gloating stretch of their mouths.

The shadows lengthening over me.

The front door bursts open, and Mimi appears, her eyes spitting black fire. My cousin, only a year older, but her rage fills the hall.

The bullies scatter like frantic ants, but this time, she is faster. A well-aimed punch, and the leader flees, his nose bloodied. She helps me up and hugs me tightly. *If anyone ever tries to hurt you again, let me know and I'll destroy them.*

She promises me.

Don't worry, Tanvi. I'll always watch out for you.

She promises me that, too.

Back then, I didn't know promises were just words. As lightweight as ash scattered by the wind.

Brittle like shattered glass.

CHAPTER 1

EVEN AFTER SUMMER break, Orin High still smells of damp clothes left too long in the washer. The sweat from so many fourteen- to eighteen-year-olds must be baked into the ancient brick building and its many moldy crevices and dusty corners. But mixing with that musty cloth smell is the scent of softeners, of sloppy joes and baked cinnamon bread, of conversations and laughter, of rushing footsteps and slamming locker doors.

So, it's not all bad. At least that's what I tell myself. And as I take in the quiet of the last week of summer vacation, I can almost believe it. Stillness pervades every hallway, every bathroom, every classroom; even the desks and chairs quiet, holding their breaths.

It's the last day to register for junior year and I managed to make it. Barely. The office secretary wasn't too happy, judging from her frequent glances at the clock, whose minute hand hovered at three minutes to three. But I came in right before the office closed for a reason. All the registrants were done and gone.

I take a deep breath and start toward the exit to the parking lot.

It wasn't always like this. I never used to dread the start of the school year. True, elementary school was hell—kids could be particularly brutal to newly minted orphans adopted and brought to Orin by their aunts. But the bullying subsided in middle school after I ceased to remain interesting, when I displayed none of the characteristics of what they thought a killer's daughter should have, when I faded into the grimy school walls and became invisible. By the time high school came around, my latent nerdiness had kicked in and I fell in love with organic chemistry and calculus, much to my cousin and fellow nerd Mimi's joy and my best friend Krista's annoyance.

But things changed last fall, the start of my sophomore year, when the invisibility cloak fell off and I was recognized again. And the shadows returned, solidifying into a new threat, a new bully.

I shake off that familiar prickling of dread and push open the front doors to walk onto the school's sprawling portico, where the soft glow of the midafternoon August sun turns the tiles a sparkling white. The oaks and maples scattered around the schoolyard remain brilliant green against the smooth blue cloudless expanse of sky, but look closely and you can see a tinge of orange, the foreshadowing of autumn.

Fall is on its way to southeastern Michigan. It's my cousin Mimi's favorite season and therefore mine, too. My fingers tingle, anticipating the feel of the smooth, velvety leaves turned crinkly and multicolored by a lack of chlorophyll. I imagine the satisfying bounce of throwing myself into a pile of dead foliage, scattering it, creating chaos. Of laughing with Mimi for hours over cider and Bollywood gossip.

But this fall will be different. Because she, my once best friend, my rock, the reason I could outrun the shadows from my past, has betrayed me to those shadows instead.

I spot her leaning against an oak, her pink halter top and faded denim shorts visible all the way across the parking lot. Looking at us, no one would think we're related. Her skin is several shades lighter than my dark brown, and her features, her aquiline nose and wide forehead, take after her white dad. Her thick black hair and dark eyes, though, are as Indian as mine.

Those eyes fall on me and she straightens. I start to lift my hand, hoping to wave, hoping she'll wave back. Hoping the widening distance between us in the last several months suddenly vanishes, like her coldness was nothing but my imagination.

But then her gaze shifts to something behind me.

My spine stiffens with the instinctive reaction of a hunted animal. I made a mistake; the school wasn't as empty as I thought. And I know who it is before I turn and meet baby blue eyes narrowing with derision, the minuscule curl of lips painted a deep scarlet.

Beth Grant. She's a senior and Mimi's classmate and the unquestioned leader of Orin High's popular clique. I chose the last possible minute before registration closed so I could avoid her, and yet she still managed to find me.

She allows the large front doors to swing shut behind her and strolls across the portico. Each click of her heels tightens the vise around my chest, my heart thudding with the same question I've asked myself a gazillion times. Why the hell did she target me? She displaced me as Mimi's best friend last year and decided to salt the earth behind her, judging from the way Mimi froze me out. She's not just a frontrunner in the race for Mimi's affections—she's won the damn thing and should fear no competition from me.

I edge toward the banister, creating a wide berth for her to pass, and lower my eyes, shame burning fire across my cheekbones, hating my fear. My breath hitches, counting the seconds as she lingers beside me. Then she swishes past, leaving the air scented with vanilla but not enough to muffle the tinge of something sharp and metallic.

I look up. Sunlight glints gold on her hair, turning blond strands into a fiery tiara. Turning her into a queen. She has everything: a castle for a home, reigning power at school—and my cousin's undivided devotion, judging from the way Mimi hurries toward her.

I bet it'd be fun to be Beth Grant, Mimi told me months before she slid into Beth's circle. *To be taken care of and waited on hand and foot. To have all the money in the world and never have to worry about stuff like college and a job and shit.*

I'll take care of you, I tried telling Mimi, but she already had that look in her eye. That determined look she gets before a track competition she desperately wants to win.

Beth's footsteps change from the clicking of heels on concrete to the muffled scrape on grass. Then they fade into the parking lot and the roar of an engine.

I stare after her blue Porsche with a bitter rage that's as intense as it is helpless. I know bullies and I know what it feels like to be bullied. After all, I was exposed to my first dose at the age of eight. They punched me, knocked me down, called me a freak and a psycho.

But what Beth did destroyed me. When she lit my mom's candles—the candles that shattered my life—and made me eight again, watching my mom turn into a monster.

Dark wisps of smoke creep into the corners of my vision, veiling the sunlight, filling my nose with an acrid scent. And above it rises the sound of Beth laughing as she recorded my meltdown on her phone while Mimi stood by, watching me throw up all over the pristine white carpet in Beth's house.

Killer, killer.

I shake off the memory, but the fact lingers, making my head spin: Beth has that video. It's all she needs to remind everyone of who I am, who my mother was—the killer who took her husband's life. Then it'll be back to square one. It'll be like when I was in elementary school.

But Mimi won't be there to fight for me this time.

She betrayed my secrets to Beth. She stole my mom's candles and showed them to her new best friend.

Why did you do that? I screamed at her after waking up in a pool of my own vomit. *You knew what I went through. You promised you'd protect me!* But she didn't care. Like she didn't care when she got into Beth's car just now and drove away without another glance at me.

The grass blurs under my feet, changes to tar, and then I'm on my bike, my face wet with tears.

I try to tell myself I'm paranoid, but the words fall flat. What else did Mimi tell Beth about me, about my past, that made Beth decide to come after me? And what if she doesn't stop?

Why would Beth record me if she wasn't going to show someone—everyone?

I can't leave Orin and run away. Where can I go? My house in Detroit, once filled with Mom and Dad's laughter, is now an empty shell, occupied by strangers. The only family I have left is my aunt and cousin.

Auntie . . .

She has stayed by my side for eight years, cried with me when the nightmares came, held my hand through every therapy session. *You're my daughter, honey, just like Mimi. We're your family, and we'll always be there for you.*

I can't leave her. I can't lose her.

I blink hard, then wipe my face on my sleeve. For Mimi, *always* is over. If Beth wants to ruin my life, Mimi won't do anything to stop her.

"THAT'S BULLSHIT, GIRL."

Krista's voice practically echoes in Peace & Love, the New Age shop where she works. I glance around for disapproving frowns or reprimands. Luckily, the only customer is a woman in her midtwenties who raises her brow at my best friend, then returns to examining the crystal collections in a display case. The store is wedged in between a bank and a pharmacy on the busiest street in downtown Orin. Narrow windows, criss-crossed with multicolored lights, flank an antique glass door, making it the quaintest place in town.

"I get why you're nervous. Everyone thinks Beth is perfect, but she's a bully. If Mimi is hanging around with her . . ." Worry darkens Krista's hazel green eyes, turning them the color of one of the beads on her rainbow necklace.

Krista and I are polar opposites: she's sociable and extroverted, practically in every club at school and an ace athlete. I'm a total nerd who'd rather spend her time watching documentaries on obscure scientific subjects. Most people can't make sense of our friendship. I can't, either. I'm just glad Krista's there to keep my shadows away. She knows about my mom, about the real reason I came to Orin. And she knew that before she walked up to me at the dojo during our Tae Kwon Do class during freshman year and invited me to her house where "a bunch of people are gonna binge on pizza and watch reruns of *Star Wars*."

Krista sighs, then drops the price scanner she's holding and wraps me in a warm embrace. "Let me make us some tea. We need fuel to think this over." Tea is her obsession; she drinks it so much, I have no idea how she doesn't have to pee twenty-four seven.

While she gets busy boiling water and rooting in the spice cabinet for hibiscus and rosehip, her favorites, I let my gaze wander over the tiny kitchenette in the back of the store. Next to the spices are tall cabinets stocked with candles, their smell almost cloying. Vanilla and eucalyptus, jasmine and rose. Along with another familiar scent. Sandalwood.

My chest squeezes painfully.

Sandalwood was Mom's favorite incense. She used it for every puja, every festival. The scent from our last Diwali eight years ago lingers in my mind: incense sticks and oil-soaked cotton wicks in little earthen pots, which Mom placed along the wraparound veranda of our two-story colonial. At night, they formed rows of tiny magical flickering flames. Dad helped me light sparklers, and we made flaming patterns in the darkness.

I close my eyes, feeling the thin metal end of the sparkler between my fingers. *Look, Daddy. I can make a star. Just like the ones in the sky.*

He lifted me up high on his shoulders. *Of course you can, princess.*

I turn away from the cabinets. I was doing so well—I tapered off my therapy sessions, (almost) forgot my past. But ever since that damned video, I've remembered more things about Mom, images that keep intruding, and I wish it'd just stop.

Drawing myself into a tighter ball in the window seat, I stare outside. This window in the store's kitchenette overlooks a little kiddie park. A little boy of about three stomps around the splash pad, giggling as the spray hits him on his bare stomach. A young woman darts toward the boy, lifting an imperious finger, her face twisted in a scowl. It's a stranger, a white woman with shoulder-length blond hair, but the familiarity of that scowl stirs a memory.

An image of Mom's expression when Daddy tried to stop her rituals. When she glared at him through the smoke from the circle of candles surrounding her.

When she insisted on going for a drive—*just the two of us, Ramesh. I'll drive.*

When the sordid information was all over front pages of the newspapers and the local channels—

Case of murder suicide shocks the Indian American community in Detroit. Local investigators found evidence indicating the woman made no attempt to apply the brakes before the vehicle hit the guardrail at eighty miles an hour. She was pronounced dead at the hospital; the passenger, her husband, was pronounced dead at the scene after being thrown from the car. His seatbelt had been cut through with a sharp instrument.

Shadowy wisps invade my vision again, veiling the families, the park, smothering the sunlight. A heaviness clamps around my chest and I turn away.

"Here." Krista places a dainty flower-patterned cup in front of me. She grabs a cup herself and sits cross-legged on the floor. "Tanvi, listen. What happened, what your mom did, was not your fault. Beth had no right to record you like that. You're the victim here. You need to tell your aunt before Beth shows anyone that damn video."

Everything in me shrinks. I can't. My sweet aunt. The strongest woman I've ever known. Who picked up the pieces of her life after her husband passed fifteen years ago and single-handedly raised Mimi while working as a nurse, and then swooped in to rescue me eight years ago. Without a second thought, she brought me into her home and never once treated me any less than her own daughter. She thinks Mimi still loves me the same way.

She'll be shattered if she knows how Mimi betrayed my friendship, let alone that my cousin stole Mom's candles.

"Did Mimi delete her social media?" Krista says.

Through the fragrant steam rising from my teacup, I find her frowning at her phone screen. "I wouldn't know. She blocked me months ago." I found that out when I tried sending her a message—one of several messages—after she'd banned me from her room and forbidden me to talk to her. Messaging her on social media was the only way to get to her until she shut me down there, too.

"Looks like she did." On Krista's screen is a post from Beth @ing Mimi, but Mimi's handle @midiva isn't clickable.

> **@iambeth: See y'all at my place, you know who you are. @midiva & I welcome you!!!**

"It's horrendous that Beth and Mimi get to have their fun bash while all you get is more psychological torture."

I raise a brow. "Fun bash?"

"Beth's got her last day of summer fling this Thursday."

Yeah, of course. Beth usually holds it before school starts. Last summer Mimi wasn't invited; Beth hadn't noticed her yet. Last summer was a different world altogether. Mimi and I were tight-knit, and Beth was just a frequent topic of our conversations—the most popular girl at school who lived in a fancy mansion and threw the most epic parties, which we knew we'd never get invited to.

Until Mimi did.

That day, my world changed. Mimi rushed over to me, saying Beth had congratulated her for making the track team. Saying how "kind and friendly" Beth was, how she asked about random stuff like her family—and invited Mimi to her house for a Halloween party next week.

Can you believe it? she said.

Mimi and I always went everywhere together. Except, apparently, to Beth's Halloween party. But Mimi didn't seem to notice it, and so I said nothing.

Now, watching Krista frown at the phone screen, I feel a familiar anxiety stir. "You going to Beth's?" Krista is part of the track team, and since several of the track kids are in Beth's inner circle even though she's not on the team, Krista some-times gets invited to Beth's parties, too.

"You kidding? After what she did to you?" She flings her phone down on a beanbag chair. "Besides, there's going to be drugs and booze, and the last thing I need is to be caught within a mile of that stuff. I don't have a trust fund to buy my way into college."

Beth? "But she heads Stay Aware." The school org is part of a citywide antidrug coalition. The funding Beth brings in is rivaled only by the football team. "Won't she lose her funding and position if she's caught with drugs?"

Krista pats my hand and sighs. "Tanvi, you are too sweet for your own good."

I wince. *You're so naïve, Tanvi.* Mimi's voice. And she's right—I am.

"Plus, who's going to dare rat out the queen?" Krista asks.

Who indeed.

I doubt Beth knew of my existence until she became friends with Mimi. But I knew her—everyone did. She was always holding court in the cafeteria or hallway, organizing some fun-draiser or the other, or on the school monitors making news announcements. And in the evenings when I hung out with Mimi and Grace, Mimi's best friend at that time, they'd gush over how perfect Beth was. By the time I made it to high school, I truly believed Beth was either a robot or a celestial being. Because no human could be that perfect.

In fact, if someone told me that Beth did *anything* illegal, I'd have laughed them off.

Which begs the question. Do any of the staff at school know about Beth's extracurricular activities?

Krista starts pacing the tiny kitchenette. "We need to figure a way to stop Beth from releasing that video."

As I stare into her anxious eyes, the steam from the tea

swirling in the air, a plan forms. Nebulous like the steam but taking shape into something concrete.

If I can get photo evidence of Beth using drugs, I can use it to take her down—or at least have mutually assured destruction. The worst for me would be another round of bullying, but Beth can lose a whole lot more. The squeaky clean, wholesome public image she's cultivated so carefully has made her the darling of the adults at school. Losing that will crush her.

Mimi won't be going to the party; she's grounded from the last time she sneaked out. But I'll be going, uninvited guest and all.

Beth thinks she can destroy my life with a video. I'll destroy hers with a photo.

CHAPTER 2

BETH GRANT'S MANSION is a humongous monstrosity of red brick and glass. At a looming four stories, it is easily five times the size of my house, a narrow colonial down a dead-end street next to Orin Woods. Medieval-style towers mark the mansion's four corners, and a sloping roof complete with ornate eaves and elaborate carvings make it look like a castle.

I hide my bike behind a hedge along the outer wall and walk through the open gates down a long driveway narrowed by parked cars. From the number of vehicles, it looks like Beth's invited the entirety of Orin High. Except me, of course.

The faint sounds of music get louder as I approach the house. It's barely three in the afternoon. It's weirdly early for a party, but with school starting tomorrow, Beth tends to time her last summer blowout from midafternoon to whenever the last straggler departs. If Krista's right and Beth does drugs at these parties, then it's a marvel how she's managed to look so put together the next day at school with not a hint of slurred speech or red-rimmed eyes to alert a suspicious teacher.

Not this time.

A sweep of marble steps leads to a front porch flanked by actual Grecian columns.

I edge over to the steps and try the door, praying it'll be open and I won't have to ring the bell. For my plan to succeed, I need to catch Beth unawares and also keep anyone from recognizing me. Mimi's grounded and at home; her door was locked when I slipped past it on my way out right after Auntie left for work. But there may be people from my classes or lab in there. I pull up my hoodie and sigh with relief when the doorknob turns easily.

The door swings open, allowing me to enter a chandelier-lit living room with sparkling marble floors and whitewashed walls. Not that I can see much of the floor or the walls with the press of human bodies, all gyrating to ear-splitting rock, fingers clutched around cups or hooked around the necks of bottles.

The place already reeks with the stench of booze and vomit, and the air is hazy with sweet, pungent smoke. This is the first party I've "been" to. Krista tried to persuade me to join her for some "tame" ones—her verbiage—but I've resisted. And looking at the packed room of mostly seniors, I don't think I've missed out. From the looks of it, half the class is going to be absent or majorly hungover tomorrow.

I catch sight of the group clustered around the drinks table giggling over a large punch bowl. One girl seems to be attempting to drink straight from the bowl. Either that, or she's going for a swim, judging from the way she's dunking her face in. Goop drips off the wet strands of her pixie cut and it takes me a second to recognize Abby from my English lit class last year. I tuck in my chin and slip through the crowd, scanning faces for Beth. And it hits me that I have no idea how exactly I'm going to get a photo once I find her. Even if she's among that pile of kids slobbering on the sofa—which she's not—how do I whip out my phone and snap a pic in full view of everyone here?

My gut twists, anxiety unfurling and diluting my earlier confidence. Maybe this wasn't the best thought-out idea.

A few minutes of searching later, it sinks in that she's not anywhere on the first floor. Her room's upstairs—I know that from the last and only time I was here—so it's possible she's there.

My breath catches. Shit, I don't want to go up. The moment is imprinted in my mind forever. My stupid heart was full of joy that morning. I was so excited, unable to believe Mimi was finally inviting me into her elite friend circle. *I missed you, Tanvi*, she said. *I want to hang out with you again, and so does Beth.*

And stupid me believed every word.

Closing my eyes, I inhale deep, trying to suppress the anxiety now burning fire in my veins before it builds into a full-on panic attack, and I space out again. My diagnosis after I came to Orin included a variety of acronyms—PTSD and GAD, as well as stress disorder—and all of it spiked after the bullying. I'd even pass out from panic attacks. And Mimi and Beth had unleashed it all again when they brought me here.

I can't let it control my life again. I can't risk the entire school being reminded of my past. One way or the other, I've got to finish what I came here for.

Chest hammering, I walk down the hall to Beth's bedroom. Inside, a four-poster queen bed in the middle is flanked by several plush sofas, and the carpet is pristine white again. I cringe thinking about the maid who must've cleaned out the stain from my puke.

A month ago, I was seated on that very same carpet, Beth and Mimi across from me. Beth had a weird gleam in her eyes, but Mimi was grinning, and so I smiled back.

A month ago, I didn't think my cousin would betray me.

Not until she placed two thick black candles on a stand. My mom's candles. The ones Mom used in her rituals. The candles Mimi stole from where she hid them in our attic.

We're just trying a little experiment. It's for school. For drama class. Mimi's voice was thick with suppressed laughter—not that I knew it then. Beside her, Beth was laughing so hard, tears rolled down her face as she recorded me on her phone.

I begged, God, I begged Mimi not to light the candles.

A strike of a match, and flames rose from the wicks.

I tried to block out the smell. But the stench crept around me, and I was eight again, watching my mom as she lit those damned candles, one by one.

The smoke rose like wisps of charred paper.

Come on, Tanvi, show us what your mom did.

Someone was puking their guts out.

Oh, shit, Mimi. Beth's voice was shrill as she scrambled away from me. *The freak's messed up the carpet.*

That night, my nightmares returned, clawing through my shut bedroom door. I huddled in bed, eyes peeled back, blanket up to my chin, waiting for that door to open. For Mom to appear.

My legs tremble, and I lean against the wall, wanting nothing more than to flee this house.

But I can't. If I do, if I walk out now and Beth releases that video tomorrow at school, I'll be the killer's daughter again. And I'll have to live with the reality that I had a chance to stop Beth from destroying my life, but I wimped out.

Sounds of laughter cut through my thoughts. The room window overlooks the patio and swimming pool, which is swarming with bodies. A girl breaks from the crowd and swims across the pool in lazy strokes. Lyla Thomas, Mimi's track co-captain.

Even Lyla was invited? She had a major fallout with Beth last year, right before Beth became friends with Mimi—rather convenient, if you ask me, but Mimi never seemed to care—and they've been like oil and water ever since. But then, why am I surprised? Lyla would never miss a party. She may lock horns with Beth, but lose out on the trendiest party of the summer? Not for someone who suffers from chronic FOMO.

A boy with light blue eyes and hair so blond it's almost white cleaves into the water and swims up to Lyla, grabbing her around the waist for a quick kiss. It's her boyfriend, Greg Waller, the quarterback of Orin High's ace varsity football team.

Good thing Mimi isn't here. She'd be pissed as hell. She can't stand the guy, and knowing his reputation around school of being a misogynist, I don't blame her. There are rumors he said something really gross about her last year, and Mimi vowed to never speak to him again. Whatever he said, the school rumor mill hasn't been able to sniff it out. My heart twists, knowing that she'd have told me if we were on speaking terms, but now I'm in the dark, too.

Lyla screeches as Greg dunks her. Others join in, some cannonballing and belly flopping hard enough to cause the water to cascade over the pool edge and spray a girl in black leggings and a saggy gray T-shirt standing alone at the edge of the patio. She spins and hurries down the steps.

I frown. That can't be Grace Warner. There's no way Beth would invite Mimi's ex-best friend to the party. Guess I'm not the only uninvited guest here.

She disappears around the corner of the house, and I return to scanning the backyard for Beth. Not that I can see much. Whoever designed this place must've been obsessed with hedge mazes, because six-foot-high hedges form an intricate, convoluted labyrinth that stretches the entire length of the yard. If Beth's in there somewhere, it's going to be impossible to find her.

Someone jostles me and I stumble, grabbing the patio steps railing. A guy with glassy eyes and a slack mouth toasts me with a can of beer. "Sup?"

Not anyone I recognize, so he's unlikely to place me, either. My assumption's confirmed when he adds, "Andrea? You look weird."

I duck my head and hurry down the steps, then glance over my shoulder. The beer guy is stumbling across the patio to the boisterous crowd around the swimming pool.

I slip into the nearest path through the maze and the party sounds are instantly muffled by the tree-sized hedges flanking me. I skulk in the shadows of the foliage, my shoes squelching on damp grass and dirt. The rugged branches rake my skin. I brace myself at every turn in the path, hoping Beth will appear but dreading it, too. There's barely any place to hide within the thick, unyielding hedges.

After one turn, the maze releases me onto a patch of lawn. Beyond this patch is a tall stone wall, which I assume signals the end of Beth's property. A square building with a sloping tiled roof and pink siding stands in one corner, hugging the wall. The pungent sickly sweet smell of weed stains the air here, with something else, something acrid and metallic blending in.

I creep toward a window with a pink-and-white frame and a crocheted curtain fluttering in the breeze. Holding my breath, my heart thundering in my ears, I peek past the frame.

Beth perches at the edge of a chair, leaning over a table and cutting a pile of white powder into thin lines.

My eyes widen. What the hell?

I was hoping to find something incriminating after what Krista said, but to find Beth snorting . . . coke? How did I get so lucky? Because there's no way she's going to be able to charm or influence her way out of this.

My hand shakes as I pull out my phone from my shorts pocket. This'll be the perfect shot. But the damn phone slips through my sweat-slick palm and tumbles to the ground.

"Shit." I bend down to pick it up, then freeze in my crouched position when I realize I cursed aloud.

I wait for what seems like an eternity until my heart stops pounding, then listen for any movement inside.

Silence. Except for the breeze fluttering the window curtains, I can't hear anything.

Staying low to the ground, I lift the phone, edging it past the window frame and angling the camera blindly toward where I'd last seen Beth and then press the button.

"What's that?" a slurred voice says.

Mimi? I gasp, then clap my hand to my mouth. Shit, Mimi's in there? She's supposed to be home, grounded.

"What?" Beth says.

"Thought I heard something outside." Definitely Mimi.

Furniture scrapes a wooden floor, followed by a soft thud.

Oh, God. I scuttle backward and into the maze, ducking behind a hedge. Its rough, knotted branches dig a groove into my shoulder as I hug its shadow and hook an eye through a break in the leaves.

Beth appears in the window. A Beth I've never seen before. Her blond hair, always elegant in a bun or French braid, is now bedraggled, the strands snarly, some stuck to her cheek. Her face is blotchy red, and she keeps wiping snot from her nose as she scans the yard with bloodshot eyes.

"There's no one here," she says.

"I heard a voice." Mimi.

"That's the weed talking." She glances behind her, then shakes her head. "What? You want me to go look?"

My heart beats like a trapped bird in my throat. She's still frowning, looking behind her, and then she disappears.

I spring to my feet and start running down the twisty path, praying it'll release me at the patio and not take me back to the cottage and Beth.

The sounds of splashing and yelling reach me, and then I'm stumbling out next to the patio where the pool party remains in full swing. Everyone who's not in the pool is crowded around it and I'm able to race across the patio to the side of the house where I saw that girl—Grace?—vanish.

There's a wide swath of lawn here that connects to the front yard. Soon, grass turns into gravel, and then I'm scrambling for the driveway. The trees and packed cars fly past me, then I'm through the gate, sobbing in relief when I spot my bike safe in its hiding spot.

Until I reach for my phone and find my pockets empty.

My heart takes a sickening plunge.

It must've slipped out of my hand again after I took the photo.

By the time I return to the backyard, I've lost all sensation to my feet.

Thankfully, my phone lies on the ground behind the patio, face up, its screen frozen on the photo I took. Beth leans over a pile of white powder cut into lines. Mimi, in a knee-length red dress with a knotted black scarf, is sprawled next to her with her head on Beth's shoulder, a joint between her fingers, the air in front of her face hazy with exhaled smoke. In her other hand is a tiny packet full of similar white powder.

Mimi, no.

My stomach flips in a wave of nausea. Not my cousin. She'd never do this.

You see them around school, T, coked up and comatose. Their trust funds will see them through life. But you and I, we can't afford this crap. We got goals, sis.

This photo was supposed to be my escape. But if I show it to anyone, it won't just be Beth who's destroyed. Mimi will be, too. The way they're sitting, it's impossible to crop Mimi out without making it obvious.

When Auntie brought me to Orin, Mimi came flying out the door with a huge smile splitting her face, her eyes dancing with joy. *I have a sister now, Mom. Tanvi will be my sister forever and ever.*

I can't hurt Mimi.

I reach for the delete button. My thumb hovers over it.

But she's the reason Beth found out about Mom.

Mimi betrayed my secrets to her.

A jumble of voices rises from the direction of the pool coming toward me. I shove the phone into my pocket and race for the road.

THE ENTIRE RIDE home passes in a blur. Once inside, I find Mimi's bedroom door still locked from the inside. There's a trellis next to her window outside; she must've used it to sneak out.

If I weren't still trembling, I'd be shaking my head at the irony. Auntie had no intention of stopping Mimi from meeting Beth, who, in her eyes, is perfect in every way. Her reasoning for grounding Mimi was to stop her from meeting her boyfriend, James, after another mom told Auntie James was a dealer.

I frown. Mimi said it wasn't true. But could it be possible that he supplied the drugs Mimi and Beth were using?

"Hey, what's up?" Krista says as soon as I call her, then gasps once I give her a rundown of everything that happened. "Fuuuuck. The queens of Orin High caught red-handed getting wasted? Oh my God, this is dope, Tanvi. No one's going to care about your video once you release this. And you can do it anonymously. We can hide your number and—"

"But it'll get Mimi in trouble. Like, huge trouble. She could lose any chance of a track scholarship and even get suspended from school or expelled."

"True. But she deserves it. She betrayed you, told Beth shit about you that was supposed to be secret. She's just as guilty as Beth."

The photo blurs as my eyes fill.

"Tanvi, listen, Mimi squealed on you. *She* stole the candles and told Beth stuff she had no right to. She called you those awful names."

"Yes, but . . ." I trail off, remembering suddenly when the bullies surrounded me in school. When Mimi broke that boy's nose for calling me a killer. Before she met Beth, she was the best sister a girl could ever ask for. A tear spills down my face and splatters on the phone screen. "I can't hurt her, Krista. It'll break me. I can't use this photo."

Krista is silent for a moment, then says, "Then what about telling Mr. Lee everything? Maybe he can talk sense into Mimi?"

Mr. Lee has been my unofficial godfather since I came to Orin. But he's also Auntie's closest friend and will insist I tell Auntie the truth. "No."

"Then what're you going to do?"

Face the bullying again? My heart thuds. I have two years of high school credits left to be able to graduate. I can't drop out now; Auntie won't let me. I could take online classes, but it'll still involve telling Auntie the reason and breaking her heart over what Mimi did.

And running away is not an option. I can't leave Auntie and the only family I know.

There's got to be a way to stop Beth from releasing my video without hurting Mimi.

And that's when it hits me. "Hey, you remember that case you told me about? About someone who videotaped a minor doing some random stuff and posted it on social media. They got into deep shit because they didn't get parental consent."

"Yeah? One of Mom's friends prosecuted the case." Krista's

mom is a top defense attorney in Orin and is well liked and respected across the table. "They won it, too."

"Could I use that against Beth?"

A choking sound comes from the other end. "Holy. Shit." She laughs. "Why didn't you think of that earlier?"

Why didn't I? It'd have been logical to confront Beth and threaten to sic any of Krista's mom's friends on her instead of sneaking around. Is it because my goal wasn't just to stop her, but to crush her totally?

To destroy her public image like she threatened to destroy mine?

Vindictive much, Tanvi?

Unease curls in the pit of my stomach, but I squelch it. "I don't know."

"Anyway, resorting to old-fashioned threats is always a great idea, but let me handle it. This's what I'll send Beth." She clears her throat and assumes a deeper tone. "Beth Grant, if you release that video, you'll be in deep shit. You're eighteen, Tanvi is not. She's a minor and you took a video of her without her permission. That's a felony. I know because my mom is friends with Orin's prosecuting attorney, and they've crushed people for less." Her voice returns to normal. "How's that?"

My eyes get wet and so does the pillow under my head. "Did I ever tell you that you're the awesomest friend ever?"

She laughs. "Maybe about a million times, but one more won't hurt." Then her tone turns serious. "You're gonna be okay, girl. Beth won't dare do anything now, you can bet on it. And Mimi . . ." The way she said Mimi's name, the doubt, the hesitation. Like she suspects Mimi will find another way to hurt me again.

Will she? And if she does, will that be the final straw that breaks my love for her?

I don't know. Krista seems to think Mimi's betrayal with

the candles was enough. I want to give Mimi another chance because I still love her.

Is it her that you love, or is it the memory of that old Mimi who loved and protected you? Who vanished when she friended Beth? And even if she returns, will you trust her again?

I rub the aching spot over my heart.

I don't know. I don't know if her backstabbing has caused a scar in my heart that'll never heal.

"Tanvi? You still there?'

"Yeah." I ignore the niggle of doubt and tap the delete button. The photo vanishes. "It's gone. It's done."

We say goodbye and after hanging up, I flop back in bed. Assuming Krista's plan works, I should be feeling relieved.

But why do I still feel this dread pressing on my chest? Like I made a mistake deleting that photo?

Like maybe I underestimated Beth?

Perfect Beth, that was how we used to talk about her. Grace, Mimi, and I, before Mimi and Beth became best friends. Grace was probably the first among us to spot a flaw in Beth. It was the winter of my freshman year, and we were in the cafeteria watching the snow pile up into a glistening silver field outside. *Did you realize there's something odd about Beth's friendship with Lyla?*

Mimi nudged her with a grin. *But you're odd, too, and we don't judge you for that. Besides, Beth and Lyla are besties.* There was just a trace of wistfulness in her voice.

Yeah, but at the winter formal last week, I walked into the restroom and Beth was there with Lyla, Grace said. *Beth was saying something about Lyla's dress, and Lyla was blubbering, shaking. Beth walked out when she saw me, and Lyla ran into a booth. I could hear her crying over my peeing.*

That was two years ago. A year later, Mimi was Beth's best friend. And Grace . . .

My heart constricts, thinking of the girl I saw skulking in the shadows beside the pool at Beth's party an hour ago. After Mimi dumped her, everyone started calling her a stalker, and since Beth would never have invited her, she must've been there to stalk Mimi as always.

My eyelids start to sag. God, I feel so lethargic. Must be from the adrenaline rush of breaking into Beth's place and almost getting caught. When was the last time I did something like that? That half a can of beer I drank at Krista's birthday last year, probably.

I can so easily fall asleep, but it's barely five and still sunny outside, and I've got to get my books and stuff ready for school and decide what to wear. Not that it's a huge decision. My dress code is T-shirt and jeans or shorts, depending on the weather, paired with sneakers.

And since tomorrow's supposed to be a sunny and perfect seventy-two, the clothes I'm wearing right now, a plain white T-shirt with black shorts, should work as long as they don't stink of sweat. I sniff the material and decide it smells okay. I'll change into my pajamas and leave the shirt and shorts on my backpack so I can grab them easily in the morning.

I settle back in my bed. With the district deciding on Friday as the first day of school for whatever cryptic reason, I doubt there's going to be much studying happening before the weekend. Which means I can take it slow and familiarize myself with my classes and any teacher quirks before the heavy stuff starts Monday. AP bio is my first class and I lucked out getting Mrs. G as the teacher. She was my homeroom teacher in freshman year and is known for giving the best recommendation letters ever. If I can ace bio and the other AP classes I've lined up, it'll weigh into my college credits and hopefully—fingers crossed—cut down on college tuition costs. I've saved the money from my job at a deli downtown, but it'll hardly pay for a semester at UMich. I'll need a scholarship, and if I can land one, I'll be in bustling Ann Arbor in two years among thousands of other students who'll barely know me and probably won't care about my past.

A thrill of excitement shoots through my heart. Two years, and I'll be totally free.

MY EYES SNAP open. Gloom fills the room and a strip of twilit sky dusky with the setting sun appears in the gap between the window curtains. The digital clock on my nightstand blinks 9 P.M. I must have fallen asleep.

Creak.

That's what woke me. A sound.

I knuckle my sleep-heavy eyes.

Another creak. Then a soft thud.

The sounds are coming from Mimi's room next door. Of course. She's sneaking back in through her window and trying to be quiet about it.

It hurts that she thinks I'll rat her out to Auntie, that she trusts me so little. But then, if she found out what I did tonight, she'd never trust me again.

Another creak, this time from a floorboard. And then silence.

My heartbeats settle into a steady rhythm. She hasn't come looking for me, pounding on my door. Which means no one spotted me taking that photo.

My eyelids droop again and the twilight filling the room turns to darkness.

CHAPTER 3

THE PAIN HITS me first. A vague annoying achy discomfort that pries me out of my sleep, intensifying rapidly into throbbing agony that refuses to be ignored. I open my eyes and am blinded with white light, painfully raw, forcing me to squeeze them shut. Once the stinging subsides, I open my eyes again, bracing myself, allowing them to adjust to the sunlight filtering through the lace window curtains.

I'm curled into a fetal position on my bed, my arms wrapped so tight around my knees they've become numb. I release my hold, letting my limbs stretch, groaning when the muscles protest.

No!

I shoot up, flinching when pain lances through my limbs. Mimi's voice feels so real; I turn to my open door, expecting to see her there. But the hall outside is empty.

You must not, Tanvi.

Her voice echoes in my head, which feels woozy, like it's spinning. I press a hand to my forehead, then do a double take.

Large blotchy red bruises wrap around my arms below the sleeves of my T-shirt. Similar marks cover my legs below my black shorts.

I stare, blinking the sleep out of my eyes.

Did I fall off my bike when I rode home from Beth's place? No, I'd remember if I did.

The hedges in Beth's backyard were nastier than I thought.

Did they have poison ivy on them? It feels fitting that something belonging to Beth would be beautiful and poisonous.

I touch a bruise on my thigh, wincing when pain stabs into my bone. The last time I got a really bad case was in middle school when Auntie took Mimi and me to the Upper Peninsula and we went hiking through the woods. I almost scratched my skin raw that day.

That rash looked different, though. Not like these angry red blotches.

I stand, grabbing for my nightstand when my legs tremble. I'm still in the white T-shirt and black shorts I wore yesterday to Beth's place. Only now the clothes are crusted with muddy stains, and so is the white bedsheet I was lying on.

Damn. How could I be so careless? Auntie hates us tracking dirt into the house, and I'm always extra careful not to do so. It's usually Mimi who she gets mad at, Mimi who breaks the rules. After changing clothes, I hide the dirt-stained materials under the bed, intending to wash them tonight without Auntie finding out, then hobble through my bedroom door.

I walk gingerly down the hall, arms extended and using the wall as support, but the floor keeps weaving like a boat caught in choppy waters. Everything seems intensified. The whisper of my bare feet on the carpet, my breaths echoing against my ribs, my thoughts ricocheting in my skull like ping-pong balls. The feel of cold plaster under my palms.

It reminds me of the panic attacks I used to get when I was bullied. When I woke up after passing out with every sensation being unbearably amplified.

I stop at Mimi's door. It's open. Her bed is empty, and her quilted blanket lies crumpled at the foot; the black and silver scarf she wore yesterday to Beth's party lies on the carpet.

Of course she's gone to meet Beth. Today's the first day of school, and as the queens of Orin High, she and Beth will need to stage their grand entrance, coordinated outfits and all.

I blink the tears away. Why am I crying? I knew a long time ago that Mimi wouldn't be coming with me to school anymore. Or anywhere, for that matter. The days are gone when we'd huddle together and excitedly plan our outfits for the first day, when we'd bike together to school, when she'd hug me before rushing off to class. Now she takes dinners in her room, forcing stilted conversations only if Auntie was around.

My phone pings. It's Auntie. **I'll be home around noon, honey. Had to take an extra shift at work.**

Guilt tightens my throat. She takes extra shifts to save up for our college expenses. She wants me to join UMich engineering and become an industrial engineer like my mom. But that's one thing I'll never do. I'll never become what my mom was. Not even for Auntie.

I got Mrs. G for AP bio & she's going to help me make a list of scholarships I can apply for.

That's great, honey. Have a marvelous first day of school, and tell Mimi I wished her one, too. She's not answering my texts. She must still be angry I grounded her.

Her pain is evident in the words, in the way little dots appear in the text box and then vanish. **I'll tell her. She's still sleeping, that's why she hasn't responded.**

A tiny lie to ease Auntie's mind.

It takes ages to get ready. Even the simple act of packing my backpack makes me dizzy and nauseous, and this headache is killing me. Is this what a hangover feels like?

I pause halfway through pulling on my jeans. There're so many things wrong with that question. That half a can of beer at Krista's birthday last year didn't even make me feel this lousy. Plus, I didn't drink last night. It's going to be totally messed up if I turn up at school looking the most smashed among the lot who were at the party yesterday.

It's while I'm brushing my hair that I discover where the headache is coming from—a bump the size of a quarter in the back of my skull. It throbs like it's on fire when I touch it. I don't remember falling on my way home from Beth's place, so the only possibility must be my scramble through the hedge maze. I could easily have hit more branches in my mad dash to escape.

After dousing my face in cold water, then downing a large cup of coffee, I feel a little more awake. I can't give Mrs. G the wrong impression. This year is critical, and I need every-thing—my grades, the scholarship apps, those prized rec letters—going exactly the way I planned.

Finally, I'm ready, lunch packed, and I open the front door.

Hazy dawn laps over the tiny strip of lawn bordered by a picket fence. Beyond the gate, the narrow road is deserted. My house is the last of four down this road, which dead-ends at Orin Woods, a sprawling acreage of dense forest.

The smell hits me as I walk down to the gate, a musty and damp smell of earth, rotting leaves, and bird droppings. The pungent aroma has been a part of me ever since Auntie brought me to this tiny town in east Michigan, an hour away from where I used to live in Detroit.

Used to live . . .

I dispel the aura, the wisp of memory of my past life, like my psychologist, Dr. Ajay, taught me to. *What happened to your father is not your fault, Tanvi.*

A chill runs down my arms. It's always colder here, the towering trees at the edge of the woods blocking out the sun, casting deep shadows over the neighborhood. Mist hangs along the tree trunks, like the combined exhalation from a million tiny animals hiding in the undergrowth.

I hug myself, wincing when I touch a red blotch on my right upper arm. The skin looks red and angry and puffed up. In the natural light, it's nothing like the poison ivy rash I had before. It looks like that time when I fell down the stairs a couple of years ago. The bruises lingered for weeks.

Maybe I fell down the stairs again last night? But wouldn't I remember that? The last thing in my memory is deleting the photo I took after talking to Krista. No, I remember waking up at nine P.M. to the sounds of Mimi sneaking back in.

An image appears in my mind. A pixelated image of several tiny mirrors. Not mirrors. Little jagged pieces of colored chips, some red, some black. They're forming something.

I frown, trying to see through the fog clouding my brain. But the headache intensifies and the image dissolves.

JUNIOR HALL IS chaotic, filled with the sounds of loud conversations, locker doors slamming, shoes thudding on the concrete floor. I shrink, drawing my bones into myself, and thread through the crowd. Now that I'm here, the relief I felt yesterday is rapidly fading. What if the plan Krista and I hatched last night didn't work and Beth posted the video somewhere? What if that pathetic sight of me cowering as Mimi lit my mother's candles, of me wailing and puking, is now available on social media for everyone to see and ridicule?

But wouldn't people be staring at me if that's the case? I lift my gaze from the dusty tiled floor. Everyone is either intent on greeting long-lost buddies or miserably surveying their locker contents. I may as well be invisible. Works for me.

But past that corner in the senior hall is where Beth and Mimi hold court every morning before class. My spine stiffens, vertebra by vertebra, as I approach the corner. By the time I turn, I'm as tense as an overstretched guitar string.

Beth leans against her locker wearing a figure-hugging

black dress with a thin blue belt and a matching knotted silk scarf. Between her outfit and her makeup, smokey eye shadow defining her baby blue eyes and a touch of pink lipstick, she's a flawless image of elegance. It's like the Beth of yesterday, snot-faced and red-eyed, never existed.

How the hell is she able to look so put together after getting wasted not even twenty-four hours ago, while I, stone-cold sober, feel like I've imbibed an entire barrel of hard liquor?

She's talking to a crowd of freshmen and hasn't spotted me. I catch some words above the clamor in the hall. *Help you reach your goals . . . strong family values . . . community partners.*

She's doing a freshman orientation session, talking about how awesome the school is and how everyone here is the model of perfection. That was the talk she and Lyla gave Krista and me two years ago. I remember hanging on to her every word, captivated by that golden image of perfection and wanting so badly to embody everything good about Orin High like she did.

Now I feel an urgent need to throw up. But there's also a deep sense of relief. It's a normal first day of school with no one paying me any attention.

But where's Mimi?

That's when I see the paper stuck to Mimi's locker door. An announcement of the track tryouts this morning. Of course. Mimi must've left home early to post the announcement.

The tension shackling my chest eases up. Not just because now I know Mimi was here this morning, but because this— getting busy with her track routine—is normal Mimi stuff. It's the Mimi I know, passionate about track, determined and ambitious; it's proof there is a part of her that hasn't changed. Track team captain and the best they have. She took Orin High to State last year with her district-record-breaking timing. If she does as well or better, she'll get an invitation to join UMich's track team, and that's been her dream since forever.

And I could've ruined everything with that photo. It's good I deleted it.

Beth's smiling blue eyes find mine through the crowd. The change in her expression is microscopic, the smile gathering an edge, a slight hardening of her jaw, the tiny curl of her lips.

And then she's back to addressing her fans.

But a thrill runs through my heart, a beat of joy. So far, I'd only been someone she could taunt, ridicule; a source of amusement. Someone she could break and then forget. She thought I'd take that video lying down, that I'd cower in fear while she made me a victim again. She didn't expect me to fight back.

Pinned to her dress is an enamel pin in the shape of a heart. I hold back a snort. There's the symbol of Stay Aware, the anti-drug coalition. When she was elected president of the org, the local newspaper *Orin Herald* ran an article over the summer describing her as a beacon of kindness and moral integrity.

My phone pings. A text from Krista. **Where's Mimi?**

I stare for a second, not comprehending. Then I answer, **She's not at the tryouts?**

Nope. Ask her to get here asap.

I frown. Mimi would never miss the tryouts. She'd been practicing all through the summer. The pain locked around my skull tightens further, inducing another wave of dizziness. Obviously, the effect of the coffee has worn off, and this annoying hangover—or whatever the heck it is—has returned full strength.

I reach for the wall to steady myself, then call Mimi. After three rings, I get her voice mail. "Hey, it's Tanvi. Where're you? Call me when you get this."

Another text pops up from Krista. **Lyla's talking to Coach.**

Shit. Lyla was co-captain last year, but it's well known that she wanted Mimi ousted from the post after the fallout between her boyfriend, Greg, and Mimi. I call Mimi again, my heart plummeting when I land in her voice mail again. "Where *are* you? The tryouts have started, and you need to get here ASAP, or you'll lose your spot to Lyla. Call me, please."

I tuck my phone in my jeans pocket and am about to head to my locker a few feet away when the back of my neck tingles. Beth's staring at my right forearm where the sleeve of my cardigan has ridden up and exposed the edge of a blotchy red bruise. I pull the sleeve back down.

Beth turns away to grab a stack of papers from her locker. "Come on, everyone. I'm volunteering all of you to help set up this morning's fundraiser." Her voice is soft, effortless, but somehow it slices through the commotion in the hall. People holding random conversations farther down stop talking and turn to face her. She has that effect on people.

Her slim, pink-tipped fingers slip to adjust her silk scarf, then she starts walking, the others following in her wake. "Who's got the cookies?"

"I do," a girl says, her voice shrill with excitement. "I came in early and set everything up."

Beth bestows a kind glance and a benevolent nod at her worker bee, and the girl giggles.

I turn away before I gag.

I'VE NEVER BEEN called to the office before. That's my first thought when they pull me out of homeroom. The thought circles in my brain as I rush down the deserted hall. There's never been any need to, not with me being a stickler for following every rule there is, always toeing the line. The only thing I can think of is they caught me; they know what I did yesterday. Maybe Mimi filed a complaint.

I check through my texts in case there's a message from her. But there's none. I text Krista. **Did Mimi ever show up to tryouts?**

Nope.

"I really can't imagine Mimi doing that." Beth's voice reaches me through the open office door.

I stiffen, every cell in my body recoiling from having to face her again. But what's she saying about Mimi? I walk into the room and am immediately assailed by the stink from whatever's molting in a basket of potpourri on the front desk. The secretary, Mrs. Patterson, a thin elderly woman with graying hair and a steady supply of polka-dot dresses, faces Beth across the desk, a deep frown ridging her forehead.

She transfers that frown to me. "Tanvi, there you are. Where's Mimi? She didn't show up for tryouts, Coach Ron just called. And she isn't in homeroom either."

My heart slams against my sternum.

"Mimi's not the type to skip school," the secretary adds in her reedy voice.

Or miss tryouts. The sense of foreboding constricts my throat further. "She didn't tell me she was going anywh—"

Beth cuts in. "She'd tell *me*. Mimi'd never go anywhere without letting me know."

I stiffen, resentment turning my throat bitter because I know what Beth said is true. Mimi would let her know before me. "Then where is she?" I blurt out. "She was at your party yesterday." Chips of blue ice form in her hardening eyes, and I realize too late that my words may imply I saw Mimi there. "I saw her return home after."

She inhales sharply, then lowers her eyes to frown at the desk.

"Where's Mimi now, Tanvi?" the secretary asks. "Have you tried calling her?"

I nod. "She left before I woke up this morning, and I thought she'd gone to Beth's."

"Well, she didn't come to my place." Beth's glare turns frigid. "She lives with you. How could you not know where she is?" She leans in closer, lowers her voice. "What happened? Your brain messed up or something? Don't tell me it's the meds making you catatonic."

I flinch. *I'm not on meds anymore*, I want to say, but my lips stay sealed. For one, I owe her no explanation. But then there is the headache clawing my skull, the mind fog I can't break. Did I have a panic attack at Beth's? Maybe while I was hiding in the hedges, which caused me to blank out for a bit?

Mrs. Patterson clears her throat. "Beth, that's uncalled for. Very inappropriate."

"Sorry," she mutters. "Just worried to death, that's all."

I'm about to snap back that I'm worried, too, but then I notice the dark edge of anguish clouding her eyes and the tremor in her hands as she grips the desk. "Something's wrong, Mrs. Patterson. You need to find Mimi, ASAP."

The secretary's face softens. "I'll call her mom. Mimi'll be okay, don't worry. I'm sure she's just running late." After a reassuring smile at Beth, she disappears into the office.

I need to call Auntie. But not here, not with Beth watching.

I head for the girls' bathroom. The walk takes me past the freshmen hall, where a group of kids are clustered, chattering and staring at their phone screens.

"*Shit*, this is brutal," one girl says.

"Wait, let me see," the boy next to her says, and she passes him the phone. There's a photo on the screen. Of a girl. No, two girls. One blond and the other dark-haired.

My fingertips go numb.

The boy looks up, locks eyes with me, then nudges his

neighbor before leaning in to whisper something in her ear. The group stops talking and turns as one to stare at me.

The scene around me shifts, blurs, except for that phone screen.

It's the photo I took yesterday. Beth and Mimi are clearly visible and so is the white powder cut into fine lines on the table next to them.

All the phones have the same photo. That same damning photo.

"Is that her? She did it?" someone says.

Their voices join the roaring in my ears.

"Oh, God, you're kidding me, her own *cousin* sent it?"

My heart slams against my ribs. Impossible. I reach for the phone, claw it out of their hand.

"Hey, what the fuck? Give that back!" They wrench the phone out of my grip.

But not before I see the social media account the photo was shared from. It's mine. Someone hacked into it to send the photo.

I turn and start running toward the exit. I have to find Mimi before she sees the photo. Explain that it's a hack. It wasn't me who sent that photo out.

God, will she believe me?

Will it matter? I took it.

The chatter resumes behind me, swelling into a crescendo, sweeping me along.

More people breaking off to stare at me.

Is it her?

She sent it?

Snitch.

Don't listen to them. Just get to the exit. The front doors are right around that corner.

Oh my God. How could she do it?

Narc.

The tall arched doors loom in front of me. I'm a few feet away when they open and Lyla and Greg rush in.

Greg throws his arms around Lyla's waist and lifts her high. Through the tears blurring my vision, I see the green band around Lyla's right upper arm. It's the band worn by Orin High's team captains. Mimi had one last year, and she was determined to get one this year, too.

Lyla sees me. Next to her, Greg smirks.

"Looks like I owe you for getting rid of my competition," Layla says.

No.

I watch them disappear around the corner. This photo is just a misunderstanding, a glitch. But how? Someone must have found my phone after I dropped it. Once Mimi returns, we'll clear everything up.

A sudden wave of wooziness hits me. I grab the wall to steady myself, then wince when the pain clamped around my skull suddenly cranks up several degrees. My vision darkens with a burst of black cotton wool.

"Tanvi." Krista. How long has she been standing there? Her hand is on my elbow, helping me up, tugging me toward the exit. My arm stings from her grip; her fingers dig into the bruise hidden under my cardigan sleeve. "Let's get you out of here."

"I deleted it." My eyes keep filling. I blink the tears away. "I swear."

"I know. I believe you. But you must come with me. Your aunt's outside, and there's a cop with her."

CHAPTER 4

THE ONLY THING saying "I'm an adult" about the young cop sitting across the table from Auntie and me is the faint shadow of mustache and a few hairs of a beard adorning his baby face.

"I know the law, and I don't need to wait twenty-four hours. My daughter is only seventeen. She's a minor. And I've already checked with her friends; she's not with any of them." Auntie glares at him over her glasses. She is still in scrubs, her RN badge on a lanyard around her neck. Her black hair is in a topknot. "You need to file a missing person's report."

The secretary had also called the police station, which is why there was a cop—this guy seated across from us—waiting with Auntie outside school when I walked out with Krista.

"Your daughter may just be lying low, ma'am." The cop's gray eyes shift to me. "Because of the photo your niece sent out to everyone in her school."

I flinch. Auntie places a comforting hand on my clenched ones. "I told you already, Tanvi didn't release that photo; some-one hacked into her account."

She believed me when I told her, hugging me tight outside school, insisting I'd never hurt Mimi.

Auntie continues, "I just want to find my child, officer." Her voice is still strong, but her chin trembles as she struggles to control her emotions.

I've never seen her crumble before. But now . . . fear is writ-ten into the furrows in her forehead and the grooves digging into the corners of her pinched mouth. It sinks in that while

I've never doubted Auntie's love for me, Mimi is her only child. Her only daughter. It was just the two of them after Uncle Dan died when Mimi was a toddler. If I'm terrified for Mimi, Auntie must be so torn up. My heart constricts hard.

The young cop straightens in his chair under her glare. "Sure, ma'am, of course." He turns to me. "When was the last time you saw your cousin?"

I look away, my gaze darting all around until it settles on my hands. The lower edge of the bruise on my right forearm is visible under the sleeve of my cardigan. Instinctively, I tug the cloth down to cover it. "At Beth's party."

"When you took the photo?"

I lower my head, unable to look at Auntie. I'd thought— for a second—about lying. Telling her someone else took the photo and hacked my account to send it so I'd get blamed. "Yes."

"You didn't see her return home?"

"No, but I heard her. And I saw the scarf she wore to the party in her room this morning."

I heard Mimi's voice, too, I remember. This morning when I woke up, I heard her say something from my door. But when I looked, she wasn't there. The voice was in my head.

Wasn't it?

My skull still throbs like an abscessed tooth, but my vision is normal now. The pain comes from the lump at the base of my skull. I search for the spot, the touch triggering another wave of pain that shoots up my head.

"So she came home, changed, then left in the morning without you seeing her?"

You must not, Tanvi.

Did Mimi say that? Did she come to my room after returning from Beth's while I was asleep? A cold sensation sinks in my stomach. That might mean she knew what I did.

"Honey?" Auntie leans over and places a hand on my knee. "Don't be scared. You don't have to hide anything." She turns to the cop. "I grounded Mimi and asked Tanvi to tell me if she sneaked out. I think Tanvi's just trying to protect her cousin."

The cop's eyes sharpen. "You said you grounded her?"

Auntie sighs. "Yes, when I found out about her boyfriend, James Surrey. He's not a good person, officer. He and his dad are drug dealers, and I was trying to keep Mimi away from him."

Auntie believed the rumors about James being a dealer, though Mimi insisted—rightfully—that he'd never been charged. I first met James in middle school, a loner, ostracized by everyone because of those rumors about his creepy dad. But Mimi ignored those rumors. She took him under her wing, too, protecting him from bullies like she protected me. He was part of her lunch group, part of her group projects at school. A year older than her, he dropped out sometime in high school, and I forgot about him until suddenly he was back in Mimi's life three months ago—as her boyfriend.

Auntie leans forward. "James is dangerous. I think you need to talk to him. What if he . . ." She shudders, leaving the question unasked. I wrap my arm around her.

The cop starts to roll his eyes but catches himself. "Your daughter is just embarrassed about that photo. Maybe she thinks she'll get into trouble, and so she's lying low."

I want to believe him, but that doesn't make any sense. The photo came out at eight-thirty this morning. Mimi missed her tryouts at seven. "Mimi couldn't have left because of the photo."

The cop frowns. "Wishing it so doesn't make it true. You may regret it all you want, but you gave your cousin a reason to hide."

My chest cracks open with guilt—and frustration. Sure, Mimi was smoking a joint in that photo, but Beth was snorting coke. Why's no one talking about that?

Auntie jumps to her feet. "Don't talk to my niece that way."

The cop says something back, and their words become a jumble in my roaring skull.

Then an image appears out of the brain fog. A pixelated image formed by the swirling red and black chips I saw earlier, just after I woke up. But now they're rearranging themselves, coalescing into a figure.

Mimi, wearing the clothes she wore to Beth's party, the red dress with the black scarf knotted around her neck. She was standing at the door to my bedroom. Scowling at me as I lay on my bed.

Then the image is gone.

"All I'm saying is that teenagers run away all the time. How do you know she's not with the boyfriend?" The derisive curl of the cop's lips reminds me of Greg. "She'll be back soon, so there's no reason to waste resources."

Auntie stiffens, her eyes flashing black fire. "My daughter didn't just *leave*, officer. She's in trouble." Her voice shakes. "I can feel it."

The fear in her words settles on my skin like chips of ice that seep inside and into my veins. I'm cold. So cold.

I'M IN MIMI'S room, sitting cross-legged on the floor. It's been a half hour since I biked home. Auntie called the school office, and they allowed me a day off, but she refused to leave the station. She insisted on talking to the cop's supervisor, an older woman. They were closeted in an office when I left.

I study the room, looking for something, some clue that'll tell me where Mimi went.

Her quilted blanket lies crumpled at the foot of the bed.

Mimi always made her bed every morning, which means she must've been in a hurry when she left.

Her gym bag, which she always brings to practice, is still in her closet. So is her backpack and all the books she'd kept ready to take to school today. When she left, she wasn't going to the tryouts or to school. How could I have missed that this morning?

I heard her sneak into her room through the window, I heard her footsteps on the wooden floor. The next thing I remember is waking up in the morning.

Except now I know she did come to my door sometime in between.

I can try and recreate it, see if it'll get any clearer.

I lie down on my bed and close my eyes. It was nine P.M. according to the clock on my nightstand when I heard the sounds from Mimi's room. A creak, then another, followed by a soft thud. Then silence.

Tanvi?

Mimi's impatient voice feels so real, I swivel my gaze to the door. I can see her standing there, the hall light washing over carefully done waves of hair waterfalling across her shoulders, as black as the scarf wrapped around her neck, the black startling against the red of her dress.

The image is clear now, pixelated red and black chips no longer swirling madly.

She was angry. Her voice was raised.

She must've known about the photo.

Did I tell her I was sorry? That I deleted it?

I don't remember saying anything. It was just her voice. *You must not!*

There was another sound. Like drums. Heavy drumming, and the house was shaking. The drumming got closer and closer.

I try latching onto the sound, holding tight so I can figure out what it is. But the memory—if that's what it is—retreats into a fog.

The sound fades. The only drumming is my head, pounding.

I return to Mimi's room. The scarf she wore to Beth's party lies on the floor where I'd glimpsed it this morning. I lift it up and find the sheer material with its silver threading caked with mud. Just like the mud I found crusted on my clothes when I woke up.

This must've come from Beth's backyard. There was mud and damp grass in the paths in the hedge maze, which could've stained my clothes. It makes sense for me since I ducked between the hedges to hide. But how would Mimi's scarf get muddied?

And didn't I check my clothes before falling asleep?

Yeah, and they seemed clean because I was planning on wearing the same ones for school today.

Why can't I remember?

I used to black out from panic attacks, but a combination of therapy and medications stopped the attacks for years. Until I had that attack again when Beth lit Mom's candles and I passed out. But I always woke up alert, aware of danger, and with full memory of what scared me.

I frown, then look around for her dress. But it's not anywhere in the room or in her closet.

A rapid clicking breaks through the fog. The click of heels on a wooden floor.

I hurry out of my bedroom and down to the living room and find it deserted.

But that clicking sound—only Mimi wore heels in this house.

I close my eyes and try to remember.

She was standing at my door in her red dress and black

scarf. And in her heels. The pretty red heels she loved. Then she must've walked down the stairs—she left the scarf in her room.

Did I see her walking down? Or was it just the sound of her heels that led me to believe that?

Why can't I see through this damned fog?

Push through it.

Noooooooooooo!

The shriek explodes behind my eyes. A sudden vise clamps around my skull, squeezing tighter and tighter, threatening to shatter the bone. The agony takes my breath away.

I gasp and open my eyes, but the world around is fading into wisps of brown and yellow that merge into a deep, deep red. A scarlet so violent, my heart breaks. I'm going to die, die, die . . .

Panting breaths fill my ears, rising above the roar of the colors, above the shrieks.

The ground under me is smooth, cool. The swirling sky solidifies into a sheet of white.

I'm flat on the floor in my room.

I hold my head between my hands, wait until I can be sure it won't explode, then stagger to my feet.

That shriek sounded so much like Mimi's voice.

CHAPTER 5

IT'S BEEN TWENTY-FOUR hours since Mimi's been gone.

A sheen of orange-gold frames the treetops, heralding day-break. The neighborhood's awakening. Taillights appear on driveways and a scattering of pajama-clad people haul trash cans to the curb. Squeaking metal joins the sounds of chirping birds and some annoyed owl hooting loudly from the woods.

But I've been awake for hours, huddled on the window seat in Mimi's room, staring outside, watching the end of the road where it vanishes beyond a red-roofed colonial, hoping Mimi will turn that corner any minute and explain everything.

Mimi never skips school. That was what the office secretary said. And that's what scares me. Mimi's behavior changed after friending Beth, but it only extended to me. Everything else remained the same, including her fixation on her perfect attendance and that 4.0 GPA. On her desk, arranged in a neat pile, are all the letters she's received from various universities asking her to apply to their programs, but she had decided on UMich sometime in freshman year. *It's in state, has a great track program and a prelaw program, and I can visit Mom as often as I want.*

Why would she just drop everything and walk away?

I lift my gaze to the ceiling where, sometime in middle school, she painted a bird, a blue jay perched at the edge of a twig, its wings spread, about to take off into the cloudless sky above.

That's me, T, she said. *One day I'm going to fly away, too, into the sky. I'm going to become famous and make so much money, Mom won't have to work again, and no one will ever dare to hurt you. We'll be untouchable.*

My phone pings. Krista, replying to a text I sent her.

Nope, checked with everyone who was at the tryouts yesterday, also with Coach. No one's heard from Mimi. & you're right. That photo was sent from your account at 8:30 AM. It was something else that made her leave. How were the cops btw?

From the way that young cop had to stop himself from rolling his eyes, I'd say not very helpful. But maybe Mimi's just lying low like he said. **They don't seem worried.**

Mimi's scarf lies drying on a clothes rack; I hand-washed it so it'll be clean for her when she returns.

I hear the click of Mimi's heels on the stairs again, but my attempts to remember keep triggering a massive headache from the bump on the back of my skull. I feel the bump gingerly.

K. We still need to figure out who knew you took that photo, Krista texts. **They went to great trouble to hack into your account just to release it.**

It has to be someone at the party who found my phone, I reply. I've already deleted my social media accounts and reported the hack, but there was that short time when I misplaced my phone and when I found it again. When the screen was frozen on the photo. They could've easily sent a screenshot to themselves, then hacked into my account to release the photo. Maybe when they realized I wasn't going to release it myself?

It must be someone who wanted to hurt Mimi and Beth. **Lyla?**

Yep, Lyla can be vicious that way.

And she has reason to hate both Beth and Mimi. Beth and Lyla had been tight through middle school and the first two years of high school, much like Mimi and Grace were. It was after Mimi ran into Beth at their junior college counseling session last year that Beth started including Mimi in her friend group. From there to completely displacing Lyla as Beth's bestie took barely two months.

Or Greg? Krista adds a thinking emoji. **After the spat he had with Mimi.**

True. It happened at a party Lyla threw in May. Krista was there as part of the track team, and she saw Mimi storm out of Lyla's house and Greg nursing a slapped jaw. According to Krista, Mimi's subsequent interactions with Lyla and Greg were *arctic*.

I remember the girl I saw skulking in the shadows, the one who couldn't have been invited. **What about Grace? She was there.**

No!!!! Beth would never!

Yep.

Grace Warren? You sure? After everything she did to Mimi?

I totally get Krista's disbelief. Sometime after Mimi's second invite to Beth's house, Mimi's missing laptop was found in Grace's backpack and Mimi cut Grace off. Grace quit talking to everyone—including me—after I asked her why she'd steal Mimi's stuff. But she became obsessed with Mimi, often following Mimi around school or hanging around the bleachers watching her at practice. *I'd look up and there she'd be*, Mimi said, *staring at me with her dead eyes. Such a weirdo. Gave me the creeps.*

From then on, the labels *weirdo*, *kook*, and *nutcase* got tagged on to Grace's *thief* label.

Though it's still hard for me to associate the friendly, cheerful person I knew with the recluse she'd become.

I'll snoop around & get back to you, Krista texts. **Chin up, girl. Mimi'll return soon.**

But when? I hug my knees and rock back and forth. The first twenty-four hours are the most critical, according to the Missing Children websites I looked at. If you can't find the missing kids by . . . My hands shake. No, don't go there.

Mimi must've contacted *someone*.

What about Beth? She said herself that Mimi'd check in with her before anyone else.

I pull up Beth's social media and the pinned post is one she made ten minutes ago, showing her tear-stained face and multiple crying emojis.

Mimi, miss you so much, come home. I need you! Call me! #sistersforever @midiva

She holds up her left wrist and the beaded bracelet with "Mimi + Beth" on it.

Bile rushes into my throat with the same intensity as when I first saw that bracelet. It was on Mimi's wrist then. She'd returned from her first visit to Beth's place, the Halloween party, her face flushed and ecstatic. She took the bracelet off after I reminded her Grace was her best friend. But then the second party happened a couple of weeks later, and Mimi never removed that bracelet after.

Then I notice the @midiva on Beth's post. Krista said Mimi had deleted her social media accounts. Beth must know that, so why's she still tagging Mimi in her post?

Hey, I text Krista, **r u sure Mimi deleted her accounts?**
Yep. Not sure when though.

That's odd. Maybe Beth did it out of force of habit.

I type in the name of Mimi's boyfriend, James Surrey, in the search bar. Several accounts pop up, but not his. He's likely not on social media.

Mimi created a collage of the two of them that she hung

above her bed. Only the wall is empty, and the collage is missing. I search the room and finally find it under Mimi's bed, face down. Auntie must've removed it just like she wanted to remove him from Mimi's life.

There are about thirty photos, all arranged neatly in chronological order. Mimi likes everything organized; she hates clutter and disorder.

The first photo shows her holding James's hand, with the caption *A new start, a promise made.* It's dated June 1st, so a few days after Lyla's party in May. The next one is dated a week later. James is leaning against a motorcycle, a smile tugging at the corner of his lips, while Mimi grins wide at the camera, her eyes dancing.

I study the next several photos, wondering at the change in him from the awkward loner I first met in middle school to this tall boy with hazel eyes and high cheekbones in a lean, strong face. Mimi found him bloodied after a fight in sixth grade and tucked him under her wing like she did me. He used to tag alongside her, watch her with adoring eyes, blush when she smiled or said something to him. Both Grace and I knew he had a crush on her, but Mimi seemed oblivious. He dropped out in high school and vanished from her life until three months ago, when they became a couple.

A hint of cloudiness is visible behind his smile, in the leashed way he holds himself, even though Mimi's eyes are full of naked love. But he's more relaxed in the next several photos, grinning wide, hugging Mimi to him.

I didn't see him at Beth's party—but would Beth have invited him? He lives with his dad in a run-down apartment above their tiny general store on the outskirts of Orin, not what Beth would consider "suitable."

I replace the collage under the bed and scan the room again, hoping to find something, a clue I missed.

My gaze falls on the framed photo on her nightstand. It's of Auntie, Uncle Dan, and Mimi taken at her birthday when she was two. They're all decked out in traditional Indian garb, Auntie in a green and gold sari, Mimi in a lehenga choli, and Uncle Dan in a kurta. Uncle Dan died of a heart attack a month later.

There used to be another photo next to it, of Auntie, Mimi, and me, taken outside the Detroit Hindu temple on my birthday last year. But it's gone.

This is my room. I only want my family here, she said when I asked her why.

I insisted I was family, too.

She stared at me for a long second before shoving past me and storming out of the room.

I lift Mimi's family photo, studying the features of my uncle, this stranger. Mimi told me years ago that he was an athlete in school—*just like me, T*—but couldn't go to college because he needed a job to take care of his ill mom. He met Auntie at the hospital when his mom was in hospice and they fell in love. Mimi looks so much like him, her skin coloring, the shape of her mouth and nose and that strong chin, but her eyes are her mom's, large and dark.

Just like mine.

Just like my mom's.

I lift my gaze and stare at the full-length mirror on the wall in front of me. At the round face and full lips, dark hair tumbling in unruly waves, inherited from the woman who birthed me.

You are so beautiful, Mom. I used to cup her face, feeling the silkiness of her long black tresses. *When will I be pretty like you?*

You're already pretty, sweetheart. You're the prettiest thing in the world.

"Liar." I hiss at the reflection. "Murderer." I can taste the hatred in the bitterness coating my teeth, the bile filling my mouth.

• • •

THE NARROW ROAD down my block dead-ends at Orin Woods, where I go when life gets unbearable. The woods and the springs were once popular trekking spots, but the trails haven't been tended in years—something about town budget cuts—and people prefer to drive the half hour to the trails in neighboring Gaston. Unless they're teens crashing the place to smoke up or transients looking for a place to sleep. Or someone like me, looking to be left alone with my thoughts.

The path is barely visible underneath my sneakers, all but disappeared under encroaching vegetation. My feet, through years of practice, find the safe spots to step on, the parts where the ground isn't going to crumble into a large rodent hole or send me tumbling down the eroding slope.

The sound of gurgling water reaches my ears, followed by the damp smell of moss, mist, and wet earth. Then there it is, a sheet of frothing water erupting from the edge of a rock face. The waterfall forms a swirling, eddying stream that continues for a length before disappearing underground. Ragged strips of tape flutter from chipped wooden posts placed along the stream and on the rocky ledge above, remnants of cordoned-off trails.

I love it here. This place was part of my therapy, my healing. For the first month after coming to Orin, I refused to leave my room, watching the door in case Mom entered. Even though I knew she had already been cremated in a ceremony only Auntie attended.

Mimi lured me out of my room on Daddy's birthday. She made a special cake—strawberry vanilla, his favorite. She was singing a birthday song on the other side of my shut door. I crawled out from my corner, past the breakfast of pancakes Auntie had left on my nightstand, and opened the door. And there she was, my cousin, wearing a brand-new churidar, holding the most perfect cake I'd ever seen in my life. "Let's celebrate Uncle Ramesh's life, Tanvi. Maybe you can't see him anymore, but he's still here, still with you. He'll want you to know that and be happy."

Soon after, I started going to therapy. It took years for the nightmares to improve, and sure, they never totally left, but every time I felt them returning, I'd come here. I'd lie on the ledge above the waterfall and talk to my dad, watching the clouds above form his face, form that grin I loved so much. He'd lift me up high and say, *I love you, Princess, to the end of the world and back.*

The mud slope leading down to the stream is choked with weeds and slick with moss. One wrong step and I could end up sliding right into the treacherous water. Treacherous because hidden under the deceptively calm surface are powerful currents that can easily drag a person down or fling them against the rocks. Two decades ago, a teen died here after slipping off the ledge. There used to be a wooden cross here with her name on it, but it vanished after a summer storm flooded the place last year.

A row of narrow stone steps leads to the edge of the stream. I lean down and run my fingers through the water, creating eddies. "Your birthday's coming up in four weeks, Daddy, and you know what that means. We're going to India Castle again."

My dad's favorite restaurant, for all its grand name, is a tiny place tucked in an alley in downtown Detroit. He loved the chole bhatura they made there, swearing it beat any of the fancier Indian restaurants around. When Mimi decided the three of us would celebrate Daddy's birthday there every year, it was hard at first. I cried through the meal, and Auntie wanted to cancel the trip the next year. But Mimi sat me down and told me about her dad. *I wish I got to know him more, but I remember nothing about him. You knew your dad, T, and all the things he loved, like chole bhatura, like India Castle. So let's keep doing what he loved, and that way, he'll always be with you.*

We haven't missed a single year since.

I pluck a leaf and place it in the water, watching it swirl downstream. "The restaurant was quite dingy when we went there last year, Daddy. The owner told us he'd lost a ton of customers since the pandemic. He even hinted the place may not survive too long." My chest tightens. "I'm going to call them like Mimi usually does . . ."

The pressure around my chest intensifies into a vise grip.

The last time we went to India Castle, Mimi arranged for them to play my dad's favorite Mohammed Rafi songs. "Jo Wada Kiya Woh" was his absolute favorite, about a dead queen promising to return to her beloved husband even if destiny tried to stop her. We all sang along. Even the staff joined in.

But Mimi won't be here this time. Because even when she returns, she'll never join me again.

I'm not family. I don't want to be your family. Not with that psycho blood you carry in your veins.

It was Beth speaking in Mimi's voice; I knew that.

It was Beth who told her that stuff, words she then used on me.

It still hurt.

The leaf I sent downstream crashes into a rock and gets caught in the sharp edges jutting through the water. Sharpened knives tearing it apart.

My fingers are numb. They're clenched tight, the knuckles bloodless.

I relax my grip and inhale deeply. I let the breeze wrap around me, leaning into the sounds of the birds, the leaves fluttering, the feel of the sunlight on my skin. Leaning away from the dark thoughts swirling in my mind.

But the restlessness intensifies, and I know there's only one way to let it out.

The place around me is not the ideal spot to practice Tae Kwon Do moves, but neither is my basement. Yet, I have a mini dojang set up there, with my belts pinned to a board on the wall, starting with my white belt all the way up to the red. Another year and a half, and I'll have my black belt up there, too.

I close my eyes and begin my salutations. Then, one by one, I go through the kicks, front, side, back, roundhouse, axe, and crescent, followed by blocks and strikes. After that comes the forms, and then I start sparring, visualizing an imaginary opponent, then step forward, kick, jump back, circle, waiting for an opening, then lunge.

My opponent takes shape. Tall, blond, with that infuriating smirk on her face.

My jaw clenches. Sweat drips off my face and drenches my tank top. My spine snaps straight. Punch, block, step back.

Then I swing, lifting my leg high, spinning right into where I imagine Beth's face to be.

If Beth hadn't started talking to Mimi that day at the college counseling session, Mimi would've been content with remaining best friends with Grace and me. Then everything would've been fine.

I knew something was off when Mimi returned from Beth's birthday party last November and shut her door on me.

I knocked on her locked door. *Come on, Mimi, you always tell me everything. What happened?*

Go away, Tanvi. Her voice was icy. *You're such a pest.*

I remember recoiling in shock. Not just because she used my full name rather than the usual *T,* but also because of the unfamiliar viciousness. She'd never been cold with me or pushed me away.

I didn't know that was just the beginning.

My fists raised to protect my head, I wait for my chance, then punch hard for Beth's face. Balance and focus on my right leg, I coil it tight like a spring, then unleash it, slamming my foot into her skull, pulverizing the bone.

Later, spent and sweating, I collapse on the grass and open Beth's post. The video of her crying and pleading for Mimi to return is still pinned to the top of her page, but the comments underneath have burgeoned since the last half hour.

>@corey_prince: I feel so bad for you, Beth.

>@i_read_books: I bet Mimi got the stuff from her drug dealer bf.

>@shitisreal: Yep, she trapped Beth & then had that freak cousin of hers take the photo. She's just jealous.

>@corey_prince: We need to stand by Beth, y'all. Don't let Mimi & her loser bf's evil plan work.

Then I see the last comment on the page.

>@trackqueen: I told you not to start collecting trash, B. Cut her out, she's not worth your tears; she's never been. #sistersforever.

I stare at the words. @trackqueen. Lyla's handle.

CHAPTER 6

I STEP THROUGH the school doors with Krista, feeling wired and wiped out at the same time. Last night was a sleepless one as I curled up on Mimi's window seat, my eyes gritty, fixed on the road, praying she'd turn the corner anytime soon. Auntie didn't sleep either; I could hear her pacing her room. This morning, I found her sobbing in the prayer room.

She's already sent me a series of texts since I left the house. They're all the same.

Message me as soon as school's done and come right home. I love you, honey, please stay safe.

She's worried I'll vanish, too. And it doesn't help that the cops aren't taking Mimi's disappearance seriously. Though the senior cop insisted they were searching for Mimi and talking to her contacts, they kept referring to the photo as the reason Mimi left. And anytime Auntie pointed out that it was released later by someone who hacked into my account, they'd switch to Auntie grounding Mimi as the reason my cousin ran away. *Teenage girls*, they'd said. It's frustrating as hell and is spiking Auntie's anxiety.

After texting Auntie back, I follow Krista down the packed senior hall. It's the only way to get to the junior hall around the corner.

Beth stands next to her locker. Dark shades hide her eyes, and her face appears paler. She leans into a tall guy with cropped blond hair who has his arm around her. The group surrounding them share matching concerned expressions, some patting her back or her arm while others reach in to give her quick hugs.

They're all supporting her. I remember the comments. They were all so quick to diss Mimi.

You and I, T, we can't afford this crap. We got goals, sis.

Resentment tastes bitter in my throat, followed by a wave of grief. I wanted Beth discredited and tarnished, shunned by everyone, but somehow Beth's become the victim here. And my cousin is still missing.

Beth lifts her head and goes still. One by one, the people in the crowd turn to look at me.

"What's she doing here?"

"She should be kicked out."

I push blindly through the crowd while Krista glares around her, one arm protective around my shoulders. Once we reach the junior hall and my locker, I yank the door open, wishing I could crawl into the narrow space and stay there forever.

"Don't listen to them, girl." She pats my forearm over my cardigan, her touch bringing the bruise underneath to stinging life. When I flinch, she jerks her hand away. "What's wrong?"

I roll up the cardigan sleeve. The bruise seems to have expanded, though it's flatter now, with the angry red edged with purple and blue.

"Shit, what happened?"

"It's from the hedges in Beth's backyard."

Her frown deepens. "Are you sure you didn't fall somewhere?"

"Yeah." *No.* I hold my arm up to the morning light streaming through a narrow window in the hall. The bruises on my legs are bigger than this one, and then there's the bump on my skull. The damn thing still throbs in nauseating waves.

"Maybe you ought to get it checked out at the doctor's. It could be a medical issue. What did your aunt say?"

Even if she is a nurse, the last thing Auntie needs is to worry about me. "I'm sure it's fine." Then I see the group in the hall and forget all about the bruises.

It's a few girls in track uniforms circling Lyla and talking in hushed whispers. The green captain's band around Lyla's upper arm contrasts with the pallor of her skin. She keeps touching it like she's making sure it's still there.

She got Mimi's captaincy, and from her comment in reply to Beth's post yesterday—#sistersforever—it's clear she wants Beth back, too. My hands clench. She's going after everything Mimi has.

"Once Mimi returns, she'll get the captaincy back, won't she?" I ask.

Krista sighs, then shakes her head gently. "Tanvi . . . Coach isn't planning on letting Mimi back into the team."

"But that's ridiculous. Mimi's got the best times. She'll make State again this year, two years in a row."

"Yeah, but you know Coach can't afford the stink of drugs anywhere near the team. He won't risk having the other schools question Mimi's times, our times."

Guilt spears through me. I messed everything up when I took that damned photo. Even if I prove I didn't release it, it won't help Mimi. Her chance at a track scholarship, at entry into the UMich program, it's all gone because of my stupid need to get back at Beth.

Muffled shouts come from outside, filtering in through the window next to me. Greg strolls across the schoolyard, followed by a cheering group carrying a large placard with the words *Greg Waller = GOAT!!!*

Lyla breaks away from her group and leans out the window, waving her arms. "Yay! You did it, babe."

Greg waves back at her, then is carried along by his fans toward the football field across the yard.

Then Lyla swings on me, her gray eyes slate hard. "Greg's back, and he's staying, and there's nothing Mimi can do to kick him out again."

What the heck's she talking about? "I have no idea . . ." But suddenly I'm talking to empty air because she's disappeared down the hall, leaving the rest of her team staring after her, confused.

"Mimi got Greg kicked off the football team?" I didn't know she had that type of influence.

"At least she tried to." Krista's busy scrolling through her phone, then holds it up. It's Greg's profile. "Look."

He posted a bunch yesterday. My eyes scan the words.

> **I'm baaaack, guys. They know they can't do shit without me, the gr8est qb in Orin history, so they come crying. Serves them right, a-holes, for dissing me! This team is NOTHIN without me.**

> **Looks like they finally figured you can't trust "evidence" from a junkie.**

Mimi must've gone after him because of whatever he said to her at Lyla's end of school party earlier this year. But how did she manage to have him sidelined? His posts mentioned something about "evidence" from a junkie.

My heart plummets as the implication sinks in. What if they used the photo against Mimi to discredit her? What if that's the reason Greg got reinstated?

That thought remains with me through the morning classes, the guilt and bitterness weighing me down. Mimi's faced every consequence of that photo being released, but the person I wanted ostracized has gotten away scot-free. Beth's in bio lab with me, her blond head bent to a microscope a few tables away. She gets to stay in school; there have been no investigations into her, no mention of suspension. Though the Stay Aware pin she's worn to school daily since appointed president is missing from her green blouse.

A quick search on my phone, and I find that her name's no longer on the website of the antidrug organization as their high school rep. That position was the feather in her cap, the reason the school staff adored her. She brought in the funds from the city and the recognition from the media during any antidrug campaign.

So she's not invincible. I eye her bent head, the tic at the corner of her mouth, which is new, the way her eyes sometimes dart around the lab like she's nervous. I've never seen Beth unsettled before, and it feels good.

But then my chest tightens again when I remember that my action cost my cousin a lot more than my enemy.

Beth's eyes fall on me and harden immediately with some dark emotion, and I remember the question she asked me in the office. *How could you not know where she is? Your brain messed up or something?*

Something has messed with it—the aftereffects of a panic attack, maybe—and the fogginess lingers, even after three days.

It's been seventy-two hours now since Mimi disappeared.

I trace the painful edge of the bruise on my forearm under my cardigan, then realize what I'm doing and snatch my hand away.

AFTER LUNCH, I head upstairs to my class on the third floor. The stairway winds past large windows that overlook the road between the schoolyard and the football field. The team's returning I assume from practice, Greg among them, still brandishing their placards and yelling. They're also blocking traffic, flipping off the driver of a pickup truck, who keeps revving his engine.

The driver looks familiar. It's James, his straggly blond hair tied back in a ponytail. An image pops in my mind of Mimi with a bag of white powder clenched in her hand. My heart twists. Did James give her and Beth the drugs?

He turns his head abruptly toward the school. His expression isn't clear, but it feels like he's staring right at me. A sudden roar of the engine, and he spins in a sharp U-turn before racing off in the opposite direction, leaving a trail of exhaust lingering in the air.

I frown, staring after the truck. Why's he hanging out outside school?

Auntie called the cops last night, insisting they search his place for Mimi, insisting he must've provided the drugs or know where she was, but they pushed back, saying they couldn't get a warrant or enter his property without valid reason. But they said they questioned him, and he told them he didn't see Mimi the night she vanished.

What if he lied? I didn't see him at Beth's party, but he could easily have met up with Mimi after she returned.

The trace of exhaust from James's truck has long dissipated by the time I turn away from the window. There's something odd about the way he sped away. I can't shake the feeling that he's hiding something.

KRISTA AND I walk out through the school doors into a cloudy damp afternoon and the first scattering of fall leaves on the grass.

My phone buzzes against my hip. I pull it out, expecting another text from Auntie—she sent me six more texts since lunch—but it's the notification I set up to check class assignments.

Krista glances at my screen and groans. "For real, Tanvi? Do you need to check your assignments every ten seconds?"

"It's been way over ten seconds." I'm about to click on the link when I spot the blank space below the reply I sent Auntie ten minutes ago. An empty space below the long column of texts starting at eight A.M. this morning.

My throat tightens.

"What's wrong?"

I turn the phone so she can see the screen. Her eyes widen. "Jeez, all those messages?"

"Yeah, I've replied to every one, and she always responds within seconds, see?" I worry my lower lip between my teeth, then tap the first number on my contact list. "Let me call her, one sec." After several rings, the call goes to voice mail. I hang up and try again, but there's no answer.

My fingers are starting to turn numb. Maybe her cell phone's not charged.

"Try the home phone," Krista says softly.

With a shaking hand, I tap out the number. After ringing for what seems like an eternity, it shuts off. Something's wrong.

"I need to get home." I fling the words over my shoulder and rush across the front lawn to the bike stand. A quick spin of the bike and I take off, weaving around people waiting for their rides and past cars double-parked along the road.

With one hand clenched on the handle, I hit the second number on the contact list, my boss at the deli and Auntie's best friend. *Pick up, Mr. Lee.*

After four rings, his deep voice comes on. *David Lee here. Leave a message and I'll return your call.*

"It's Tanvi." I blurt out. "I tried calling Auntie and she isn't answering. Call me. I'm on my way home."

Twenty minutes later, I skid around the corner to my block. My legs feel leaden and numb by the time I reach my gate. The bike clatters to the pavement behind me and I race across the yard to the front porch. The window curtains are drawn tight. That's new. Auntie always leaves the curtains open to catch as much natural light as possible.

I try the knob. Locked. We don't have a key hidden under a flowerpot or doormat, but I have one somewhere in my backpack. For the odd chance that Auntie wasn't home.

Or for emergencies. Shit.

Okay, calm down. Just find the damn key. I dig through my textbooks and finally, my fingers brush cool metal. I yank out the key and open the door.

A heavy silence fills the living room, broken by the steady ticking from the clock on the display cabinet. Auntie's favorite armchair is empty, her shawl draped over its back. A thick volume of the Bhagavad Gita rests on the coffee table, her prayer beads marking the spot where she stopped reading. Next to the book is an untouched plate of pancakes.

My stomach lurches. Her breakfast.

The scent of incense reaches me. I bolt toward the tiny alcove behind the dining room, which functions as a prayer room. Her blue slippers lie on the floor outside the alcove. Her bare feet protrude from the doorway.

My heart slams against my ribs.

Inside the prayer room, Auntie lies on the floor in front of the idols, curled up, her five-foot-nothing frame crumpled inside her robe.

I drop to the floor. "Auntie?" Oh, God. I shake her shoulder, then brush her hair from her face. "Auntie, please!" Is she breathing? Fragments of the CPR class from school float into my mind. I should check for breaths, for a pulse. But I can't remember how to start.

Call 911.

I reach for my phone with shaking hands, then notice a slight flicker of her eyelashes. "Auntie?" I turn her face toward me and pat her cheek. "Oh, please, please wake up."

She opens her eyes, stares vacantly around, before fixing on me. "Tanvi?"

Thank God. "What happened?" I hug her tight, and my throat aches from keeping my own sobs silent. "Are you okay?"

"Yeah, just . . . fainted, I think."

Around me, the smell of incense mixes with that of burning oil from the charred wick in the foot-high bronze lamp. The incense sticks are halfway burned through, dropping a small pile of ash in front of Lord Krishna. Wisps of smoke rise in the air from the burning wicks and reach the ceiling. The lower walls are now a dull gray from soot from the pujas for Mimi's safe return.

"We need to go get you checked out."

"No." Her voice is stronger, emphatic. "I'll be fine; just help me to the sofa."

An arm around her shoulders, I do so, fluffing the pillows so she can lean back.

A grating, choppy sound drifts in through the open door. Someone's pushing their vehicle to the limit on the road. A yellow Beetle stops hard in front of the gate, brakes squealing.

My boss jumps out, still wearing his green apron, with the words *Lee's Deli, the best in Orin* scrawled across the front. Six-foot-two, straggly salt-and-pepper hair falling across his wide forehead, Mr. Lee barrels down the front yard.

My boss never hurries; everything about him says *relax, the world's not going to end in the next fifteen minutes*, but I know the fierce love he carries for Auntie, Mimi, and me.

The ache in my throat eases, and I'm able to breathe.

Mr. Lee has been like a father to both Mimi and me. Me more than Mimi, probably because he saw the darkness I brought with me to Orin. He enrolled me into Tae Kwon Do after the first bullying incident—*so you can always stand up when they try and bring you down, don't take any crap from anyone*—and pays me way more than he should for working at his deli.

His anxious eyes find me. "Kiddo . . ."

"She fainted."

"David," Auntie says, lifting her hands toward him. "It was my fault; I hadn't eaten anything since morning, and now I've gone and scared both of you."

"Let's take you to the ER. Just a quick—"

"No." This time accompanied by a strong shake of her head. "I'm a nurse, remember? I know what needs medical attention, and this is just dehydration. I can move all my limbs, see?" She wiggles her toes and fingers, the corner of her lips curving. "So quit worrying, both of you."

It's the first time she's tried to smile since Mimi disappeared. I capture one of her hands between mine and press it to my face. "I'm going to get you something to drink."

"Thanks, honey."

Mr. Lee's broad shoulders relax. He lowers himself beside her, taking her hands in his. They've been best friends for nearly two decades. Platonic friends; I found that out when I tried setting them up. They had the best laugh ever that day.

In the kitchen, I add a pinch of salt and sugar to fresh-squeezed lemonade, and then watch as she downs the whole glass.

That's when I see the scrapbook lying open on the coffee table. Titled *Sisters Forever*, Auntie made it last month to celebrate eight years since I came to Orin.

The first photo in the scrapbook reflects the horror ingrained in my psyche. The one from Daddy's birthday, when Mimi hugged me while I stood still, arms limp by my sides, staring at the strawberry vanilla cake placed on the dining table.

Ten pages down is the photo from when I won a math competition in middle school. Auntie came to school that day and snapped a photo of me holding the certificate while

Mimi made a victory sign, grinning wide. I tried to smile for that photo, forced my lips to curve, but my eyes remained opaque.

I can beat you in math any day, Ramesh, Mom would joke. *You can tutor Tanvi in all the other stuff, but my daughter has my math skills, don't you, sweetheart?*

An engineering whiz in the making. Daddy's eyes twinkled as he leaned down and kissed Mom's forehead.

That was six months before Mom miscarried, before the trip to India, and . . .

Paper tears. I look down, find my fingers digging a hole in a page, and relax my grip. Auntie and Mr. Lee are talking quietly among themselves.

I turn the page. The next photo is from Gaston Beach. There are about twenty photos in this section, titled *Gaston Getaway*. Mimi and I in bathing suits splashing in the water, eating ice cream cones, sunbathing, burying each other in sand. The last one was taken a year ago on the beach, my smile was as wide as Mimi's, my face flushed with happiness as I hugged her tight, eyes no longer opaque.

Not totally, though. There's a shadow in my eyes even in this one, and I'm hugging Mimi tighter than she's hugging me. Like I knew I could lose her, too.

Families are so fragile. There one second, gone the next.

My hands are numb now. I can't feel the pages. I place the scrapbook on the coffee table gingerly, like it's made of glass.

". . . put more pressure on the police," Mr. Lee's saying, frowning at his phone screen.

Auntie wipes her eyes. "They keep saying she ran away and will return on her own. But she'd never do that—right, Tanvi? She'd never leave you. She loves you so much."

Loved. My throat is constricted, but I force out the words Auntie wants to hear. "She does, Auntie. Totally." Another lie to join the others I've told already. Another lie widening the distance I created between my aunt and me.

"I have a contact in the Detroit PD. I'll reach out to him, see if he can put some urgency into these guys." He pats her head. "We'll find Mimi, don't worry."

Upstairs in Mimi's room, I return to my pastime of watching the road.

I know my cousin. She had her gym bag packed for tryouts; she wanted that captaincy. She's never skipped school and had her schoolbag ready as well.

I lean my aching forehead against the cool glass of the windowpane, my fingers searching for the bump on the back of my head.

Something happened after Beth's party. Something that made her leave.

CHAPTER 7

"SERIOUSLY?" WITH HER lower lip between her teeth and hands clenched around the steering wheel, Krista is crazy maneuvering her car to try and fit into the only remaining spot at Gaston Beach. "You'd think they'd have more parking available at such a busy spot."

Busy is an understatement. The beach, located on the shore of Lake Huron, is packed. With a cloudless blue sky, full-on sun, and seventy-five-degree weather, it's a perfect summer day, probably one of our last ones with fall arriving. The view through the passenger window rivals a picture postcard: silver-tipped waves leave patterns of froth on glistening white sand.

It's the ideal setting for the beach party Lyla organized for the track team. But that's not why I'm here. An hour ago, Lyla posted on her social media page:

> **Y'all who're planning on skipping the party may want to rethink!! Heard a rumor that a certain missing someone might show themselves!!!**

My heart nearly stopped when I saw it. She had to be referring to Mimi. Krista replied immediately to my frantic message, and together we scoured the accounts of everyone in Mimi's circle. There was no mention of Mimi on any other posts, and Lyla ignored the messages Krista sent her. And our phone calls.

So I joined Krista and spent the drive from Orin at the edge of my seat, hands clenched in my lap. Determined to confront Lyla about her post. Was she talking about Mimi? Was she lying?

Or will Mimi really be at the party?

Hope pumps through my blood, but it's edged with fear—what if Lyla lied? And if she didn't and Mimi's going to be at the party, then why is she torturing us this way?

The car jerks, the seat belt automatically tightening across my chest. Krista's got the hood of her car sniffing the butt of a black sedan in front. Behind, there's maybe a half foot between us and a scowling pickup. "Wow. How'd you manage that?"

She grins, flexes her fingers tipped with green to match her spiky green hair. "Magic, baby."

My pulse scrambles at a frantic pace as I hurry ahead of Krista down a grassy shoulder toward the sand.

The party's in full swing. The sounds of crashing waves compete with laughter and shouted conversations. Someone's converted several large drawstring sports bags into containers stuffed with a gazillion snack boxes, and the coolers are over-flowing with cans of pop. There are people sprawled on blankets with the rest wading in the water or throwing a frisbee around.

No Mimi.

I catch my breath, fighting against a crushing grief. After steadying my voice, I say, "Let's split up and look. If you see Lyla, ask her."

Krista nods and starts down the sand toward a group clustered around a table while I turn left. Several yards down the beach this way, the sand gives way to pebbles and then boulders. When Auntie used to bring Mimi and me here for our weekend getaways, we preferred the rocks to the sand, spending our time skipping around or pretending there was treasure hidden under the stones. We'd make promises to return when we're older and dig for it and become super rich.

Tears spill down my face.

Our last trip here was a year ago. Months later, Mimi was betraying my secrets to Beth, showing her the candles she stole from my house. Reviving my nightmares of my mom, reviving the panic attacks, the cold sweat breaking out on my skin, and the overwhelming numbing crushing terror that took over my mind.

I can sense it returning now, my skin prickling, turning numb. My vision blurs as the scene shifts. The beach takes on an eerie gloom, the sky no longer blue, but blanketed with storm-dark clouds, the water choppy, seething with anger.

I close my eyes, forcing the fear down, letting the sun heat up my skin, reminding myself I'm on a beach with tons of people and there's no way my mom can hurt me.

When I open my eyes, my gaze falls on the girl sitting on the rocks. She wasn't there a few minutes ago.

A girl with thick black hair straight down her back, with bangs framing her round face.

Grace Warner, Mimi's ex-best friend. She's staring at me, but her eyes are blank, vacant, like she's looking right through me.

The hair on the back of my neck rises. *Dead eyes*, Mimi said. A vacant unblinking stare. It's so weird to think she used to be friendly, easygoing, probably the most upbeat of our trio. Grace, Mimi, and I were inseparable before Mimi friended Beth. We introduced Grace to everything Bollywood while she dragged us into gaming (which we sucked at) and K-pop.

I return Grace's stare, wondering when she started changing. Was it after Mimi returned from Beth's Halloween party and FaceTimed Grace and for two hours straight told us how Beth never left her side the entire time and listened to her every word? Even I got Beth-fatigued by the end, and I could sense Grace getting quieter and quieter during the call. That was the last call between the three of us I remember.

"Grace *Warner*?"

Abby wades out of the water. I'm about to reply when she looks over her shoulder at a girl floating several feet away. The sunlight glinting on the water obscures her features, but I recognize the long blond hair. Beth.

So Beth gets to hang out with her friends and enjoy the party. But Mimi was part of this clique, too, and it's been four days since she left, and I haven't heard any support from them for her. Except for Beth's recurring tear-filled posts about how much she misses Mimi, all while her supporters slam Mimi for "the drama" in the comments.

Beth begins swimming toward the sand, angling toward where I stand. I stiffen. She hasn't confronted me about the photo or the threat to sue that Krista sent her, which I found surprising, but maybe she's about to correct that error now. A second later though, I realize it's not Beth. This girl's face is thinner and she's shorter—I shade my eyes against the blinding sunlight.

It's Lyla.

She's dyed her brown hair blond and cut it in the exact style as Beth's.

Weird. She'd been Beth's best friend for years until they split last year, and I don't remember her ever copying Beth.

"What's she doing here?" Lyla wades out of the water onto the sand. "Don't tell me someone sent her an invite."

"Maybe she's obsessed with us now that Mimi's abandoned her," Abby says.

Grace must've heard them—their shrill voices carry well in the breeze, and they're not trying to be quiet—but she remains expressionless, her body still. If it weren't for the breeze swirling her hair, she could be mistaken for a statue. *An avenging angel.* The thought pops into my mind. Maybe a bit dramatic, but that's what she looks like as she watches us on the beach.

Then, in one fluid motion, she's up on her feet.

I stiffen, wondering if she's going to confront us. But about what?

My worry turns pointless because she walks across the rocks to where a faded sign reads WARNING! THIS AREA IS CLOSED OFF. DO NOT ENTER. She steps around the sign and disappears.

"Where'd she go?" Abby says, squinting down the beach.

"Probably back to whatever hole she came from," Lyla says. "What a ghoul."

Irritation crawls down my spine. "She has as much right to be here as you. And where's Mimi?"

Lyla flinches, then gapes at me. "Why the hell are you asking me? I did noth—"

"Your post." I snap. "You said she'd be here."

She grimaces. "I, um—it was just something I wrote, I didn't mean *her*."

"Of course you did." Lyla's been one of those frequent posters on Beth's page, supporting Beth and calling Mimi out for "going missing because she's dramatic and wanted attention" and in the next post saying Mimi was "a wimp" and "a backstabber for leaving Beth to face the consequences."

"You meant Mimi. So, where *is* she?" My voice rises over the waves splashing on the sand and the laughter and shouts from the others partying. Some of them are turning to look at us.

"Keep your voice down," Lyla hisses.

"Look," Abby says, casting a nervous glance toward Lyla. "We don't know anything about Mimi. Lyla just wrote that so people would want to come to the party because no one was really interested . . ." Her face falls when Lyla glares at her, and she takes a hurried step back. "Sorry."

"Way to go, Abby. Throw me to the lions, why don't you?" Lyla turns to me. "There you have it. Go away now."

My lower lip trembles and I catch it between my teeth. I

want to be angry, I want to tear into her, but all I feel is an overwhelming grief crashing over me like one of the waves. "Why did you do that? Do you know how cruel it is to say something like that? I came here hoping . . ."

Lyla's pencil-thin brows draw together in a scowl. "I'll delete it, okay? And why're you here anyway? I didn't invite you."

"Krista invited me."

She glances around her, then pitches her voice low. "You have a habit of crashing parties uninvited, don't you? I saw you at Beth's sneaking through the yard."

I flinch. And then it hits me.

"It was you." The words are out before I can think better of it.

"Me what?"

"You found my phone. You hacked into my account to send that photo around and get Mimi in trouble so she'd get kicked out of the team."

Lyla's eyes flicker. "You took the photo, not me."

Is that a confession?

Her face hardens. "You're just like your cousin, spying on people, finding stuff to use against them. If you're not careful, you'll end up just like her."

Abby nudges her hard, an urgent flash of warning in her eyes, and Lyla scowls, turning away from me.

"What do you mean by that?" I catch the glance between them. "Lyla, do you know where Mimi is?"

Abby steps between Lyla and me. "You don't belong here, Tanvi. Why don't you go find Grace, since you care so much about her?"

I step around her and plant myself in front of Lyla. "No, I'm not leaving until you tell me what you meant by that."

"Why're you acting so destroyed, anyway?" Lyla shakes away Abby's restraining hand and gets in my face. "Everyone knows you hate Mimi."

"I do not!"

"That's why you took that photo. So you could chase her away. You wanted what Mimi had, what you didn't have. A family, a house, a mom. She was scared of you, *freak*."

Her words feel like an iron fist on my chest. The pain wraps around my lungs until I can't breathe.

A triumphant gleam lights Lyla's eyes, and she strides away. Abby opens her mouth, then closes it and follows Lyla.

Scared of me?

She's just making stuff up. Mimi wasn't scared of me; she knew I loved her.

I'm not family. I don't want to be your family. Not with that psycho blood you carry in your veins.

Beth's words, coming from Mimi's mouth. But the words slip like ice into my blood until I'm shivering.

I turn away from the beach and start toward the rocks.

The sand gets grittier under my sandals, then becomes pebbly and hard and then slick stone. I step past the danger sign beyond which Grace had disappeared, past pools left by the waves, bottomless abysses of murky water, trapped between stone circles glinting in the sunlight.

Something sticks out from a rocky crevice. A fragment of faded red cloth.

I reach down and tug on it, pulling out a tattered part of a moldy dress. A black purse crusted with sand tumbles out after. It's waterlogged, ripped open like a fish's belly, filled with algae and dirt and a laminated card.

When I wipe off the mud, Mimi's face smiles back at me from her driver's license.

CHAPTER 8

FLICKERING BLUE AND white lights reflect off the sand. They reflect off the dark blue uniforms of the cops and the yellow tape surrounding the pile of rocks where I found Mimi's discarded dress and purse. And the curious faces of beachgoers straining against the cordoning tape, ignoring the shouts from a cop to back off. Lyla's there, and Greg, and other familiar faces, all slack-jawed, avid eyes, phones out.

"Back away from the crime scene, please," the cop yells.

The crime scene.

God, I feel so cold. The numbness wraps around my chest and seeps into my bones, though the sun shines overhead, a blazing ball of heat. Several feet away, the waves push onto the rocks, splintering into a million shards against jagged granite, but all I hear is a weird whooshing, like someone's pushed me underwater.

Another car pulls to a screeching halt next to the row of cop cars blocking the road. Someone in protective gear gets out and walks to the rocks. They climb up just like I did, one step after the next, getting closer to . . .

Someone screams Mimi's name repeatedly; it seems to be me, my own voice, but my throat's closed to a pinhole.

Krista pulls me in for a hug scented with lake water. But her hug doesn't stop the steady chattering filling my ears, like someone going crazy on a keyboard. It's my teeth. My bones, rattling wildly.

Was it just minutes ago that I climbed those rocks?

If only I hadn't done that. I wouldn't have seen what I did.

My chest hurts like someone's slit it open with a blunt knife.

Krista produces a blanket from somewhere and wraps it around me. "Let's go sit in the car."

People surround me, a blur of bodies, closing in. Lyla's staring at the rocks, her irises almost wiping out the white of her eyes.

I hug my knees tight, rocking back and forth, trying to shut out the lights. Blue, white piercing through my eyelids. The sounds are pressing in, too, ripping through my eardrums. Cops shouting, the hum of conversations from the audience. The hum of excitement. They're all so excited, craning their necks to see beyond the press of cops. Morbid curiosity in their wide eyes, hoping for a glimpse.

Mimi.

I drop my head on my knees and rock harder.

"Tanvi!" shouts a high, worried voice. My heart leaps.

Mr. Lee lumbers across the sand, arms outstretched. The tears come then, like a dam let loose. I'm on my feet and enveloped in his hug. His warmth seeps through and reaches my bones. The numbness eases and on its heels comes a terrible grief. "I want her to come home now."

He inhales deeply, rolling his shoulders like he's shifting a huge weight. "I know, kiddo. I know."

"We need to search for her." I grab his arm, tugging him toward the rocks, but he stays put. "We can't leave her. She needs us."

Mr. Lee leans down and looks me in the eye, and I see the expression. The helplessness carving lines of misery into his face.

In the distance, the guy in protective gear is putting something into plastic bags.

They're bagging Mimi's dress.

"I'm going to talk to them, okay?" Mr. Lee says. "I'll find out more. But I think you need to go home."

"No . . ."

"Your aunt will want you home when they come to talk to her, kiddo." His eyes glitter with tears. "She'll need you with her."

My heart breaks again. I remember how she fainted in the prayer room, the fear I felt when she didn't respond to my voice initially. She's living off hope right now, believing Mimi left of her own free will.

But now . . .

The hopelessness in Mr. Lee's eyes, in Krista's slumped shoulders, the way they're carefully avoiding looking at the rocks.

"Get to your aunt before they get to her," Mr. Lee says before turning toward the closest cop.

And so, I let Krista lead me away from the rocks, focusing on putting one foot in front of the next, though tears keep blurring my vision.

"Shit," Krista says.

Lyla sits straight-backed on a bench at the edge of the sand. Shoulders square, chin up, her posture regal. And it strikes me that she has truly changed. Not just in her appearance. She's adopted Beth's posture and body language. No longer slouching, no longer the shadow next to Beth or Mimi. No longer the second-in-command to Mimi in the track team, or Beth's wingman and wannabe queen bee.

She sits there like she owns the place.

She's the queen.

Her expression shifts. It's a minute change, a slight tilt of her lips, a tiny gleam in her eyes, a spark of life. She stands and walks away down the beach before I can really register it.

But for a second, I thought I glimpsed gloating triumph in those eyes.

IT'S BEEN TWENTY-FOUR hours since I found Mimi's dress and purse on Gaston Beach. And every time hope flares in my heart—hope that she deliberately left it there, a red herring, to make it seem like she's dead, so we'll stop searching for her—I see the man in white overalls sliding her purse into an evidence bag.

I see the despairing acceptance in Mr. Lee's eyes.

I see Auntie slipping deeper and deeper into silence. I haven't left her side, staying with her while she watched the door, waiting for the bell to ring with news—any news—from the cops.

She's sleeping on the sofa next to the door with the phone clutched in her hand while I sit on the floor next to her, my body dead tired but my eyes wide awake and wired as I scroll through my phone for anything to do with Mimi.

The last post from Beth was before the beach party. It's a picture of a heart sign drawn around her sisters bracelet with their names on it. Underneath it, she's written, **Mimi, I forgive you, please come home.** The replies were all toxic versions of calling Mimi a narc, a dopehead, a traitor for trapping her best friend.

But that was before the beach party. Before her clothes were found on the rocks.

There've been several replies to Beth's post since.

@shitisreal: Her dress was covered in stuff like it's been there for a few days.

@corey_prince: Man, someone killed her there & dumped her in the water.

@abbylovescake: I saw her leave Beth's party with her bf, guys! I bet it was him!!

@iambeth: stop it!! We don't know that for certain, she may still be okay.

@corey_prince: I saw them dragging the water. she's gone.

@shitisreal: girl, why the hell r u crying for her?? after all that crap???

@iambeth: because she was my friend. 💔💔💔💔 💔💔💔

@i_read_books: Bodies dumped in the waves can be lost forever.

They all think Mimi's gone. Even Beth.

I drop my phone and pace the floor.

She can't be gone. She can't. How can someone so alive be gone?

I wrap my arms around my shaking body, feeling again the way she used to hug me whenever I was sad or scared or hurting. Embedded in my palm is the memory of her grip as she walked me into school on my first day, making her nine-year-old frame larger to shield me. I can still hear her yell, *That's my cousin you're bullying, jerk*, as she punched the guy who shoved me.

Above me, the blue jay Mimi painted on the ceiling perches at the edge of a twig, wings spread wide. The colors are vibrant, powerful, though it has been years. I can still see her, standing on a ladder, carefully edging the bird's feathers, the tip of her tongue caught between her teeth, as she did when she focused on something.

She was supposed to be that bird. Perched and ready to take off, to fly free with no restraints. Orin was too small for her. Maybe *I* was too small for her. She wanted so much more.

And she had it all planned out. Methodical, organized, so nothing would go wrong.

In a cabinet downstairs are all the trophies she accumulated over the years in academics and track. But she was proud of her track awards the most, ecstatic after she won an event in eighth grade. That was when she told me about her dad being an athlete and how he couldn't go to college due to finances. *But I'll make it, T. I'll run in college, and I'll get a scholarship so Mom won't have to worry.*

My phone pings. It's the notification I set for any new information on Mimi. A breaking news alert from *Orin Daily News* pops up on the screen.

There has been a development in the search for the teen runaway from Orin. A dress and purse positively identified as belonging to Lakshmi (Mimi) Taylor was found on Gaston Beach yesterday afternoon, leading the authorities to open a criminal investigation into the teen's disappearance. We reached out to Lieutenant Williams, the lead investigator at Orin PD, for comment on the status of the investigation. Does this mean diminished hope of finding the teen alive? The lieutenant refused to comment, but a source, who preferred to be anonymous due to the ongoing investigation, told us that the situation is indeed grim. The state of the clothes indicates they had been in the water for most if not all of the five days since Mimi disappeared, and the chance of the teen being found alive has shrunk significantly. Lieutenant Williams has requested that anyone who has information about Mimi Taylor's disappearance should reach out to Orin PD immediately.

My throat feels raw with tears—and rage. The cops could've taken this seriously a lot earlier, like when Auntie and I went to them the day Mimi vanished. Instead, that young cop ignored us, even laughed us off. I told him Mimi couldn't have run away due to the photo. I told him I saw her scarf lying on her bedroom floor, meaning she changed her clothes and left.

Hold on. She didn't change.

The red dress she wore to Beth's party is the same one I found on Gaston Beach. She left behind the scarf, though.

Or did she?

Her scarf was clean when it was wrapped around her neck that night five days ago, the silver threads glinting in the hall-way light as she stood at my bedroom door. This was after she returned from Beth's party.

Then I heard the click of heels on wooden floorboards. She was downstairs, heading across the living room for the front door.

Click, click. I remember the haste in her steps. I lean into the sound, praying it'll lead me, show me a path through the fog.

Her footsteps stopped.

Squeak. And then a thud.

That's new. What was that sound?

The front door. The hinges squeak when it's opened, and it always thuds against the wall; there's a dent in the plaster where the knob hits it.

So she opened the door. But the sound was cut short by a thundering roar.

The roar drowned out her words. *Don't you dare . . .*

Then I can't hear anything else.

But I can see her. She's standing at the front door, silhouetted against the night, which was black as the scarf around her neck.

She took the scarf with her. That thought settles in my chest like a heavy rock. Because if she left with the scarf, clean—then how did it land in her room, crusted with damp mud?

I assumed it got muddy the same way my clothes did, from the dirt in the hedge maze. But my clothes were clean when I returned from Beth's place.

Which means my clothes got muddy afterwards.

I feel the bump on the back of my skull. It's still tender but has decreased to the size of a dime, and the waves of nausea and pain aren't as blinding. The bruise on my right forearm has faded to a yellowish tinge, but the ones on my thighs are still swollen and tender. I assumed all my injuries were from the sharp branches in the hedge maze at Beth's.

But what if they weren't?

Did I follow Mimi out of the house?

I try willing a memory out of the fog clouding my brain. But the fog doesn't comply. It swirls, thickening, darkening, blocking the image.

Blocking out the sounds.

Why can't I remember?

Something's wrong. Like, terribly wrong.

My lips turn numb and prickly, then panic starts to beat in my chest like the wings of a trapped bird.

I stand up, energy coursing through my body that I'm not sure what to do with. I need to tell the cops all this. About the scarf, my injuries, the mud-stained clothes. After making sure Auntie's still asleep, I tiptoe to the kitchen and call the station.

"Officer Laney here, how can I help you?" a nasal tone answers.

Shit, it's the young cop we talked to at the station that morning Mimi left. My jaw tightens. "Hi, this's Tanvi Nair. Could I talk to Lieutenant Williams, please? It's about . . ." I steady my voice when it catches. "About my cousin, Mimi Taylor. I have some information for him."

His voice sharpens. "You can give it to me."

I'd rather not. "Sorry, but could I speak to him directly?"

"No, you may not. He's busy."

I grit my teeth, knowing I can't afford to show my anger or my distrust. "Something happened that night after Mimi returned from Beth's party that the lieutenant needs to know about. Please."

"You can either tell me what you know, or we can forget the whole thing."

I recount everything, starting with hearing Mimi return through the window in her room, including my injuries and how I thought they came from the hedge maze at Beth's, the mud-stained scarf, my memory being foggy.

He sighs. "Anything else? Is there a reason you didn't share any of this *important stuff* the first time?"

"I, um, I didn't remember until later—"

"Thank you, miss. I'll give the lieutenant your message." The line dead-ends.

God, what a moron. Did he even bother to listen?

My breath shudders. I know I should stop scrolling through my phone for any more news about Mimi. I definitely know I shouldn't scroll my social feeds when I run out of news. But I do anyway, and something drives me to click on a video titled *My version of #MimiTaylor*.

A brunette with a narrow face and a receding chin appears. I recognize her from Beth's entourage during freshman orientation, but I've never interacted with her before.

She begins to speed through a monologue, eyes glinting.

"Hey everyone, I'm Melissa, welcome to my first post. I managed to get all the details so I can fill y'all in. It all started with a photo and a girl backstabbing her cousin out of greed and jealousy and has now ended with the cousin's stuff washed onto a beach. And a missing body. Stay with me, friends, while—"

I shut off the video and curl up on the floor, but not before seeing it has like over 10K views. Did she even *know* Mimi?

My hands clench around Mimi's scarf, the scent of her vanilla perfume rising over the hand soap I used to wash it.

CHAPTER 9

AFTER ANOTHER NIGHT of fitful sleep, I wake up to sunlight and my phone beside me. There's been no calls from the police station about the information I gave Officer Laney. It must mean something, so why hasn't Lieutenant Williams called me back?

What if Laney thought it was nothing and didn't give my message to the lieutenant?

Mimi's scarf remains clutched in my hand. I press it to my face. I miss her so much. I miss that she won't come tearing through that front door, sweating and grimy and exultant, yelling about how she beat the boys' track team in a dare in freshman year. Or flopping on my bed to tell me how she'd gotten to talk to the UMich track coach, and how she had a chance if she improved her times. *Then Grace and you and me, we'll all be in Ann Arbor!*

Or struggling to straighten my thick black curls into a silky waterfall like her hair, though I told her I liked mine natural.

My hand steals to my hair, to the snarls I haven't bothered brushing out since Mimi left. She won't be returning to style my hair. She won't be returning to give me a chance to bridge the chasm that split us apart.

The sound of voices comes from downstairs. The cops? I jump out of bed and race down the stairs, then stop dead.

Beth sits next to Auntie on the couch. A fruit basket wrapped with condolence ribbons rests on the coffee table.

Shit, no. I clench my hands. This girl here is the last thing I need right now.

Auntie's eyes are closed, her face creased with new lines of grief in the two days since Mimi's clothes were found on Gaston Beach.

I take a step toward her but stop when Beth's eyes lift, zero in on me, and narrow. Something dark shadows the blue irises. Her arms tighten, and she angles her body, curving her shoulders around Auntie and tucking Auntie's head under her chin.

She's excluding me, as if only she and Auntie have shared grief.

A shiver runs down my spine, a memory. I drop my gaze to my clenched fists, feeling Mimi's hand, clammy with excitement, in mine. Her voice throbbed with that same excitement when we went past the wrought-iron gates barricading Beth's mansion and she told me how much she wanted to be Beth, even for a day. I knew she craved something else. Something that made her paint that blue jay on the ceiling of her room.

Something that made her cut me out of her life so she could keep Beth.

"Mimi wouldn't want you to feel sad, Mrs. Taylor," Beth says. "All her life she'd only wanted to keep you happy, to protect you, to be strong for you." Auntie shudders, and Beth pats her shoulder. "I'm here now. I'll watch out for you because Mimi would want that. Because Mimi was more than a friend to me; she was my sister."

I flinch. Beth's hand stills, her gaze slides for an instant toward me, and then she continues patting Auntie's hands.

My sister.

Within weeks of that Halloween party, Mimi and Beth were calling each other sisters, and Grace came to me sobbing after Mimi refused to sit with her for lunch for the first time since middle school. A day later, Mimi stopped biking home with Grace and me and instead opted for a ride in Beth's Porsche.

"I'll always be here for you." Beth's still talking, a trace of impatience in her voice. Probably because Auntie hasn't responded to her and instead remains still, eyes closed, tears slipping past her lashes. "Please think of me as family, Mrs. Taylor."

No. Not her. Not this girl. I unglue my feet from the floor and take another step toward them. "Auntie." My voice is a croak, my throat stiff from tears.

Auntie's eyes snap open. Then she straightens and lifts her hands toward me, the movement dislodging Beth's hold. Beth's hands clench, her eyes lower to the floor but not before I catch the sudden flint hardening them.

I kneel in front of Auntie and melt into her embrace as she hugs me tight. She begins sobbing again, tears soaking into the sleeves of my pajama shirt, my own tears flowing in response. Then her arms relax, and she wipes the tears from my face before kissing me on the forehead. "That dress on the beach, it's not Mimi's, honey. That police officer can say what he wants; he can say that Mimi's gone. But she's not. I know it in my heart. She will return home."

A heavy weight presses hard on my heart. She's still in denial.

Then over her shoulder I catch Beth's stare. "I'm sure the cops will find out what happened to Mimi, Mrs. Taylor," she says, her gaze locked on me. "And if *someone* is hiding information on what happened to her, they'll be found out for certain."

She's looking at me like *I'm* hiding information. But I didn't hide . . . Is she talking about my not remembering?

Blood leaves my face in a rush. She couldn't have known, not unless Officer Laney told her, and he wouldn't have.

Would he?

She raises her brow a fraction, like she's waiting for me to say something.

Ice slithers into my veins, and I can't look away, hating this feeling of being trapped, hating how she can reduce me to mindless terror, and how she knows it judging from the gleam in her eyes. Then her face smooths out and she turns to Auntie with a gentle smile before reaching for the *Sisters Forever* scrapbook. "This is so beautiful, Mrs. Taylor." Her voice is soft, reverent. "Did you make this?"

Auntie nods, her arms still around me.

"I wish I had something like this, memories of my childhood stored so beautifully. But my parents weren't like you. They couldn't get rid of me fast enough."

"Oh, honey." Auntie grasps Beth's hands between her own. "I'm sure that's not true."

Now I'm the one displaced. I get up from where I'd been kneeling in front of Auntie and move over to a chair. Over Auntie's shoulder, I catch the same satisfied gleam in Beth's eyes before she lowers them. Her lower lip trembles. "It is, Mrs. Taylor. I've often envied what you and Mimi had. That type of love, not everyone has it."

"But your mom?"

"She left when I was in middle school. I haven't seen or heard from her since. I'm sure she's forgotten that I exist."

Did Mimi tell me anything about Beth's mom? All I remember is my cousin gushing over how perfect Beth was. Though once—after I called Beth shallow—Mimi blew up on me and said no one ever understood the stuff Beth had been through.

Beth grips Auntie's hands like they're a lifeline, and her eyes, always either brittle hard or cool and reserved, are now liquid soft. "And you know my dad. Even before the factory closed, he barely knew I existed. But now he's withdrawn into his wing of the house. I didn't have anyone who was there for me until Mimi became my best friend."

I almost snort. Did Lyla not count? And if so, why is this her first visit here to Mimi's house? I clench my hands, my knuckles turning bloodless. Grace used to practically live here when she was friends with Mimi, but Beth never came over.

"Oh, child." Auntie throws her arms open and Beth melts into them.

Okay, I'm going to throw up. I jump to my feet and stride over to the window.

After they hug, Auntie turns to the photo on the scrapbook page—the strawberry vanilla cake—and she's smiling through her tears like I am. "My Mimi. So strong. I asked her to be Tanvi's big sister, honey, to protect her. And she did."

Beth glances at me, scorn flattening her lips. The expression is gone in an instant, her voice sympathetic as she says, "Mimi always put family first, even before herself. Whenever she hung out with me, she talked about Tanvi. She didn't want anything bad happening to her little cousin ever again."

I can destroy Beth's lie with one stroke. All I need to do is tell Auntie about the candles Mimi stole and how Beth recorded my meltdown and threatened to release the video. But it would shatter Auntie. So I keep my mouth shut and meet Beth's stare without averting my burning eyes.

"It was Grace and Mimi watching out for Tanvi," Auntie says, hiccupping through her sobs, then turns the scrapbook page to a photo of Mimi, Grace, and me at the waterfall in the woods. We're holding up victory signs, pouting at the camera, eyes dancing. "You must know Grace; she was Mimi's best friend. I thought she'd come by like you did, or at least call . . ."

Beth's fingers tighten around the photo, and for a second it feels like she's going to rip it out. Then she closes the book and stands. "I think I'll take my leave, Mrs. Taylor. I'm so sorry for . . ." She seems to choke up. "For everything." After hugging Auntie, she turns to me. "A quick word?"

Once we're outside on the front porch, she turns to me. Any previous softness wiped clean from her face, her eyes are back to cold blue and assessing. "You got your aunt convinced you loved Mimi, but you put her through hell, didn't you? She suffered so much because of you. She told me everything."

What's she talking about? "Suffered?"

"She couldn't trust you, not with her deepest feelings, because she *knew* you'd rat her out to her mom."

"I'd never do that." My jaw clenches. "Mimi could tell me anything; she knew that."

"Then why did she come looking for me? For my friendship?" Her lips curl. She reaches into her jacket pocket and brings out a small journal bound with brown leather wrap. On the cover are the words *Mimi Taylor*.

My mouth dries. Mimi's journal? But she never kept them; she said she found the whole "writing down your emotions" thing so boring. I reach for the book, but Beth slips it back into her pocket. "What's that?"

"Of course, you wouldn't know. It's not like Mimi could confide in you or anything, could she? This is all she had."

I remember stopping outside Mimi's room one night. She was writing something in a small book about the size of this one. I caught the glint of tears in her eyes, but before I could say a word, she snapped, *Don't you ever sneak up on me like that*, and slammed the door shut.

Was it this journal she didn't want me to see? "Why're you keeping Mimi's stuff? You have no right—"

"She gave it to me! Because she knew she couldn't trust you not to read it." A tic develops in the corner of her jaw. "Do you know how sick she was of constantly having to be strong for you, of constantly being reminded by her mom that she had no worth other than as your *protector*?"

My throat tightens. "That's not true." Beth's lying, she has to be. True, Auntie did tell Mimi to be my big sister, but Mimi liked being my protector, standing up to my bullies on her own. She never mentioned being tired of it.

But I didn't ask her, either. I didn't ask her how she felt being the strong one in our relationship. I leaned on her without a second thought.

Is that why she went looking for Beth? To find someone she could lean on?

Is that why she pushed me away afterward?

Beth's watching me. She's seen the way I'm shaking, and the gleam in her eyes makes me sick.

"She knew what you were." Beth's still talking, her words stinging like icepicks on my flesh. "How much you wanted her gone."

"I didn't . . ."

"That's why you wrote those threatening notes. So you could have her home, her mom, all to yourself."

My muscles turn to stone. I stiffen.

She gasps. "I knew it! I knew it was you who wrote them."

"What? No!" Did she read my instinctive reaction as a sign of guilt?

She takes a step toward me. "You left them in her locker so she'd think someone in school did it. But she knew it was you all along. Her *family*." Her voice is tinged with disgust. "What do you think will happen once I tell the cops about them?"

I fall back, away from her, away from that awful knowing smile. A wave, and she's gone, her blue Porsche gliding down the road until it vanishes around the corner.

I fly upstairs to Mimi's room and rummage through her desk, her backpack, her books, but find nothing.

A cardboard box is stuck under the lowest shelf in her closet. I drag it out. It contains everything from Mimi's locker: folders and textbooks, and a crumped wad of paper.

I smooth it out. The letters are printed and in all caps.

YOU WILL PAY WITH YOUR LIFE.

My legs turn numb, and I drop down on the bed.

So Beth was telling the truth about Mimi receiving threatening letters. God, how could my cousin believe this was me? How could she think I'd do this?

I didn't know she was writing her journal when she shut the door on me that day. Or even think of searching for any journals. Why would I when I thought she loathed keeping them?

You don't get it, T, she told me when I asked her why she never talked to me anymore.

Grief washes through me. I wish I knew what she was going through. I could've talked to her, convinced her that I loved her, that she could lean on me, too.

But I did love her. And that's the truth. So whatever Beth might say, I know I'd never threaten Mimi. I'd never write this note.

Whoever wrote this hated Mimi.

They hated her enough to want her dead.

I remember Grace staring at Mimi and Beth as they drove off after school, her face hard. *Mimi's gone, T. She betrayed us. She'd rather be part of the popular crowd, hanging out with the rich kids. She doesn't have time for us anymore.*

Mimi wouldn't do that, I said.

She's changed, and you better accept it fast.

Grace never hung out with me after that, and days later, they found Mimi's stolen laptop in her backpack. She turned pariah after that, withdrawing into herself, but always watching Mimi—at school, at sports events.

Following her down the school halls.

Her locker was just a few doors from Mimi's.

Could it be Grace who wrote this note?

CHAPTER 10

A FAINT CHILL hangs in the afternoon air. I rub the goose-bumps from my arms, then continue pedaling.

I've been searching for Grace for an hour. I checked her apartment, combed through downtown Orin, and now am biking toward the strip mall on the outskirts of Orin right next to the highway exit. It used to be our favorite haunt. We'd go there after school or on the weekends, sometimes to buy stuff for cheap, but mostly just to chill. Everything has changed, but maybe—hopefully—not that. Maybe Grace misses it just as much as I do.

The mall consists of only four stores, the largest of which is a sprawling dollar store, with a diner, an arcade, and a pharmacy next to it. The parking lot has a few cars, a collection of bikes—and there's a small red scooter with pink handles parked in front of the dollar store.

I don't need to see the GW stamped on the side to know that's Grace's scooter. Her dad bought it for her in seventh grade, and it became our favorite mode of transportation; we'd all pile on the scooter and Grace would give us a ride wherever we needed to go until Auntie forbade it. I remember Mimi teasing her last year when we found her trying to oil the squeak out of the handlebars, telling Grace it was time to get rid of that rust bucket.

Shh, Grace said. *It'll hear ya. Besides, you don't get rid of things you love after they get old.*

I push the door of the dollar store open. The cashier, a

thin guy with straggly brown hair, barely glances at me before returning to whatever's on his phone screen.

Tall, overflowing shelves line the room. You can get anything here, from cheap jewelry and accessories to school supplies and home appliances. I remember spending hours walking the aisles with Mimi and Grace, rooting around for stuff before heading to the diner in the back for subs and pop.

The muffled hum of voices and laughter fills the place, with an occasional rattle from the pipes along the walls. I grab a basket and head for the first aisle. A couple of preteens lie on the floor, their heads buried in a comic book. In the next aisle is an old man, stooped over a cart, mumbling to himself. The aisle next to it is empty.

Grace's scooter's right outside; she must be in here somewhere.

The tingling in the back of my neck is the first sign that I'm being watched. I glance behind me and catch a blur of movement. I hurry down, then stop dead.

Grace stands in front of me. A gray cap shadows her face, hiding her expression, but her eyes are wide and fixed on me. She holds herself still, hands clenched at her sides.

I stare at her, my heart thundering in my throat. The change in her since she quit being Mimi's friend still hits me hard. Those cold gray eyes used to be always warm, always kind, never mad or impatient with me for tagging along with her and Mimi. The one time she unintentionally hurt me—when I fell off a swing she was pushing—she cried more than I did.

But now I sense something dark and ominous in her stance. It reminds me of the way she watched me from the rocks on Gaston Beach.

The same rocks where I later found Mimi's clothes and purse.

I slip my hand into my jeans pocket, close my trembling fingers around the crumpled note I found in Mimi's closet.

Her eyes drop to the paper in my hand, to the printed letters dark against the white background. She draws in a quick breath. "How did you get that?"

Not *Hi, what is that*, or *I have no idea what you're holding*. She knows about this note. "I found it with the things from Mimi's locker."

"You think I wrote it?"

"Did you?"

She turns and starts to walk away.

I slip around and block her path. "I want to know the truth, Grace."

"The truth?" She lifts her head, the fluorescent lighting falling on the glint in her eyes. "That's rich coming from you."

"What do you mean?"

She's silent, a muscle twitching in the corner of her mouth. "What do you want from me, Tanvi?"

So many things. I want to know why she walked away from me when I confronted her about Mimi's laptop. She could've explained why she stole it; I wanted to hear her side of the story. Instead, she cut me off, just like Mimi did. I swallow the lump in my throat. "Why did you threaten Mimi? Why did you hate her so much?"

"Me? If you're looking for people who hated Mimi, look in the mirror."

Beth said something similar. My lips turn numb. "I didn't hate Mimi. How could you say that?"

She falls silent again. My heartbeat counts out the space before she speaks again, her voice sounding faraway. "Hate is such a weird thing. Often when people use the word hate, they mean love. But you know that, don't you? You loved Mimi, but then I heard the story you told the cops, that you woke up and found Mimi gone."

Story? And how'd she know what I told the cops? "It wasn't

a story." It was though, wasn't it? Because I did see Mimi after she returned from Beth's party.

She tilts her head. "You slept through all that rain?"

Rain? I frown.

"It was raining that night. We had a thunderstorm."

I stare at her, my stomach plummeting. Oh my God. That's true. That was the thundering sound I remembered hearing right after the clicking sound of Mimi's heels and after the squeak of the front door opening. It was the rain silhouetting Mimi when she stood at the front door. I could barely hear my own voice though I was shouting.

Mimi, don't!

I have to. Don't you dare . . . The sudden gust of wind and the thundering sound of rain drowned out her words.

I can see the scene so clearly. How could I have forgotten that? What's wrong with me?

"Why didn't you tell the cops the truth, Tanvi?"

Ice bleeds into my veins. "What do you mean? I told them everything; *they* chose to believe Mimi ran away because of the photo." Officer Laney has all my information, but it's been radio silence from him or the cops since.

She raises a brow. "You told them everything?"

"Yes!" The force of my response sends a sharp clamp of pain up the back of my skull. Instinctively, I reach for the lump. Though it's down to less than a dime now, it still throbs, pulsating like a live thing under my fingers.

"So now you're a liar, too. I thought I knew you, Tanvi."

My mouth dries to dust. "I never hated Mimi. Not even when she cut me off for Beth, not even when she said all those mean things, not even when she . . ." *betrayed my secrets about Mom to Beth and lit those candles.* "And why're you asking me these questions? It's you who left weird, threatening notes in her locker."

Her eyes flicker, then she pulls her cap down, shadowing her expression. "If that's what you believe, I can't help you, Tanvi. Maybe you should have told the cops what really happened the night Mimi vanished."

GRACE'S WORDS KEEP echoing in my mind, mingling with Auntie's gentle snoring. She's asleep next to me on her bed, the residue of tear tracks on her face.

Grace thinks I lied to the cops. But I told them everything I remembered. Not initially, but later when I called Laney back. Except for the rain. I didn't know that odd drumming sound was the rain until Grace reminded me.

And now I can see the heavy sheets of water soaking Mimi as she raced out of the house. It soaked her red dress and black scarf. And that must be how my own clothes got damp and mud-stained. I must've followed her out.

But what happened afterward? Why can't I remember more?

Grace made it seem like I *knew* what happened that night. Why would she say that unless she knows something herself?

She wasn't surprised or shocked when she saw the threatening note. And then there was that stuff she said about hate and love being the same. Maybe her love for Mimi turned to hate when Mimi broke up with her for Beth.

She has a motive.

As do the others who hated Mimi: Lyla, Greg . . .

And they were all there at Beth's party.

Did one of them follow Mimi home that night?

The sounds I heard that night, the creak and the thud—I thought it was Mimi entering her room through the window. But what if they were made by whoever followed her home from the party?

Hold on. There was a post I'd seen on Beth's profile . . . something about Mimi leaving the party.

Moving as quietly as possible so as not to wake up Auntie, I reach for my phone on the nightstand.

Yes, there it is. Abby replying to Beth's post about missing Mimi.

@abbylovescake: I saw her leave Beth's party with her bf, guys! I bet it was him!!

I hadn't realized its significance earlier, but if this is true and James and Mimi left Beth's place together, then it means he lied when he told the cops he hadn't seen Mimi the day she vanished.

Why lie unless you have something to hide?

From Mimi's room, I retrieve the collage Mimi made of the two of them.

Her expression in all the photos contrasts starkly to how she regarded him in middle school. She was friendly and kind to him then while he worshipped the ground she walked on. But now the feelings seem reversed. There's love in Mimi's eyes while his expression is shuttered, cloudy, like he's holding himself back even when he hugs her. That naked love he used to regard her with in middle school is missing. But so is the beaten, bullied, cowed posture he had, cringing when anyone except Mimi approached him. Instead, he's developed a defiance in the steady stare of his hazel eyes, the lift of his chin. Like he wants to take on the world.

Was it love that made him return to her life? Or did he have an ulterior motive?

My phone pings, and the screen lights up with a text. It's from Mr. Lee.

Hey kiddo, Lieutenant Williams from Orin PD wants to

talk to you. They just want to clarify a few points, nothing to worry. We'll set up a time.

My heart stops.

Clarify a few points.

Like in questioning me?

Dots appear, then, **No, not at all. He said it was just a casual talk.**

I doubt it. **Have they found anything new?**

No. They're still looking.

I start to type **Is there a chance**, but my fingers tremble and I can't continue with my question—Is there a chance, even the teensiest one, that they'll find Mimi alive?

But he seems to have guessed what I wanted to ask. **Sorry, kiddo. The lieutenant talked to your aunt and me. They think she drowned in the lake probably that night or by the next morning.**

My tremors worsen until my entire body's shaking. When Beth was here earlier, Auntie said the police officer told her Mimi was gone. She must've been talking about the lieutenant.

Are you okay?

Yes. I'll be fine, I add because I can sense him watching the text box, worried, his heart aching like mine.

An article in the *Orin Daily* confirms Mr. Lee's words.

Hopes dim further of finding the missing teen from Orin alive. According to a source connected to the investigation who spoke on condition of anonymity, the condition of the clothes indicates they were stuck under the rocks on Gaston Beach for several days. The assumption steadily gaining ground is that the teen drowned in the lake within hours after going missing, and her clothes and her personal belongings ended up on the rocks while the body was washed away. Per the source, the investigation is now in a "recovery phase," indicating they're focusing on finding the body.

As for the main investigator, Lieutenant Williams remains tight-lipped beyond saying "some new evidence has come to light that this is not just a runaway teenager who had an unfortunate accident. We are working diligently toward uncovering the truth and determining any possibility of foul play."

New evidence. Could that be the information I gave Officer Laney? But all I told him was about my bruises from the hedges in Beth's yard and how I didn't have a clear memory of Mimi leaving since I was half asleep at that time.

And I told him about Mimi's mud-stained scarf. She was wearing that scarf—then clean—when I saw her walk out of the front door.

The lieutenant will want to know how it landed back in her room.

And I'll have no answers to give him.

He'll want to know what happened after I followed Mimi out into the rain. Did I do something to her? Something that caused her disappearance?

What if he doesn't believe that my bruises and the bump on my head came from the hedges in Beth's yard?

What if I see that look in his eyes? The look the Detroit cops gave Auntie when she was trying to tell them my mom couldn't have killed Daddy? No one looking at our family photo displayed all over the news, at the beautiful dark-haired woman with the shy smile and kind eyes, could believe she was a killer.

That was what Auntie said, too, in the police station, her trembling hands clutching a coffee cup, her face wan and crumpled. *That can't be my sister who did this, not my sweet sis. It wasn't premeditated.*

I watched them through the blinds in the playroom window, the crayon crushed in my hand. None of the cops believed Auntie; they all had the same expression. And so did the social worker with me. As if they already knew the answer to their questions.

They'd already decided my mom was guilty.

The lieutenant will look at my bruises, the bump on my skull, and wonder if my injuries came from me . . . attacking Mimi?

It feels like a fist squeezing my neck. God, he'll think I lied about not remembering.

Can evil can be inherited?

What if the cops think so? Will they think that whatever made my mom kill my dad made me hurt my cousin?

Will they focus all their attention on me?

My breaths are getting shredded; my vision's fading. I'm hyperventilating into a panic attack.

I can't space out. Not now.

The wooden edge of the bed frame digs into my palms as I focus and steady my breathing, using the techniques my psychologist taught me during my earlier sessions.

You're not responsible for what happened to your father, Tanvi.

I inhale deep and slow, fill my lungs, then exhale.

I need to take control, separate the facts from my fear. Spiraling into a meltdown will mean Mimi won't get justice. Because then the person who hurt Mimi will get away.

And whatever Beth or Grace or the cops may think, Mimi was my family. I'd sooner cut my own heart out than cut her out of my life.

James.

He has a place he shares with his dad, an apartment above his store. I'm going to check it out.

CHAPTER 11

EVER SINCE MIMI'S clothes were found on Gaston Beach, there's been a dramatic flip in the general attitude at school, where she's gone from being "a dopehead who couldn't take the heat and ran away to escape the shame she brought on the rest of us at Orin High and this community," to "oh my God, she was such a good person who just happened to make a wrong choice, and we all miss her terribly."

Every time I see a post that talks of Mimi in the past tense, it hits me again that Mimi's gone. The wave of agony sweeps through me again, leaving an intense fatigue in its wake. This morning before she left for her therapy appointment, Auntie told me we just needed to search harder because Mimi was out there somewhere waiting to be rescued. But what Mr. Lee told me echoed the news articles. About the investigation being in the recovery phase, about recovering a body.

The fatigue intensifies and I close my eyes, blotting out the classroom. *Focus, stay on track.* Ten minutes left for my bio class to be done and then I can go over to James's place like I planned. But first I need to finish my notes. We have a huge test in two days, and I need to ace it. Lately, it feels like bio is the only thing I understand.

Right on the heels of that thought comes the sinking realization, that awful pincer-grip of loss. It doesn't matter anymore. I'm not leaving Auntie and going off to college. Not if Mimi isn't coming home again.

I reread the paragraph, something about neurons and the

brain stem, but the words don't make any sense. The kids around me seem to be getting it, though, their heads buried in their notes, scrawling furiously.

". . . need this done right." Mrs. G's voice cuts through my thoughts. "I'm here after class if you need any help. Understand?"

The class gives a collective nod.

"This test is your chance to start this class on the right foot. Some of you I know will do fine." Mrs. G smiles at me.

I force a smile. She'll be disappointed in me, but none of it matters anymore.

There's a sudden rush of footsteps outside and Abby appears at the door, her face flushed and sweaty.

Mrs. G frowns at her. "The class is done, Abby. Where were you?"

"Sorry. Track practice ran late."

"Your coach knows that you need to pass this class to stay in track, doesn't he?"

Abby grimaces and hurries over to the empty seat next to me.

Once she's seated and the teacher turns away, I whisper. "You said you saw James and Mimi leave Beth's party together."

She frowns. "I never said anything—"

"In your reply to Beth's post."

Her hand stills halfway through reaching for her book. Then she opens the book and flips through the pages. "No idea what you're talking about."

I glance at Mrs. G—she's busy with one of the other kids— then scroll through my phone under cover of my desk. Abby's comment has been deleted. I search her profile, page after page. It's gone. Am I losing my mind? No, I'm sure I saw it yesterday. Why'd Abby delete it?

"I totally fucked up." Abby mutters, looking miserable,

mascara smudging her wet eyes. For a second, I think she's talking about the social media posts, but then she says, "Mrs. G's had it in for me ever since I flunked her class last year. I bet she's gonna tell Coach if I flunk this stupid test, too, and then he'll kick me out of track for sure."

"I'll give you my notes if you tell me about James."

"There's nothing to tell."

"Abby, please."

The teacher lifts her head and looks at us. I pretend I'm reading and after she turns away, I slide my notes over to Abby, hoping I wasn't making a mistake, hoping her comments and the fact that she didn't join Beth and Lyla in demonizing me meant she wasn't totally against me. "Just change things around so it doesn't look obvious to Mrs. G."

She gathers the papers, her fingers trembling. "Thank you, but there's nothing to tell. I didn't see anything." Her voice is so low, I barely hear it. Then the bell rings, and she jumps to her feet and streaks for the door.

Crap. I grab my books and push through the crowd streaming toward the door.

"Hey, Tanvi?" Mrs. G calls out. "Hold on."

So close. I clutch my binder and face the teacher. "Yeah, Mrs. G?"

Sympathy gentles her expression. "I'm so sorry about your cousin. Have you given any thought about my offer?"

She wanted me to take time off—bereavement time, she called it—and offered to help me make up for the classes and credits afterwards so I can still graduate on time. It's been two years since she was my homeroom teacher, but she's still got me under her wing.

"It won't hurt your chance to get into the UMich premed program."

She knows my dream. But UMich was Mimi's dream, too,

and if she doesn't get to go there, then I won't be going, either. So the grades don't matter, credits don't matter. The only thing that matters is finding who hurt Mimi. Who hated Mimi enough to make her go missing that night.

"Tanvi?" Mrs. G is still waiting patiently for my reply.

Why can't I accept her offer? Is it because then I'll have to accept once and for all that Mimi's gone? "Thanks, Mrs. G. I'll think about it."

That seems to satisfy her, because she nods and turns to her computer screen.

Outside, a river of bodies and backpacks cram the hall, but Abby's gone.

BY THE TIME I reach downtown Orin, it's packed with the evening rush. A pall of gloom hangs over the place with heavy gray clouds blanketing the sky, threatening rain, and giving the air a weird twilight aura.

The aura intensifies the prickling ball of anxiety in my gut. The image I have of James as the awkward loner in middle school is a total contrast to that man in Mimi's collage. I remember the tall, gangly kid forever in Mimi's shadow, whose eyes never left Mimi's face, his shy smile only appearing if Mimi coaxed it out. His barriers fell only around Mimi, though she never gave the slightest hint she saw him as anything other than a friend, one with a broken wing she needed to protect.

But one thing's for sure. I wouldn't have feared that kid, but the man in the photo, the stranger, is a different matter.

The traffic light ahead turns green, and I join the line of vehicles pushing forward, nudging each other's taillights. The dark blue SUV next to me revs its engine, and the sidewalk trembles as the traffic restarts. Or maybe that's my pulse drumming hard. I take off, cutting across the road, ignoring angry horns.

With the business district behind me, the traffic starts thinning out, and then I'm flying past residential areas until I reach a fork onto a narrow road identified by a chipped wood sign as Tinder Avenue. Thick brush and towering trees crowd the road. The twilight aura is more pronounced here, with shadows cast by low-lying clouds and fog rising from the dank ground.

Another half a mile down Tinder Avenue and I'll be at James's.

A squeaking noise comes from behind me. I look over my shoulder.

There's someone on a bike way back, a slim person in dark clothing. Before I can get a better look, the person veers off the road and down the shoulder to vanish into the trees.

That's weird. I shrug off the paranoia and continue, slowing down when a two-story building, stark and rectangular, appears through the trees.

The store, Surrey Antiques, is on the first floor. James lives with his dad on the floor above. A white pickup truck is parked out in the front next to a bike, and a faint rectangle of light shows through the grimy glass panel on the shop's front door.

I hide my bike behind some undergrowth and creep over. After rubbing out a circle of dirt on the glass, I peek through. Light from a fluorescent bulb, hanging askew off one wall, falls on shelves overflowing with lamps, picture frames, chipped statuettes, and other junk. But otherwise, the place seems empty.

A movement from the cupboards along the back wall catches my eye.

One of them is opening.

It swings out like a door would, and James's dad, Mr. Surrey, appears from behind. A shorter, wider version of his son, a scowl twists his fleshy face and draws down his overhanging brows. He scans the room, his gaze thankfully slipping past the front door, then he edges out and shuts the cupboard.

The way he looked around . . . Like he's doing something he shouldn't be.

The cupboard door is inching open again, and this time, James appears. His T-shirt hangs loose on his thin frame, and deep hollows cut under his cheekbones, that strong face in the collage now sallow and sagging. Has he lost weight recently, or is that just how he looks now?

Mr. Surrey says something and James stops dead, like he's walked into an invisible wall. He drops into a chair next to the desk.

Mr. Surrey slaps him on the back of the head, the sound loud enough to be heard through the shut door.

I wince, remembering the days he'd show up in middle school with a black eye and tell the school counselor he "fell down some steps at home." Mimi protected him at school but couldn't get him to speak up against his dad.

How's he going to react? As the timid kid I knew or the man in the collage?

The latter, I realize, when James shoves his dad, then faces him, hands clenched, looking like he'd give anything to take a swing.

They glare at each other. Mr. Surrey breaks first. He grabs a jacket lying on the desk and trudges toward the door.

Crap. I dash around the corner of the building.

The door slams shut. Footsteps fade away, followed by an engine's roar. The pickup truck shoots past me and down the road, its taillights fading into the haze.

I edge back to the door and peer in. James sits at the table, his head in his hands. What do I do now? I came here intending to find out why he didn't tell the cops he and Mimi left Beth's place together after the party. Why lie if he had nothing to hide? I can't wimp out now.

I lick my dry lips and reach for the door.

That rage twisting his face when he glared at his dad . . .

Be careful.

There's something on the floor next to him. A duffel bag, hot pink leather with wraparound pockets and chain link straps.

Mimi's bag? Did she leave it here when she stayed over? But why hasn't he returned it?

He hefts the bag over his shoulder and disappears through the cupboard. Before I can think it through, I push open the front door and slip inside the shop.

His low voice reaches me from behind the cupboard door. He's talking to someone, their voice too low for me to make out.

Mimi?

My heart leaps for my throat. Oh, God, is that why he has her bag? She's here?

But then why would she leave her purse and clothes on the beach? Why is she letting us think she's hurt? Or putting Auntie through this torture?

My heart beats out of my chest.

Scuttling forward to a long table, I duck underneath it just as James's long legs appear. I hold my breath, staying totally still as he walks past my hiding place and across the shop to the front. A register clangs, followed by coins clinking, before he strides to the door.

Through the furniture, I catch sight of his tall figure before the door shuts behind him. An engine roars to life. Then it recedes into silence.

He's gone.

I race to the back of the shop.

The cupboard door is narrow, about a couple of feet wide, with shelves ten inches deep. I tug on it, but the thing doesn't budge. I shove it hard, first with my shoulder, then using my whole body. Nothing. Not even a squeak of hinges.

"Mimi! Mimi, are you in there?" Placing an ear to the frame, I listen for anything, a cry, a gasp.

Total silence, broken only by my shuddering breaths.

I feel along the dusty shelves for an edge to open it until my searching fingers brush an indent. There's a click. I tug again. The cupboard swings open, revealing a wall of darkness and a musty smell. No, more of an earthy, pungent stink of weed.

"Mimi? Where are you?"

My voice echoes before fading into whispers, then quiet.

I slip inside and play the light from my phone around, hoping, praying it'll fall on a familiar figure. That even though Mimi isn't replying to my call, she's here.

Please let her be here. Please. *Please*.

The light washes over empty earthen pots, metal tubes, and a few clear plastic bags filled with crumbled green leaves, all stacked against the walls.

But no Mimi.

I clap a hand to my mouth, but a whimper escapes me. It grows to a sob. She's got to be here. She has to!

Someone's crying. Deep, long wails. *Oh, Mimi, Mimi.*

The sound comes from my mouth. An awful emptiness is building inside me, threatening to swallow me whole.

Shit. I slam my hand against the wall. Again and again, until my skin is raw, my bones throbbing.

This isn't fair. I want her back. She should be here, not some stupid stash of weed.

None of this makes sense. Who was James talking to in here? And why did he have Mimi's bag?

Her bag. He wasn't carrying it when he left, so it must be in here somewhere. I've got to find it before he returns. There may be some clue inside, some clue as to what he did to her.

After easing the secret door closed behind me, leaving a

small gap to keep the latch from locking, I search through and find the bag behind a stack of pots.

The tag on the handle still has the words *Happy Birthday* in my handwriting.

I pull it close, running my thumb over the words, and slip into the past.

Auntie and Mimi were having another argument. Mimi wanted this duffle bag, and Auntie was having none of it. "Five hundred and sixty dollars, Mimi? You know I can't afford that."

Tears filled Mimi's eyes. "Beth gets stuff like that all the time. Do you know how hard it is when my friends have everything and I have *nothing*?"

"We can never compete with Beth's money, sweetheart. How about a compromise? Ask David for a job at his deli and earn half the money. I'll pay the rest. And it'll be your graduation gift, how about that?"

"Work at the deli? Seriously, Mom? I'll be the laughingstock of the entire school. I know why you never have money for me anymore. You're spending it all on *her*." She glared at me through her tears while my heart shredded to bits.

It took me weeks to scrape the money together between my job at Mr. Lee's deli and cleaning out yards around the neighborhood. But it was all worth it when I biked home from the mall, holding on to my precious burden.

I set the bag in front of her and said, "Happy birthday, Mimi. I love you." I waited for her face to light up.

But she grabbed the bag and, without a glance my way, raced up the steps. "Beth, I got the bag. I'm so excited!" Her door slamming shut felt like a slap in the face.

Look, Mimi, look at the bag I got you. No, it wasn't any trouble at all, thank you for asking.

Of course, I'll do the dishes, take out the trash, and clean the bathrooms for you. And no, I won't tell Auntie I did your chores.

Do your homework for you? You don't even have to ask.

I'll crawl through glass for you, cousin. Just be my family. I have no one left.

I drag in a breath and choke on dank, musty air. The rancid stink jerks me back to the dusty, cold floor I'm kneeling on. With a shaking hand, I unzip the bag. It's stuffed with clothes: black leggings, jeans, and T-shirts. I don't recognize any of it as Mimi's. James's got someone else's clothes in Mimi's bag?

A thud cuts into the silence. I freeze.

It comes again, a thump on the wooden floorboards, followed by another. Footsteps.

There's someone inside the shop.

Sweat breaks out in a clammy film on my forehead. I need a place to hide. Now. But the small room is completely exposed.

I squeeze into a corner of the cupboard and curl into a tight ball.

Don't breathe. Don't move.

The shrill note of a phone breaks the silence. My stomach clutches painfully before I remember my phone ringer is turned off. The sound came from a few feet away.

"Hello?"

I recognize James's deep voice. The hair rises on the back of my neck.

"What are you doing here?" he says. "I told you not to come around."

I crane forward to catch his words.

"No, I told the cops I didn't see Mimi that Thursday."

He lied; I knew it! I tiptoe forward, closer to the gap in the cupboard door, and peek outside.

James paces the front of the shop, phone clamped to his ear. "Yeah, I know," he snaps. "But Dad's getting worse. I'm gonna need more money to take him to the hospital." He drums his fingers on a tabletop. "He's my dad, okay? His infusion is scheduled for tomorrow, so I need the cash now." Then he stops dead. "What do you mean? Outside the shop?" He strides to the front door and opens it. "Whose bike is it?"

Oh, God. Ice trickles down my spine. Whoever he's talking to has found my bike.

The front door thuds shut behind him.

In a flash, I slide the cupboard door open, race for the long tables in the middle of the shop, and duck underneath one.

The front door opens. James's boots appear. "There's no one h—What the fuck?" He races across the room, past the table I'm hiding under, and toward the cupboard I left open. His boots disappear into the secret room.

I jump up and flee for the front door. He'll know it's empty in seconds. He'll come after me.

I yank the door open.

Something crashes in the back of the shop, behind the secret door.

My heart thumps against my ribs. I rush across the road and throw myself on my bike. Crouching low, pedaling hard, I fly down the road.

"Hey!"

My gut clenches. I glance over my shoulder.

He's out of the shop and coming after me. His eyes are narrowed in a flushed, angry face, his hands fisted and ready.

This isn't the awkward middle schooler I might've known. This is the guy who knows what happened to Mimi but lied to the cops about it. The guy who could've hurt Mimi.

He starts running toward me.

No, no. I pump my legs harder, streaking past the towering trees.

Behind me, an engine roars to life.

CHAPTER 12

THE TREES FLANKING the narrow winding road push in, casting deep shadows I'm grateful for. I glance over my shoulder. I can't see James anymore, or his place. But I can hear him. The low growl of an engine. And it's getting louder.

I force a burst of speed from my aching legs and bike harder. My breath comes ragged and short. The wind whips my hood off and grabs my hair in wild swirls, but I duck my head and push, willing my bike to fly.

The growl of the engine becomes a deep rumble, growing by the second. Light flickers through the trees behind me, illuminating the brush. Soon, it'll fall on me. There's no way I can outrun him if I stay on the road.

Does he know it's me? Has he seen my face?

I need to hide.

Angling off the pavement, I ride into the undergrowth. Leaves crunch under the tires. Hopping off the bike, I haul it into a thick cluster of bushes and duck behind it, feeling my way deeper into the growth. The waning sunlight barely penetrates the branches overhead. Hopefully, the shadows will hide me, too.

Over the smell of mulch and earth, I catch the stink of oil. The powerful beam of a motorcycle lights the road.

I can see him, hunched in the seat. He's inching along, the headlight sweeping the undergrowth flanking the road.

The pounding of my heart almost drowns out the bike's rumble.

Then the engine cuts off. The sudden silence is deafening, a feeling of cotton balls stuffed in my ears.

He swings a long leg off the bike and strides to the tree edge barely fifteen feet from where I'm hiding.

I cover my mouth with a shaking hand to muffle my panicked breaths. Every beat of my heart, every rustle of the leaves under me, feels like a thunderclap.

The flashlight in his hand comes alive, washing over him. The deep hollows of his eyes, the thinned lips, and the carved granite of his visage. Then the beam glints off something in his hand.

My ribs constrict. Every bit of air rushes out of my lungs.

A gun is tucked into his palm.

The beam falls on the trunk next to me, then plays along the ground mere inches from my feet.

I brace myself. Ready to make a break for it. Ready for the gun to go off.

After what feels like an eternity, the light disappears. Footsteps recede. The engine kicks up again.

I risk another peek around the bush.

James rides his bike down the road, still going slow, still searching.

I wait, staying still until the taillight vanishes through the trees and gloom settles on the road and forest. Once I'm sure he's gone, I slump against the tree, exhaling through gritted teeth.

That was way too close. I'm shaking so hard, my knees practically knock out a rhythm.

I came looking for James, and now he's looking for me. The realization sinks in and sends my heart plunging to the pit of my stomach.

AFTER PREPARING AUNTIE her dinner of chapati and potato bhaji, I sit with her until she's done eating and fallen asleep. Back in my room, I collapse on the bed.

James has a gun.

He came after me with it. Did he intend to shoot me?

Why would he do that unless he's involved somehow?

I must tell the cops.

But it'll be my word against James's. What if they don't believe me? My stomach twists. No, I need to approach this differently. Anonymously. I can leave an anonymous tip about James on Crime Stoppers.

Yeah, that'll work.

It takes me a minute to go to the online site at Crime Stoppers and find the submission form. What should I add? After debating, I say that someone I knew saw James with Mimi the Thursday before she disappeared and that James had a gun tucked into his belt. According to the website, they'll send the info to the appropriate police department—so, Orin PD and the cop now in charge of Mimi's case. Lieutenant Williams. Good.

I'm about to log off when a floorboard creaks outside my room. Then, stumbling footsteps shuffle past my door—and then stop.

"Auntie?"

From the hallway, I see Mimi's bedroom door standing open. A low murmur escapes through the gap.

My pulse stutters. Mimi? The carpet whizzes past my feet, and I come to a stumbling stop at the door.

Auntie sits on Mimi's bed, a pillow on her lap, smoothing the cloth with a shaking hand, her lips moving.

The spike of adrenaline fizzles out and I'm left with an awful sinking feeling. I try shaking it off and lean into Auntie's words. She's singing a lullaby in Malayalam. The song is familiar to me. It's from a Malayalam movie in the nineties, sung by a mother to soothe her crying baby. Auntie used to sing it when we were kids, when I'd wake up with the stink of smoke and the sounds of screeching metal, and she'd draw me into her lap and cuddle me close.

I sit beside her and hug her tight. Her arm circles me, and she starts rocking, her voice falling silent, the words drifting into echoes in my memory. My eyes fill.

"She's angry at me, honey," Auntie says, her voice ragged. "Because I wanted her to stay away from that boy. I thought she was listening to me. I didn't know . . ." Her voice breaks. "About the drugs."

It was my fault for taking that photo, for ratting my cousin out. "I'm sorry I took that picture, Auntie." My tears drench the cloth of her pajama shirt.

"Shh, don't cry, sweetheart." She frames my face between callused palms. "I know you love her; I know you'll do anything for her. She'll come back, see? One day that front door will open, and there she'll be, my sweet Mimi."

My chest feels like it's getting crushed. I take her hands between mine. "We'll find Mimi and bring her home."

She pats my head, then lies back. I lift her feet up onto the bed. "Why don't you go to sleep?" She hasn't been sleeping well and her psychiatrist prescribed a sleeping pill yesterday.

"Okay." She turns to her side and reaches for my hand. "Stay here with me."

"I will."

Her eyes drift closed.

She needs me now. But will that change after the lieutenant questions me? Once she knows there were so many things about the day Mimi vanished that I haven't told her?

I text Mr. Lee. **Any idea when the lieutenant will be by to question me? Not that I'm stressed about it or anything.** As soon as I hit send, I realize how weird my words may sound because it'll be natural for me to be stressed.

Even if I have nothing to hide.

If? I flinch. I'm not hiding anything. I *want* to know what happened to Mimi. I want the cops to find who hurt her. No matter what Grace or Beth think.

In a day or two, Mr. Lee texts. **It's an informal meeting, kiddo, just to get your input on the last time you saw Mimi.**

A knot of dread forms in my belly. The last time I saw—I *remember* seeing—Mimi, she was opening the front door and walking into the night. Even if the cop believes I have no memory beyond that up until I woke up the next morning in my bed, he'll want to know why I didn't tell Officer Laney that right away. Why I waited until days later to call the station and give the cop the information.

Grace said I should've told the cops what really happened the night Mimi vanished.

It implies she knows what happened and that I should, too. Do I?

In front of the mirror, I part my hair to look at the small bump on my skull. It's barely visible, though still painful to touch.

A few years ago, someone in my class fell off their trampoline and got knocked out. He was diagnosed with a concussion, was out of school for days, and told me later that he had trouble remembering events around the time of his fall.

Could this be similar?

An injury I can't remember happening . . .

An injury that somehow made Mimi disappear . . .

My hands tremble. I grip them tight, my knuckles turning bloodless.

If the foggy memory and the bump on my head was caused by a concussion, the lieutenant's gonna want to know why I didn't go to the doctor's. And I'll have no good answer for that.

He'll be coming to that interview with all the information gathered from the investigation so far. Including Mimi's journal, if Beth's given it to him.

The dread in my gut grows tentacles. I'd give anything to say Beth was bluffing about the journal, but why'd Mimi slam her door on me that day when I found her writing at her desk? She'd kept her room locked since then. And I know she blamed me for Auntie not having the money to buy the duffel for her.

If Mimi wrote down that I wanted everything she had—money, a stable home, a mom—the lieutenant will buy into it, too. He'll believe I wanted Mimi gone, just like Beth does.

And then there's my past. The violence in my mother which'd remained hidden until one day it surfaced through her gentle façade and killed my dad.

Are homicidal traits hereditary?

My gaze strays to the closet in my room. Somewhere underneath the junk on the floor is the brown envelope Auntie gave me a few weeks after she brought me to Orin. It contains the letters Mom wrote her. Auntie wanted me to read the letters so I'd know what happened to my mom.

Mimi wanted me to read the letters, too. She insisted it was the only way I could properly heal, that therapy and medications would only go so far.

Your mom's mind was broken after the miscarriage, T. Don't judge her because you don't know what horrors she must've gone through.

My head feels heavy, weighed down with a ton of bricks. I curl up next to Auntie, gripping her hands between mine, and watch her sweet face. Watch it dissolve as my eyes fill.

I didn't want to understand my mother's actions. How could I after she took my daddy away from me?

You have courage, T. Real courage. Fight for what's true. Look for the truth.

Mimi was talking about my mother, but her words remind me that there was a time she saw courage in me.

Now I need to find that courage again and figure out what happened to her.

I need to focus on this new information about James. Mimi loved him, and it's possible he loved her, too, but that doesn't mean he didn't hurt her.

Earlier at his shop, I overheard James say he was taking his dad in for an infusion at the hospital tomorrow morning. The only hospital around here is Orin Community Hospital. And with Auntie still off from work per her psychologist's recommendation, I won't run into her there.

A quick search of the hospital layout map on my laptop shows me a large room labelled OUTPATIENT INFUSION CENTER on the third floor. There's a lobby next to it for family to wait. Since I don't know when Mr. Surrey's infusion is scheduled for, I'll need to get there right when they open and then hang out until James gets there, too. It's not an ideal place for a confrontation, but at least it's a public space.

Hopefully it has a "no guns allowed" policy.

CHAPTER 13

A CIRCULAR DRIVEWAY leads to the front doors of the six-story sprawling hospital located in the heart of Orin. Mimi and I used to hang out here often when Auntie had to work and Mr. Lee wasn't available to babysit.

Though I haven't been here in five years—since Mimi and I were old enough to stay home by ourselves—a feeling of familiarity sweeps over me when I walk through the glass double doors and enter the sweeping lobby. Back then, Mimi would tug me along, eager to show me the cool spots, like the nurses' lounges where Auntie's friends would ply us with snacks, and an abandoned wing of the hospital with musty rooms, which we'd pretend was haunted. But now the absence of Mimi's warm hand in mine pulling me along, or her excited voice urging me to *hurry up, T, before they kick us out* leaves me with a gut-wrenching sense of loss.

The lobby is packed—I must've hit peak visiting hours—and a row of elevators in the back lead to the floors above, including the third-floor infusion center where I'm hoping to find James. But then I spot him waiting at the elevators, hands clenched around the handles of a wheelchair in which his dad sits, slumped. A nurse in scrubs and blond topknot stands with him, talking in a low murmur.

I thread through the crowd until I'm behind them, but with a couple of people between us as a shield in case James decides to look over his shoulder.

"What if he doesn't improve?" he says. "His oncologist said his last CT scan showed spread to the liver."

The nurse shakes her head. "Think positive. They'll repeat his CT after this round of chemotherapy. Hopefully, it'll work, and you'll get some good news."

So his dad does have cancer. That's why he said he needed money. An odd feeling wraps around my chest, like a vest that's a bit too tight. I saw his dad slap him—Mr. Surrey is obviously abusive, but here his son's taking care of the guy, worrying about him.

But then I remember how James came after me with a gun and any pity drains away. If Mimi's gone because of him, he'll need to pay.

The elevator door dings. I step back into the crowd while James enters the elevator, then hurry to the stairs. Taking the steps two at a time, I burst out through the doors on the third floor and into a narrow winding hall flanked by shut doors. It's deserted. I glance to both sides, then follow the echo of voices to my left.

James stands with his back to me down the hall, watching the nurse push his dad toward a pair of closed doors marked with the words INFUSION CENTER. The nurse and wheelchair disappear through the doors.

James exhales and his shoulders slump.

My heart drums frantically in my chest. If he recognized me yesterday, how's he going to react now? What if he turns aggressive again? Though the hospital does have a "no guns allowed" policy—I checked—he can still get to me before help does.

I plant my feet, limbs ready to launch or pivot, whatever's needed per the defensive Tae Kwon Do moves I've learned. I can't let him see my fear. If I wimp out now, I'll lose this chance of finding out if he hurt Mimi.

Taking a deep breath, I shift through various scenarios of starting this conversation. Challenge him outright? No. He'll either clam up or attack me. My heartbeat surges. *Stay strong, start with something unrelated, maybe inquire about his dad.* "James."

He starts, then spins around. "Tanvi? What're you doing here?"

I study his expression, looking for signs of the anger he displayed when he followed me yesterday. But instead, he looks trapped, his eyes flicking to the exit. I force a steady tone. "I came to see my aunt. I'm sorry about your dad. How're you managing?"

He stares at me. "Managing?"

"With Mimi gone and all, and now your dad sick. If you need anything, I'll be glad to help."

"I'm fine." He's silent for a beat, then he says, his voice low, "Why did you take that photo of Mimi? Why hurt her that way?"

I flinch. That was the last question I expected from him. "I didn't mean to hurt her." And how dare he talk about hurt when he likely supplied the drugs? "I didn't know she was there."

"What?" Then his frown clears. "You were trying to get a photo of Beth? Did you tell Mimi that?"

"No, I didn't see her afterward," I say automatically, feeling a sting of guilt. Yes, I did, but I don't remember if I told her or if that was why she was mad at me. "But you did. You picked Mimi up from Beth's party, didn't you?"

James starts again, but I rush on, keeping my voice clear of the agitated turmoil in my heart. "I know you did. How did she seem at that time?" In my murky memory, there's the image of Mimi standing at my bedroom door, her tone and expression angry. She had to have known I took the photo. "Was she mad? Upset? Angry?" *At me?*

"She was upset, yes."

My hands clench. God, I'd give anything for a chance to apologize to Mimi.

Then the rest of the implication of his words hits me. He *knew* her state of mind. Meaning Abby was right. James saw Mimi after the party but lied to the cops about it.

"But she wasn't mad at you," he adds. "Not at anything you did."

I inhale sharply. "How do you know? Did she tell you what was upsetting her?"

He shrugs, his face closing off. "No, just that she had to talk to you right away. She wouldn't let me slow down until I reached your place and dropped her off."

So that part of my memory was right. She did come home. But what was she trying to tell me so urgently? All I remember are bits and pieces, like snips of a reel.

Mimi standing at my bedroom door. *You must not, Tanvi.*

Mimi's voice drowned out by the rain as she left the house after. *Don't you dare . . .*

But that's where the memory stops. I don't remember anything critical, anything she would need to tell me.

But I do remember she left wearing her red dress, the same one found in a decomposed state on Gaston Beach. And according to the news article I read, the state of the clothes led the cops to believe Mimi drowned within hours after going missing.

Did she go to Gaston that same night?

And was it willingly, or was she taken against her will?

I harden my voice. "Did you pick Mimi up from my house after that?"

"What do you mean?"

The double doors leading to the infusion center open with a soft click, and a white-haired guy in a lab coat with a stethoscope draped around his neck strides out, eyes us curiously, then heads to the stairs. I wait for the door to slam shut behind him. "She left the house after you dropped her off. Someone must've picked her up; she didn't have a vehicle."

"It wasn't me." Then realization dawns in his widening eyes. "What's with all these questions? Hold on, is this a fucking interrogation?"

I steady myself. "You told the cops you didn't see Mimi the day she vanished."

He goes still, the color receding from his face. "I didn't . . . I had to . . ."

"You waited for her outside after dropping her off. What did you do to her?"

A muscle jumps in the corner of his jaw. "Nothing. I did nothing, okay?"

He lied to the cops, and from what I overheard at his shop, he's involved somehow in what happened to Mimi. "You have a gun."

He frowns. "What the hell are you talking about? I'd never . . ." Then his jaw goes slack. "Fuck, was that you at the shop yesterday?"

Why does he look so shocked? He couldn't have *not* recognized me.

His jaw stays dropped, his eyes so full of shock and something else. Grief? Pain? But then he visibly gathers himself, closes his mouth, and turns away. "I have to go."

"Please, James."

"I didn't intend to shoot *you*, okay? I thought you were someone else."

So he intended to shoot *someone*? "You're lying." Again.

"No!" He pushes his hand through his hair. "You're Mimi's little cousin. Fuck, I've known you since middle school."

Does he mean that? His hazel irises are turbulent with

some strong emotion, but I can't read them. So if it wasn't me he meant to hurt, then who? Who was he going after? "What happened to my cousin, James?"

His eyes lower and he turns away. "I don't know."

He knows. I can see it in the nervous tic in the corner of his mouth. "James, please. You owe it to Mimi for everything she's done for you."

The tic worsens. His hands are shaking now; he stuffs them in his pockets. "What the hell do you want me to say? I was locked up that night, okay? I was stupid enough to get into a fight at Orin Tavern and they kept me in until Saturday. Mimi was gone by the time I got out. So go ask your fucking questions to someone else because I got an alibi, and it's ironclad." He spins on his heels and strides down the tiled floor toward the doors leading to the infusion center.

No, that's impossible. He's involved. It's got to be him.

Sweat breaks out along the back of my neck.

But if it's not him . . .

How did I get hurt?

My clothes weren't damp or mud-stained when I returned home from Beth's place. They got that way after. After I saw Mimi walk out into the rain.

After I followed her . . .

Did I hurt Mimi?

A clicking sound jerks me out of my thoughts. James stands in front of the double doors to the infusion center, which are opening. He glances at me over his shoulder, then vanishes through.

My phone pings. A text from Mr. Lee lights up the screen.

Are you good with talking to Lieutenant Williams tomorrow?

My chin trembles. I bite down on my lower lip to stop the tears.

It could still be James. He's lied already; he could be lying about the being locked up part as well.

I need to find out if he really has an alibi for the time Mimi vanished.

ORIN TAVERN IS a bar that used to operate in the older part of town. Years ago, they started serving food as well, and now it's mostly a diner with a bar, but the name stuck and remains imprinted on a wooden placard above the low ranch-style building. It's located at the entrance to the winding road dead-ending at Orin Tool Works, Beth's dad's factory. The factory, like the rest of the shops on the road, closed months ago, and the tavern is the only functioning business here now.

When I arrive, the place is silent except for the breeze rustling the brush alongside the parking lot. If it weren't for the beat-up car next to the front door and the light shining through the rectangular glass pane on the door, I'd think it was deserted.

An elderly man with thick silver hair atop a lean brown face sits at a desk, marking something on a large ledger. He lifts his head when I knock, then opens the door. "Miss, we're not open yet."

"I just needed to ask you something. Sorry, but I'll be quick."

"Sure." He tucks a pen behind his right ear. "Go ahead."

"Do you remember a fight here last week?" He frowns, and I add, "Where the cops got called and someone was arrested?"

"Of course I do. It was terrible. Happened Thursday around nine-thirty, I think."

"Who did they arrest?"

"That boy, James Surrey. Got locked up, I heard."

James wasn't lying, then. My heart sinks like a stone in water. "Do you know how long he was locked up?"

"The weekend?" He nods. "Yes. He was mad as hell when

he came around here two days later because he thought it was me who called the cops on him."

If James hadn't been released until two days later, he couldn't have hurt Mimi. Then why did he lie to the cops about seeing her? I remember the conversation I overheard at his shop. He, and whomever he was talking to, knew something about Mimi they wanted to keep hidden. "Did he come here alone? Was there a girl along with him? Dark hair, in a red dress. Hold on." I dig out my phone and show the screen where Mimi and I hug each other. It was that last photo in the *Sisters Forever* scrapbook. "This girl."

"Hmm, I don't know. Maybe? It was all so fast, you know, with that Grace calling the cops and them—"

"Grace? Grace Warner?"

"Yep. She didn't like that they cuffed James, though. Fought with the cops to release him and almost got arrested herself."

That's odd. But then Grace knew James well from when he was part of our group in middle school. It'd explain why she tried to protect him. I feel sick at the thought of having to talk to her again, but if she was here, she'd know if Mimi was here with James.

After thanking the elderly guy, I close the tavern door behind me. Sharp electricity stings my fingertips from the metal doorknob. I snatch my hand away, then wince when a similar pain shoots up my scalp.

I feel for the source, my fingers brushing the bump on the back of my head. It's shrunk to the size of a pea.

A wave of dizziness sweeps through me. I brace my hands on the door to stay upright. The lights are hurting my head, making me nauseated. The flickering lights through the glass pane on the door.

Disco lights.

The music playing inside the tavern is too loud. Drums and

guitar, pounding out a rock beat. I rest my aching head against the glass pane.

Shadows gyrate inside the tavern, people dancing on the floor, their figures a jumbled mash of silver and shadow.

I close my eyes to shut them out, to stop the pain.

When I open my eyes, it's gone. The rectangular pane of glass is clear, showing chairs stacked on tables. The place is deserted. The only music I hear is my harsh panting breaths.

What the hell was that? A memory?

CHAPTER 14

I SIT ON a bar stool behind the cash register at Mr. Lee's deli, surrounded by the familiar smells of lunch meats and sauces, mixed with the scent of coffee from the steaming cup in front of me. The deli normally is my comfort zone—I've been helping out here for over two years—but the usually soothing atmosphere does nothing to quiet my nerves. It's been an hour since my shift started, an hour and a half since I left the tavern, but my legs still tremble every time I think of that bizarre episode. My English lit notes lie scattered on the table next to the register. I have an essay due Monday, but I can't focus on the pages.

I return to the last memory I have of Mimi—the fragments of her words, *Don't you dare*—followed by her walking into the rain in her red dress.

Think. Imagine the thundering rain, Mimi walking away. She must've gotten to the road. Which direction did she turn? Or did someone pick her up?

I wait for an answer, a break in the fog, for other sounds to appear over the incessant drumming of the rain. But there's nothing, just emptiness and the throbbing ache in the back of my head, which brings along another wave of dizziness.

I close my eyes and wait for the dizziness to pass. The lieutenant will be coming by here to talk to me in an hour. Mr. Lee texted to let me know they decided on the deli rather than home to not upset Auntie. The cop will want answers, but all I have are scraps of memories and a whole lot of fog.

But hidden in that fog is the reason for my injuries. For some reason, my mind's not letting me see.

What's it hiding from me?

The sharp thud of the front door closing yanks me out of my thoughts. A girl about eight years of age skips to the counter displaying a row of deli meats and condiments and leans on the glass, anticipation lighting her face. A couple in their thirties follow her, the woman reaching for her hand. "So, what do you want, honey?"

Mother and daughter, I assume, from the similar thick, wavy black hair and large dark eyes. The guy has his arm around the mom's shoulders.

The skin on my arms prickles as a wave of familiarity hits me. I've seen this image before.

The photo taken at the airport on our trip to India. The last time Daddy, Mom, and I posed together for a photo. The one I hid in my closet because I couldn't bring myself to tear Mom out, though I wanted to so badly. But every time I looked at her face, the kind smiling eyes, the gentle expression, it reminded me of the way she used to love me, and my heart broke into a million pieces.

The shakes start deep inside me.

"Hi there," the girl says. "Can I have a BLT?"

I stare at her. God, she looks just like I did at her age. Her eyes are bright with joy. There is no grief, no shadows darkening her expression. No fear of what is to come. She has no idea how one day she'll wake up and find her dad is dead. How she'll have to stand by while strangers call her mom a killer.

Her sweet, beautiful mom.

My chest is on fire.

"Excuse me?"

The voice drifts to me. A fog surrounds me, and through the swirling mist, an image appears. Three people. Three strangers.

"Are you okay?" The male voice is louder, edged with concern.

The adults are frowning. The woman reaches a hand out to me. "Honey, what's wrong? Do you need help?"

Get a grip. I swallow, then force a smile. "Sorry. No, I'm okay. What can I get you all?"

"A BLT." The kid is still grinning wide and dancing around and jabbing at the glass, while the parents study me with matching frowns. "I love BLTs. With loads of bacon and lots of tomatoes. I love tomatoes, too. And they're good for you. Aren't they, Daddy?"

I hang onto my smile like a life buoy. "Your daughter is so cute."

My words achieve their purpose. The parents' expressions change from concerned to happy, and then they're ordering, and my hands are busy, toasting bread, stacking subs, then wrapping them. The crinkling of paper and the kid's laughter fill the deli, and all I want to do is crawl into a dark corner and cry.

But I watch them walk out, my eyes dry and burning, watch them talking among themselves, laughing, watch the father lift his child up high and hug her. Just like Daddy used to lift me.

My throat hurts from the tears held back. My mom and dad loved each other; my childhood memories are full of them in love, joking, having fun. But she still killed him. She decided one day to deliberately drive off the road and kill the two of them.

How does someone change like that? How does love change to homicidal intent?

That thought is followed by an immediate rush of nausea.

I loved Mimi. I loved her so much, it tore me apart when she betrayed me to Beth.

Did that anger, that grief, make me change, too?

Somewhere in the time span of memory loss, did I become someone else?

James said Mimi wanted to tell me something critical, something so urgent he had to rush her home. She must've told me what it was—it must be in the words she said when she was standing at my bedroom door or when she was walking away from me into the night. Submerged in the recesses of my brain.

What if it was something that made me angry? Something that made me follow her?

That made me . . . hurt her?

The bell above the front door buzzes. I hurry from around the counter, thinking it's the family returning, then stop dead.

A stocky white man with sparse salt-and-pepper hair and a rugged square face walks toward me. Behind him is Mr. Lee.

"Hey, kiddo." Mr. Lee leans down for a quick hug. "This is Lieutenant Williams."

He wasn't supposed to be here for an hour—that's my first thought, followed by a sensation of being unable to breathe. Recognizing an incoming panic attack, I grip the metal edge of the counter and meet the cop's smiling hazel eyes. Aware of the cool assessment behind the smile, the way he's noted my white-knuckled grip.

I release the counter and force my lips to curve.

"I won't take too much of your time, Ms. Nair. Just a follow-up on what you told Officer Laney." He walks toward a table in the corner and draws a chair out for me. "Why don't we sit and talk?"

I sink into the chair, my legs suddenly numb. What exactly did I tell Laney? I told him about my injuries and how I thought they came from the hedge maze at Beth's, the mud-stained scarf, my memory being foggy. And how Mimi was wearing the scarf when she left, and I didn't know how it ended up in her room afterwards. The cop seemed underwhelmed by the information; he barely listened to me before hanging up.

But not the lieutenant. That analytical expression makes it clear this isn't a casual visit; it's an interrogation. He's seen the holes in my story, the holes I hadn't noticed in my naivete when I called Laney. I feel the ground disintegrate under me.

A warm hand clasps my clenched ones. Mr. Lee's seated next to me. "You'll be fine, kiddo. I'm here."

I nod, my throat tight. There's so much unconditional love in his eyes, but then I don't think he'd ever believe I'm capable of doing anything bad, or that anyone else would, either. Once, I accidentally broke our neighbor's flowerpot while biking and then freaked out, spiraling into an anxiety attack. This was a month after coming to Orin—I assumed I'd get taken away from Auntie and Mimi, so I denied culpability. Mr. Lee chose to believe me rather than the neighbor's eyewitness account. I'm glad he's here with me now with that promise of unflinching support.

The lieutenant clears his throat. "Ms. Nair, you told Officer Laney that you woke up the morning your cousin went missing with injuries and you couldn't remember how you sustained these injuries."

"I . . . yes." I wait for the flicker of skepticism but get an encouraging nod instead. "I thought I couldn't remember because I was half asleep."

"What injuries did you notice?"

I told Laney this already. "Bruises on my arms and legs, and a bump on my head."

"How big of a bump?" When I measure out an inch on my finger, his brows raise. "You told Officer Laney this happened from the hedges at Beth Grant's house."

I nod.

"I looked at the Grants' yard. The hedges are tree-sized, and some of the branches are thick enough to bruise." Relief wakens in my heart, then dies at his next words. "But to cause a head injury and memory loss, something that sounds a lot like a concussion? Must have been a rough night."

He says it with a soft chuckle, but it does nothing to ease my mind. My arm itches. The bruise there is fading, the purple retreating into my brown skin.

"You told Officer Laney you remembered seeing your cousin leaving the house again, later that same night. Did she say anything to you before she left?"

Yes, words that made no sense. Words that I'm terrified to remember now because what if I reacted to them—and that's why Mimi's gone?

What did I do?

"Ms. Nair?"

"Yes, um, no, she didn't."

"So there was nothing? No words exchanged?"

The disbelief in his voice rubs raw on my skin like salt on a wound. "Just, maybe goodnight, things like that." I cringe at how absurd my words sound and wait for him to call me out.

"Okay. You also said you believe she was wearing the dress found on Gaston Beach, and a black scarf when she left." His voice has changed, an edge creeping into the even tone. "But then you found her scarf in her room the next morning. How do you explain that?"

Mr. Lee shifts in his chair. "Mimi could easily have returned home while Tanvi was sleeping, Lieutenant. And then left again."

A shadow crosses the lieutenant's face. Then it's gone, and he leans back in the chair. "Forgive my misstep. I should've first asked you how you were doing with the concussion. You didn't seek any medical treatment?"

I notice he doesn't respond to Mr. Lee's explanation. Does

that mean he believes it? I lick my suddenly dry lips. "No. It, um, the bump is almost gone."

"And the headache?"

It's back now, clawing at the base of my skull. Making it hard to think, to evade his questions.

"You do realize that it would've been extremely hard for you to bike home from Beth Grant's house after a concussion. Impossible, I'd say." He leans forward, his eyes suddenly sharp. "What do you truly think caused that injury, Ms. Nair?"

My mouth's dry as dust and I can't speak because I know the real question he wants to ask me. I feel it on every inch of my skin.

Did you hurt your cousin?

Icy fingers walk down my spine.

She's a killer, too. The kids laughed and poked at my arms when I tried fending them off. *It runs in the family. Psycho.*

Psycho, psycho, they chanted, circling me as I cried, scattering only when Mimi got there to rescue me.

"Ms. Nair?"

My lips are numb and stiff, and it's hard to make them move, but I know I need to. "I squeezed into the hedges to hide, and a branch caused the injury." I can't recognize the voice as mine. It's like someone's in my head, manipulating my voice.

Telling me to lie.

And I need to listen to that someone because I want the lieutenant to stop looking at me that way. Like he knows I was uninjured and not concussed when I returned home from Beth's place. Like he knows my injuries came from attacking Mimi afterwards.

And he thinks I'm lying through my teeth to protect myself.

Then he nods and stands, the chair legs scraping the tiled floor. "Okay, I think that'll do for now. Here." He slides a business card across the table. "Call me anytime if you think of anything that may help us find your cousin." He exchanges a few words with Mr. Lee—words that I can't make out with the ringing in my ears—then he's gone, the deli door swinging shut behind him, followed by the revving of a car engine outside.

Mr. Lee's saying something, but all I can think is *He'll be back.*

If Dr. Ajay were here, he'd tell me the human brain is complicated, that I can't force myself to remember that missing night just like I can't force myself to forget Daddy's death. But I don't have the luxury of waiting because the lieutenant's not done with me yet.

He knows I couldn't have biked home concussed.

I know I wasn't hurt when I returned home. I got hurt after I watched Mimi leave the house again. After I followed her into the rain.

I love her. I know that in every fiber in my body. But I also know Mom's love for Dad turned to hatred vicious enough to kill.

My face feels so tight, my skin crackles like dry parchment. Then I see the text on my phone screen. It's from an unknown number.

I saw you that night.

A weird buzzing fills my ears, like a thousand angry bees locked in my skull. Mr. Lee's staring out through the window and hasn't seen the message.

Bubbles appear in the text bar, then:

LIKE MOTHER, LIKE DAUGHTER.

CHAPTER 15

EVERYTHING'S BEEN A blur since the text. I deleted it right after I saw it, and two days later, the sentences burn bright in my brain like fluorescence patterns in a dark night.

Like mother, like daughter.

A terrible weight presses down on my heart, crushing, crushing until it feels like it'll implode.

"You okay?" Krista says. "You're shivering."

"Just cold." Which is obviously a lie because it's one of those last hot September days where the temperature has climbed to eighty already, though it's barely nine A.M. and the school's AC isn't working.

Krista nods, sympathy in her green eyes, and wraps an arm around my shoulders. "They'll find out who did this, Tanvi."

Someone thinks it's me.

The hair rises on the back of my neck. I pored through social media after receiving that text to look for any chatter about me or my mom. Anyone posting about what my mom did or linking in the news article from eight years ago, or even—and my blood ran cold at this—if Beth's released the video she took of Mom's candles and my passing out. But I couldn't find anything. There wasn't anything about the photo I took, either. Most comments were about the investigation itself.

The first post that popped up was from someone called Melissa. It took me a second to remember the freshman from Beth's orientation group who'd posted previously right after

Mimi's clothes were found. I didn't know her popularity had skyrocketed until I saw she'd gained over 30K followers. Her second video was uploaded last night.

While Krista's busy talking to a couple of her track friends in the hall, I click on the video again. This one is titled *My take on #MimiTaylor part 2.*

"Hey everyone, I'm Melissa, welcome to my recap. There's been fresh movement since I talked to you last. The investigation into Mimi's disappearance has taken a new turn. Initially, the understanding was that this was a case of a runaway who landed on Gaston Beach at the wrong time and unfortunately was targeted by a random person who saw her there. But I've heard from sources that certain people we know have been called in for questioning. Now I'm talking about well-known figures—a jock whose athletic career could be in jeopardy, a reigning queen now in danger of losing her crown, a wannabe who landed a prized captaincy spot after her competition vanished. So why are the investigators focusing on Orin and on Mimi's friends and acquaintances and not sweeping Gaston for a psycho? Could this be a premeditated crime? The investigators seem to think so. Stay with me, friends, for the next edition of Melissa's recap where I'll have all the deets."

A jock, a queen, and a wannabe. She's talking about Greg, Beth, and Lyla. So they've all been questioned? The weight crushing my chest eases a bit. It isn't just me that the cops have in their sights.

After leaving Krista in her homeroom, I head to mine at the end of the hall, threading past stragglers. On the way, I check my phone again for any posts from the three. Beth's been uncharacteristically silent since Mimi's clothes were found on the beach and Greg has made his media private. But Lyla's posted overnight.

> @trackqueen: what the hell r the c*ps doing? get the shithead in Gaston who did this to Mimi & leave us be!!! Why r they harassing us?

> @i_read_books: what's going on???

> @shitisreal: she's freaking out cause they questioned her bf about you know what. Seeing Mimi got missing right after she talked to Coach, it's clear SOMEONE wanted her out of the way!!

> @trackqueen: stfu, we did nothing wrong.

> @shitisreal: hahahaha yeah right.

Once I reach my homeroom, I settle into a seat next to the windows, my thoughts returning to the anonymous text I received. Could the texter be someone who wanted to divert attention from themselves and onto me? Like one of the others who had been questioned? But if that's the case, they're more likely to tell the cops about my past rather than text *me*.

What if it's someone who knows what my mind is hiding from me? Someone who saw me do something that night . . .

"Hey," Abby says from the seat next to me.

I nod and open my notebook, a clear hint that I don't want to talk.

But she says, "Thanks for the notes." Clearly, she's not good at taking hints.

It feels like years have passed since I gave her my notes to try and buy information about James. I nod again.

After a couple of minutes of silence filled with the annoying scratch of her fingernail on the desktop, she says, "Sorry about everything. I don't think I told you that yet, but I'm so terribly sorry about Mimi and everything."

My eyes fill with tears. She actually sounds genuine. I lower my gaze to the desk, refusing to let her see.

"I really miss Mimi," she says. "She was a great captain, tough but fair. She worked hard to make all of us better. All Lyla thinks about is her own times. She'll sink the team to prop herself up." Abby's lips thin into an angry line. "But then she got what she wanted, didn't she?"

Thankfully, the teacher walks in and the class settles, with conversations tapering off and the scrape of chair legs on the floor. Abby's not done though. She whispers, "I have something to tell you after class."

More apologies? She's waiting for an answer, so I nod again. My head's gonna snap off with the amount of nodding.

The second the bell rings and class is done, she's up, grabbing her books and tugging on my arm. "Come with me. Hurry," she adds when I frown at her. "If I don't make it to practice in five minutes, Lyla will get suspicious."

"Of what?"

But she's already at the door. I follow her out, gritting my teeth when she continues down the hall. "Why are you acting so mysterious?"

Her gaze slips past me and widens. Before I can say a word, she pulls me into an alcove at the end of the hall.

A group of girls in tracksuits are walking toward us with Lyla in the lead.

I study Lyla and am struck again by the drastic change in her. Her customary hunched shoulders and shrinking demeanor are gone, and she walks with Beth's confident strides. Her silk blouse and skirt outfit with a scarf around her neck and the dyed blond hair complete her Beth transformation. But on her it looks fake, like a watered-down reflection of Beth.

Once Lyla and her entourage disappear around the corner, Abby says, "It's been Lyla all along."

I frown, eyeing her. "What're you talking about?"

"Hacking into your account and releasing that photo, for one. She hated Mimi ever since Beth unfriended her for Mimi. Then Mimi was made captain and man, was Lyla livid." A gleam of satisfaction lights Abby's eyes. "But what really set her off was Mimi telling Coach she saw Greg use drugs before his games last year."

"What?" I gasp. "He did?"

"At least that's what Mimi said. Coach was going to investigate, and if her accusations were proven right, then every game Greg played would be called into question. He'd never be able to play again. Lyla and Greg knew they had to discredit Mimi so no one would believe anything she said." She glances around at the stragglers in the hall—it's the lull between classes—but lowers her voice anyway. "They planned to do something at Beth's party; I heard them whispering among themselves."

I should feel relieved at this news because it may mean it's not me, but the feeling that wrenches my heart is grief and anger. Lyla and Greg planned to hurt my cousin, but I knew nothing of this, nothing of what Mimi was going through. If Mimi hadn't cut me off on Beth's instigation, I'd have been able to help her.

"But then Beth stopped the party, like, suddenly," Abby says. "And Mimi left with James on his bike. Lyla and Greg wanted to follow them. We'd all come to the party in my car, so Greg told me to sit in the backseat and he drove with Lyla next to him." She shudders, staring at her clenched hands.

"Greg was driving like a maniac, following the bike so closely I thought he meant to run them over. Every time James sped up, he'd speed up, too, and a couple of times he almost bumped the bike off the road. Mimi kept looking back at us, and she looked terrified."

My mouth dries. I've never seen my cousin scared of anything. She had a spine tougher than anyone I knew.

"Greg backed off once James turned down your block. They kicked me out of my own car and drove off. Which pissed me off. Especially since it was all messed up when they returned it, like muddy and the insides all wet."

What the hell? Just like my damp, mud-stained clothes. "Did they tell you how it got like that?"

"Nope. But before they kicked me out, I heard Lyla say she knew where Mimi would be later that night, and they could get her then."

"Where?" My heart thunders so loud, it nearly drowns out my words. "Where did she think Mimi would be?"

"I don't know."

"You must tell the cops what you told me. Once they question Lyla and Greg—"

"I can't. You don't understand. I just told you so you'll know it's not your fault, it wasn't the photo you took that led to Mimi disappearing. Lyla and Greg would have found another way to get her . . ."

Did they? Is that how the car got messed up? According to the news article I read, the investigators believed Mimi drowned within hours of her going missing. What if Greg and Lyla found her right after she left our house, forced her into the car, and took her to Gaston? It's forty-five minutes to Gaston if you bike real fast. Mimi and I did that a few times, biking to Gaston Beach when Auntie couldn't drive us. But it's only fifteen minutes by car. Once they got Mimi there, they . . .

Every drop of saliva in my mouth dries. "The cops need to know, Abby."

She shakes her head so hard, her red bangs fly across her eyes. She pushes the strands away with an impatient hand. "If you tell the cops, I'll deny the whole thing."

My stomach drops in a sickening manner. "Abby, please."

She backs away from me. "You don't know Lyla; she's vicious."

"Abby, wait . . ."

She shakes her head again and races off down the hall and around the corner. In the direction of Lyla and her group.

I thought for a brief few seconds that I had an ally, a chance at righting this, finding who hurt Mimi, but Abby—for all her words—has still chosen Lyla. I want to be angry, brave—but all I can do is slump against the wall, the rough plaster scraping my back through my thin shirt. Greg and Lyla had a motive, and the lieutenant needs to know this so he can interrogate them. But if I tell him and Abby denies everything, he might think I'm making things up to throw suspicion off me.

No, I need to find proof that Lyla went after Mimi.

My phone buzzes. It's Auntie. "Tanvi," she says as soon as I connect. "Are you okay?"

Recognizing the anxiety threading through her voice, I steady my own. "Yes, Auntie, are you home?" Mr. Lee was going to take her to the park. Her psychologist, Dr. Ajay, suggested it as a distraction.

"Yes. I don't want to go to the park." There's a restlessness edging the anxiety and sharpening her tone. "How long will it be before school's done, honey?"

Considering I'm only done with my first class, there's the whole day left, and I was planning to tackle Lyla and Greg today, it'll be a while. But Auntie needs me more. "I'll come home right now, Auntie."

"Good. Come home soon, honey."

"I will. A half hour tops." She'll start the countdown until I walk in through the door. Greg and Lyla will have to wait until tomorrow.

AUNTIE SITS AT the kitchen table, a brown envelope stamped with Orin PD's address in front of her.

My heart thuds. She clutches Mimi's license, her eyes lowered to it as she caresses Mimi's photo with a trembling finger.

Oh, God. "Auntie . . ."

"The police dropped it off. They said her phone and house key weren't in the purse." She lifts her eyes, and they're shining but not with tears. "You know what that means? She's going to return, honey. Otherwise, why would she keep the key?"

I throw my arms around her, and Auntie hugs me tight, but my insides are a block of ice. If Mimi planned to return, she wouldn't have dumped her cards. But I don't have the heart to say that to Auntie. Instead, I call Mr. Lee from my room, who confirms that the cops didn't find Mimi's phone or key in her purse.

"I know Indira thinks it means Mimi will return, but the purse was ripped open when it was found on the beach. The phone and key must've gotten washed away, just like . . ." His voice catches.

Just like Mimi. His sob creates an echo of agony in my heart, a reminder that there's no way to ease it, not without Mimi returning unharmed. "Could whoever, um, hurt Mimi have taken it?"

"Then they would've taken the debit card. There's been no movement in her bank account, and her phone's never been used since." There's a pause. "Kiddo, don't worry too much about the way the lieutenant questioned you, okay? He knows you loved her. It's just that the cops seem to think the suspect is someone who knew her."

Which is what that Melissa person said on her video as well. "Do you know who all they've questioned?"

"Well, James, for one. The others I'm not sure."

So, if Melissa's sources are right, it'll mean Greg, Lyla, Beth, and now James, too.

Downstairs, Auntie is in the prayer room again, with Mimi's photo placed in front of Lord Krishna's idol.

She lights the lamp and sits cross-legged. I follow suit, intensely aware of the empty space beside me where Mimi sat during special festivals while Auntie did her pujas. Before we'd get decked out in our traditional Indian clothing and head to the temple in downtown Detroit.

Auntie closes her eyes, folds her hands, and starts chanting. I join her, murmuring the Sanskrit words invoking Durga's blessings, familiar to me since childhood, since Mom taught it to me. I would sit on Mom's lap while she held my folded hands between hers and I'd repeat the words after her. Feeling her heart beating in rhythm to mine, feeling the safety of my mom's embrace, the steady flames from the oil lamps and the scent of incense create a sense of peace and rightness inside me.

The low murmur of prayers and the hiss of burning from the oiled wick blend into a song, while smoke swirls to the ceiling, and the scent of camphor and incense surrounds me. I lower my gaze to Mimi's photo and don't wipe away the tears that slip down my face.

HOURS LATER, ONCE Auntie is asleep, I slump on the sofa in the living room. Night has fallen outside, and the neighborhood has quieted, the evening sounds of people returning from work, screeching kids and excitable dogs having petered out.

With the house being the last on the block and the closest to the woods, the only sounds are an occasional owl hooting.

A squeak cuts through my jumbled thoughts. It sounded like the rusted hinges of the gate.

I peer through the window. Weak yellow light from the front porch falls on the deserted yard and barely penetrates the darkness beyond. But the gate seems to be closed. I'm about to turn away when I notice the front door is cracked open.

But I'd locked it when I returned from school. I'm positive.

With trembling fingers, I lock it and slide the double bolts in.

The thuds of the bolts falling in place echoes into silence, and then I hear it again. *Squeak.*

Shadows move beyond the edge of the light on the road outside.

One shadow. A figure standing still.

A jolt runs through me, and a memory appears out of the fog in my mind.

There was someone standing there the night Mimi left. I saw Mimi walking through the rain toward them. Then she turned, looked over her shoulder. *Stay home, Tanvi. Don't follow us.*

Us.

My pulse begins a frantic beat in my neck.

But not loud enough to drown out the roar of an engine. The beam from a single headlight penetrated the rain and lit up the road.

It was a motorcycle.

Mimi climbed on behind the driver. They disappeared into the gloom, then the engine died down, replaced by rain drumming on the pavement. Night descended like an inky black curtain.

Sweat breaks out in a clammy film across my forehead. I

back away from the window, my shaking hand reaching for the flashlight kept on the console table next to the sofa. Cool metal sinks into my palm, a click and a beam of brilliant light slips through the windowpane, lighting a wedge of lawn, the gate, and the strip of road the shadow was on.

There's no one there now. But there was then. On that night.

James has a bike. After bringing her home from Beth's, he must've then waited to pick her up before going to the tavern.

I heard her enter her room at nine P.M., and per the guy at the tavern, the fight happened at nine-thirty. Which means she must've stepped in for just a few minutes before going off with him again. Mimi wanted to tell me something important. That was why she returned. Though why didn't she text? Or call me? True, she'd blocked me after friending Beth, but she could've easily unblocked me.

Shit, if only I could remember what she said. Or why I followed her.

I start pacing, then stop dead. I still haven't been able to find out from Grace if Mimi was at the tavern during the fight.

Or if James hurt her on the way there.

Could he have?

If James did, he couldn't have taken her to Gaston and gotten to the tavern by nine-thirty. Besides, there was real grief in his expression when he talked about Mimi at the hospital. He also seemed genuinely taken aback when I told him it was me he'd chased down with a gun.

If it's not him, then . . . Greg and Lyla? If only I could convince Abby to tell the cops what she told me. Maybe I can still get her to. There's another bio test coming up in a week; I'll offer to get her notes for that.

I reach for my phone intending to text her but see a message on my screen. It's a text from Krista. **WTF is wrong with Beth? What's she talking about??**

A sick feeling rises in my gut.
Beth can't have released the video. She can't . . .
But it's not the video.

**sorry for the silence, but I needed time to process
what happened to my best friend. I see all these stupid videos trying to capitalize off Mimi, I'm looking
at you, Melissa, but none of you know anything
about Mimi. Only I know the darkness in her life,
the horrible stuff she lived through, all because she
took in a parasite, a snake, into her house & who
ruined her life. And if y'all think it's a lie, I have
proof. In Mimi's own words.**

Mimi's journal.
I feel like puking. Even Krista realized Beth was referring
to me, and so will everyone who reads this.
Once Beth gives the journal to the cops, they'll have the
strongest motive possible against me—one written by Mimi
herself.

CHAPTER 16

MY STEPS DRAG as I walk across the schoolyard to the front doors while Beth's voice keeps echoing in my brain.

Do you know how sick she was of constantly having to be strong for you, of constantly being reminded by her mom that she had no other worth?

Auntie never said that. She'd never say that. But she did go above and beyond to make me feel at home. I don't know if my psychologist ever told Auntie how terrified I was of losing my new home, how the slightest harshness or raised voice on her part made me freeze in terror that she'd turn me out. But Auntie made it a point to always show her love for me, much more than she did for Mimi.

Mimi never gave off any vibes that she felt overlooked. I don't remember the slightest indication that she resented me—at least, until she ditched me. But was I so blinded by my own grief that I missed the clues?

You never cried with her for her father.

That thought makes my throat tighten. She didn't either. Did she?

I don't remember him at all, T, so I can't really miss him or cry for him.

But maybe she was hurting in a different way, hurting that she didn't have any memories.

It was just her and Auntie until I came along. And then she had to suddenly step into the role of protector. She was just a year older than me; she was only nine, and she did it. She became my bodyguard, my confidante, supporting me all the way through. She centered her life around me. Oblivious as I was in my grief, I never bothered to ask if she wanted to lean on me for a change.

Did she feel crowded out? Like she was losing her own identity?

Is that why she confided in her journal and in Beth rather than hash it out with me?

A knife twists in my heart. I hurry through the front doors and the girls' restroom down the hall to find an empty stall. Then I sink down on the toilet seat, muffling my sobs whenever someone enters.

I should've known. I should have . . .

But she told me everything else: her dreams, her goals, how we'd go on trips together when we were older and had the money. We were inseparable up until we weren't. I only saw the love she had for me.

Which means I missed the clues.

My butt's numb from the toilet seat and my eyes are gritty by the time a text pops up on my phone. I stiffen, thinking it's a repeat of the anonymous threat. But it's from Krista.

Going to the vigil?

What vigil?

An attachment appears. It's of Beth's post from this morning.

Hi friends, I'm organizing a vigil for my best friend, Mimi Taylor. It'll be on the football field right after school's done at 3:15 sharp tomorrow. Please attend so we can all pray for Mimi & her family.

I wonder if you can taste hatred. Because that's what the ache in my teeth feels like.

I hurry out of the stall and wash my hands in a trickle of water from the rusty faucet.

A click of heels approaches the restroom door. It's thrust open and Lyla enters.

Her Beth persona has slipped a bit. The signature silk scarf is missing, and her makeup must've been applied by a sloppy hand considering the clumped mascara on her lashes. Her eyes widen when she sees me, but the surprise transitions immediately to a scowl. She strides to the sink.

Abby said Greg and Lyla followed Mimi that night, that Greg almost bumped their bike off the road. It's impossible to imagine Mimi's terrified look—my cousin's never feared anything. I watch as Lyla takes out a makeup kit from her purse, tempted to rip it out of her hand and force her to tell me if she hurt Mimi. But that won't work, and so I hide my clenched fists in my pockets. If I want answers, I'll need to be subtle about it. "Congrats on your making captain."

She pauses midway through pressing cold water to her eyes. "Hypocrite, much? I know exactly what you're thinking."

So much for subtle. "Then you'd know I'm wondering if you got rid of Mimi so you'd make captain and so any investigation into your boyfriend's drug use would get stalled."

Her lips curl. "Yeah? Well, I heard the cops have you on the top of the suspect list. Something about the initial story you gave them having gaping holes in it?"

The blood drains out of my face. She can't have found out. There was nothing revealed on my social media search, and even Melissa, the freshman who's appointed herself as the ultimate source of information on Mimi, hadn't mentioned my name as one of the people questioned.

"And so now you're like a cornered rat, trying to blame someone else. Because of you, they got Greg in for questioning. You told them Greg followed Mimi after Beth's party."

What? "I didn't say that." *I only wanted to.* Did Abby grow a spine and say something?

"Liar," she snarls. "You're such a phony. I know you wanted Mimi gone, too."

"You're delusional."

"Though I understand why you hated her." She continues like I hadn't spoken. "She was a bitch, the way she framed Grace by planting her laptop in Grace's backpack so everyone'd think she was a thief."

"What the hell are you talking about? Mimi would never do that to Grace."

"You really that stupid? Mimi couldn't have weirdos like Grace around when she was trying to get into Beth's inner circle. She lied about Grace just like she lied about Greg. Just because he called her out at my party last summer, saying she was a gold digger. And that was exactly what she was. A gold digger who'd willingly destroy everyone else to get what *she* wanted!" Lyla glares at me, her makeup kit forgotten on the sink.

My first reaction is to lash out at her and deny everything. The cousin I knew would never frame Grace and treat her so cruelly.

But she also wouldn't have betrayed my secrets to Beth.

Which she did.

I force myself to meet the accusation in Lyla's eyes. "I didn't hate my cousin; I didn't hurt her, either. But I think you did, you and Greg. You followed her after Beth's party all the way to my house. Then you tracked her down afterward and—"

"She was fine when we saw her at the tavern." Lyla's lips thin into white lines. "And she was fine when we left right after the cops took her loser boyfriend away in cuffs."

Is she telling the truth? If she is, then it means James couldn't have hurt Mimi. "You didn't see where Mimi went afterward?"

"No!" She glances at the door and lowers her voice. "We all scattered when the cops got there, and she did, too. You should know."

I stiffen. "How would I know?" Did Lyla see me at the tavern? Is that why she mentioned gaping holes in my story? "I didn't lie to the cops."

She shrugs. "Who's gonna believe you? You're the one with the twisted gene. Mimi made a mistake taking you in and making you part of her family."

She took in a snake, a parasite, into her house, Beth said in her post. *I have proof in Mimi's own words*. She was referring to Mimi's journal.

Did she show it to Lyla?

"You're just like your crazy mom, and everyone in Orin knows that."

Like mother, like daughter.

I could ask her if she sent me that text, but does it matter anymore? After Beth's post, they'll be believing the same thing. I slip past her and to the door.

"The cops ought to lock you up so the rest of us can be safe."

The door swings shut behind me, cutting off her scowling face.

The vise crushing my heart feels like a physical thing. The rest of them get to stay innocent until proven guilty; I'll stay guilty until proven innocent. My feelings for my cousin, the belief I have that I'd never hurt her—none of that will cut it anymore.

I must remember what happened. That's the only way out.

THE VIGIL BETH organized for Mimi the next day is underway by the time Krista and I exit the school building. A makeshift podium is set up in the middle of the football field on which Beth stands while a growing crowd gathers around her.

"Most of you here know Mimi Taylor as the ace athlete, the star who put Orin High on the map for track, and also as the fellow senior you could borrow notes from and know they'd be super detailed enough to get you past that next quiz." A smattering of laughter and nods from the crowd follow her words. "But I also knew her as the best friend anyone can have." She dabs her eyes with a tissue, then waves.

I follow her gaze to a brunette in a gray suit who waves back. Michelle Bitt, a news reporter for WCBB-TV, our local news channel.

"Mimi Taylor was my best friend," Beth says. "I feel like I lost a piece of my soul. No one wants the truth about what happened to her more than me."

Really? Auntie's life is now split between deep bouts of depression and intermittent bouts of severe anxiety, and she's popping meds just to sleep. And this girl thinks she's suffering the worst? First she was the "victim" trapped by Mimi's drug habits, and now she's the grief-stricken friend.

She touches a tissue delicately to her eyes. "You all know how inseparable Mimi and I were." She reaches into her bag for another tissue, and I wonder if she has Mimi's journal in there. If only I could read it and find out what Mimi said about me. "She often said she believed we were sisters in another life."

Did I push my cousin toward Beth by not being the sister she needed?

Beth's so kind. She wanted to know about me, my life, and listened to every word like it was the most important thing to her. Like I was important.

The day after Beth's Halloween party, we were walking past Beth in the school hall when her gaze skimmed past Grace and me, but instead of skimming past Mimi, too—we'd always been invisible to her—she smiled. *I know you now, Mimi*, that smile said. Weeks later, we knew how much Mimi had changed when she walked past our usual table in the cafeteria toward Beth waiting with an empty space next to her.

She's Beth's now, Grace said.

No, I said fiercely. *I know Mimi; she'll return to us.*

But she's changed, Tanvi. That's not our Mimi.

Should I have tried harder to get Mimi back then? But I had no clue then that she had been feeling overlooked or that she was starting to resent me. Entrusting her innermost feelings to a journal instead of telling me the truth.

I blink away tears, then spot Abby at the back of the crowd. She's staring at Beth with a frown. Lowering my voice, I tell Krista the stuff Abby said about Greg and Lyla following Mimi after the party and then add everything Lyla told me in the restroom yesterday. "Lyla insists Mimi framed Grace," I finish.

Her eyes widen. "There was a rumor going around that Grace was framed."

"What?" I gasp. "You *knew*?"

"Not really. Sorry, Tanvi, but I wasn't sure if it was true and didn't want to mess up things between you and Mimi if it wasn't."

My stomach turns. God, I can't believe it. How could Mimi do something so awful to Grace? And if she did do that, then I really messed up by not being there for Grace.

"Let's talk to Abby," Krista says. "She better hope she was the one to send in that anonymous tip about Greg and Lyla, or else we *will* be going to the cops right now."

I don't bother trying to stop Krista. Abby's face pales when she sees the two of us approaching her. "Shit, you can't ask me to do anything else."

For the first time since Mimi went missing, I feel a burst of relief. "You told the cops."

"Shh." Abby strides away from the crowd and we join her. She glances at the crowd to see if anyone is looking, but everyone's attention is fixed on Beth. "Yeah. What you said messed me up, and I couldn't sleep. I'm totally fucked if Lyla finds out."

"Thanks, Abby. I owe you." Buoyed by her honesty—however brief—I tell her what Lyla told me about Mimi framing Grace. Abby's the only person in that circle who will actually talk to me, and who knows how long that will last. "Is it true?"

Abby worries her lower lip between her teeth. "Well . . . okay, Mimi told me the laptop was missing and she was certain it was in Grace's bag. We were at the girls' lockers, and Grace's gym bag was lying on the bench along with everyone else's. And Mimi's laptop was sticking out of Grace's bag. Everyone saw it. But when Mimi confronted Grace, Grace didn't deny anything." Abby shivers theatrically. "She just looked at Mimi like Mimi stabbed her or something. She's always been kind of weird, but . . ."

"What?" My chest aches so hard for Grace.

"I wouldn't be surprised if Mimi wanted to get rid of her because Beth wouldn't have it otherwise." When I raise my brows, she shrugs. "That was why Beth dumped Lyla—Lyla refused to break up with Greg. There are no divided loyalties with Beth. Once you're selected as her bestie, it's like you're not allowed to have any other close friends or relationships."

Krista scowls. "God, I hate that girl. Did she even care for Mimi?"

"To be fair, she's been totally cut up since Mimi left," Abby says. "And the cops questioning her didn't help any."

Melissa implied this in her video. My stomach flips.

"But we all saw Mimi leave her place after the party," Abby says. "Beth remained home after that. I saw her when I was walking past her house after Lyla and Greg kicked me out of my car that night."

"I really wish I could do more," Beth says in response to another question from the reporter. We all turn back to her, meld our attention back with the crowd's. "My heart is crushed with grief," she says.

Beth's audience has grown since Krista and I started talking to Abby. They watch her, rapt, held bound to her as if by magnetism.

". . . love all people, all human beings," she says, angling herself so her words are delivered directly into the mic held out by the reporter but still somehow keeping eye contact with everyone in the crowd. "My heart is full of love and hope for all of us."

There's pin-drop silence, except for people sniffing and a few muffled sobs. They're hanging on with bated breath to every word she says. Absorbing it like a sponge absorbs water.

She makes me feel important, like I'm important to her, Mimi said.

She cares deeply for me.

I bet every person in this crowd—except Krista, me, and Abby, probably, since she's still frowning—believe completely that Beth cares intensely for them.

She's managed to convince them with her presence, her words, her way of addressing them.

I think I know why Mimi changed.

She didn't do what she did to Grace and me just because of Beth's demand for full allegiance. Or to be popular. Mimi was strong-willed; she wouldn't give in or hurt Grace so awfully unless there was something that overrode her usual sensibility, her ethics, her sense of fairness.

And that something was Beth's charisma, her ability to convince people that her words are the truth. She made Mimi into a loyal follower. Not with force, but with persuasion and hypnotizing charisma.

I stare at her, reluctantly aware that if I didn't remember her laughing as she lit Mom's candles over my begging her not to, if she didn't record my breakdown and threaten to publicize it, I'd have also started believing that she was as pure and gentle as she professes to be.

But Mimi was not the person Beth transformed her into. Underneath that exterior was the cousin I knew and loved, the cousin who once loved me. Despite logic or reason, I know it as sure as I know my heart inside my chest is beating.

That's what I must remember and hang on to.

The back of my neck tingles. I turn and lock eyes with Grace in the back of the crowd. Unlike the others who stare at Beth wide-eyed, Grace's watching me, her gaze hard and assessing.

Uneasiness coils in the pit of my stomach. If what Abby told me about Mimi framing Grace is true, then Grace must really hate Mimi. Grace didn't deny writing that threatening note when I asked her during the run-in at the dollar store. Then there's the fact that I overheard James talking to someone at his place, someone who also was aware of what happened to Mimi.

The elderly guy at the tavern told me Grace fought the cops to keep them from cuffing James after the fight at the tavern.

I move toward her, pushing through the crowd.

She stiffens, then stumbles back and darts behind the bleachers.

I run after her, slipping through the wooden posts until I'm on the grass beyond. And find it deserted. She's gone.

A gray pallor covers the field and the road ahead, with dark clouds hanging low. A fat drop of water falls on my knee, instantly absorbed into my jeans.

It's starting to rain.

No, it's not. The sky remains overcast, but the air is dry.

But it was raining that Thursday night, the drops drenching my shirt and shorts within seconds of leaving the porch.

The memory is so vivid, I freeze.

The rain formed a sheet of water, the drops so heavy it hurt my skin. *Mimi, wait*, I yelled, running down the yard to the gate. *I'm coming with you.*

She stopped. *Don't follow us.* Her waves of black hair, her skin, her dress, brilliantly silhouetted in a beam of headlight from the bike.

No, something's not right about that image.

The headlight . . . It came from a scooter, a red scooter. Mimi climbed on the scooter, behind . . .

Grace.

It wasn't James who picked Mimi up the night she vanished. It was Grace.

CHAPTER 17

THE CHIPPED WOOD on the gate digs into my palms as I study the strip of road in front of my house. This was where I saw Mimi leaving with Grace that Thursday night. She climbed on the scooter behind the girl she called a thief, a stalker. The girl she framed.

Grace must've known that. Yet, she gave Mimi a ride.

Why'd she do that? Mimi could've easily called James or had him wait if she needed a ride. Maybe Grace offered a ride as some sort of compromise between them—an innocent action on her part.

Only, on the night Mimi disappeared, no action would be innocent or coincidental.

I swing the gate open and step onto the road. Lyla said she saw Mimi at the tavern. And if that memory fragment I had of looking through the tavern door is real, then it meant I followed my cousin and Grace there.

When Mimi, Grace, and I used to hang out, we'd sometimes go to Old Orin where the tavern is located. After Auntie forbade the three of us from riding on Grace's scooter together, Grace would take her scooter with Mimi riding behind, and I rode my bike. They usually got there within twenty minutes, and I'd take double that when I used the road, so about forty minutes.

The elderly guy at the tavern told me the fight started at nine-thirty. Enough time for Grace and Mimi to get there right when the fight broke out. If I followed them on my bike,

I'd have arrived after the fight. The knot in my stomach tightens. I would have missed them.

But there is a shortcut through the woods to Old Orin. We discovered it by accident while exploring the place and finding a track leading to Orin Tool Works, the factory owned by Beth's dad. The factory was in use then—it was shut down right before the holidays last year—but we'd wait until there were no workers around and then cut through to get to Old Orin.

That shortcut through the trees took only about twenty minutes or so.

We'd race down the path I'm running down now, scattering leaves like I'm doing, hurdling tree roots, scrambling for balance on slick rock, racing each other to see who had the best time. Mimi was always the fastest; I had the worst. I can see her running ahead of me, glancing over her shoulder, then slowing down to allow me to catch up. *Come on, T, you got this.*

Mimi.

My hand trembles as I reach for her, the memory of her fingers slipping through mine.

The path ahead of me splits; one fork leads to Orin Springs with the muted sound of thundering water in the distance, and the other isn't a true path. But my feet unerringly know the way, threading past gigantic tree trunks and over stones sharp enough to bite through my sneakers. Soon, the trees start thinning, and then I'm out of the woods and behind Beth's dad's factory.

Wire netting fences off the factory, but there's a gap in one corner we used to get through. I approach the gap, chills running down my spine, feeling Mimi's presence beside me. The coarse wires of the netting scrape the bare skin of my hands as I squeeze through.

Did I do this exact same thing on that Thursday night when Mimi vanished? I wait for the memory to hit, but though the chills intensify, my mind remains blank.

Large pieces of construction equipment—a bulldozer, a couple of excavators—lie on a sea of weeds and twisted creepers in the factory's backyard, which is swallowed by overgrown vegetation. The factory itself, a sprawling three-story rectangular structure made of red bricks, looms over me. The rows of windows are all boarded shut, and, except for an occasional creak or rustle, the place is silent. But I listen hard, and I can hear voices, conversations, milling footsteps, from the hundreds of employees who used to work here.

Now it's just waiting, skulking, watching me in brooding silence.

I start across the yard. The knee-high weeds brush my jeans and I wonder if they'll leave green stains. The closer I get to the building, the stronger the stink of rotting vegetation and animal poop is until it's almost cloying. I circle the side of the building and reach the overgrown front yard.

But something's trampled the weeds here, creating a path from the gate to the front door of the factory. It seems to be recent—the broken stems of the weeds still ooze a sticky liquid, and there are footprints on the dirt-carpeted concrete steps leading to the front door, which is firmly shut.

That's odd. Who'd want to enter an abandoned factory?

The narrow windows along the three floors are all boarded shut. The place is deathly still. My gaze tracks to the window next to the front door. Darkness fills the thin gaps between the wooden boards, but even though nothing's visible, the hairs on the back of my neck rise. Like there's someone in there. An eye pressed to the gap watching me.

Maybe it's just a squatter taking advantage of an abandoned

place. I take a step away, then another, the unnerving tingling in my back refusing to let go until I'm through the front gate and on a deserted strip of potholed road outside.

Farther down, a row of shops appear, mainly eateries, coffee shops, a few convenience stores, a couple of dry cleaners. They used to service the workers at the factory, but they're all abandoned now. People prefer shopping in the newer part of downtown, where Krista's store and Mr. Lee's deli are located. If it weren't for Orin Tavern, Old Orin would truly have been forgotten.

Remembering my task, I glance at the time on my phone. It took me eighteen minutes to get here from home. If I had taken this route that Thursday night, I'd have gotten here by around nine twenty-five P.M. Which would've been about when Mimi and Grace got here on Grace's scooter.

My breath shortens as I approach the tavern. It's quiet—it won't open until much later—and the inside is deserted, chairs turned upside down on tables, a vacuum cleaner next to the wall, the bar bare of any utensils.

But it would've been bustling that night. There would've been cars parked in the now empty parking lot, and Grace's red scooter would have been among them. And the glass pane on the front door would have been brilliantly lit from inside, with rock or probably jazz music throbbing in the air.

I touch the cool glass pane and try to coax out the memory I had earlier of standing here and seeing people dancing under the lights. The fight would've broken out about five minutes after I got here. I close my eyes and imagine the scene unfolding, the dancers scattering, people yelling. The swelling sound of sirens followed by flickering blue and white lights and screeching tires. The thudding of boots on the ground and the door flying open as people raced out and scattered to get away. Loud cop voices shouting orders.

A cop reaching for James, Grace trying to stop them from cuffing him.

Why wasn't Mimi helping James?

My eyes fly open.

My cousin wouldn't have hesitated to step in and protect her boyfriend. But the elderly bartender didn't remember seeing her. Instead, he distinctly remembered Grace fighting the cops to keep James from being arrested.

Where was Mimi during this time? She had to have been inside.

What happened to her after the fight?

I remember how destroyed James looked at the hospital when he talked about Mimi, but he knows more than he's letting on judging from that phone call I overheard at his shop.

He might not have hurt Mimi, but the person he was talking to could have. The person who fought the cops for him.

Who took Mimi to the tavern that night.

I need to find Grace.

IT TOOK ME an hour to track Grace down this time, and it happened purely by chance. Thank God for small towns because I was biking past Orin Café, a popular downtown coffee shop where most people congregate to hang out and get caffeinated. And there it was, Grace's red scooter, parked outside the doors.

The crush of conversations, laughter, the scent of coffee and baked bread hits me as soon as I enter. A thin guy with lanky brown hair handles the long line of customers snaking around the foyer while four employees scurry around, their hands flying, preparing orders, yelling out names.

I look around, then spot Grace cleaning a table in the far corner, an apron tied around her uniform. Ah, so she works here.

Her back is to me, but she must've sensed something, because her spine stiffens and the hand wiping down the table stills. Then she turns, her eyes narrowed, assessing and not at all surprised. "You again? What do you want from me, Tanvi?"

Guilt twists through my heart. If Mimi framed her, she has reason to hate Mimi—and me for not being there for her. But I can't think of that now. I need to find out if she acted on that hate and did something to hurt Mimi. "I need to ask you some questions."

She shrugs and returns to wiping down the table, the rag clenched in her right hand.

"Hey."

"I heard you." She glances at me over her shoulder. "Meet me by the back door. I have a break in five minutes."

I blink, surprised at how quickly she agreed. I was expecting more resistance.

Impatience flashes in her eyes. "I can't talk when I'm working. Not if I want to keep this job. My boss is the worst."

"Fine." I make my way around the café to the back door and wait there, surrounded by the stink of garbage from the nearby dumpster blending in with that of weed and cigarette smoke.

Shortly after, the door opens, and Grace appears. "Okay, get on with it."

I take a deep breath. "I know you picked Mimi up from my house after Beth's party and took her to the tavern. Why would you do that when you hated her?"

She stares at me, then turns to the door.

I block her way. "I need to know."

"Why? You know everything already. Hell, you know more than me."

"What're you talking about?"

Her expression changes, becomes shuttered. "You're such a secretive person, aren't you? Even when we were friends, it was like I never really got to know you. Like you were terrified people would see you for what you really were."

I was going through therapy when Mimi introduced me to Grace and wasn't in any condition to trust anyone new. It took me over a year to start trusting Grace enough to not be on guard around her and another two before I trusted her enough to tell her everything about my past, including Mom's rituals and the candles. "You knew about me, about everything that'd happened." My voice is stiff, resentful that she's bringing this up when we'd moved past this already.

"Yeah, I did, and the irony is I felt terrible for you. I never thought you'd turn out to be like your mom because I didn't believe shit like that. But now . . ." She takes a deep breath. "Now I know."

"Know what?"

"That maybe I was wrong to trust you. That maybe you *are* like her." Her jaw flinches, then hardens. "You know exactly what happened to Mimi."

Blood leaves my face, leaving it prickly and numb. "No, I . . . I don't."

She flushes, her freckles standing out against the brick-red blush covering her cheekbones. "You *followed* us. Mimi told you not to, but you did anyway. You took the shortcut through the woods."

"How . . ." The words stick to my dry throat. She must've seen me.

"You were right there outside the tavern door, looking in through the glass. Watching the fight." She rolls her eyes. "Yet I'm the one who gets called a stalker."

The numbness creeps down my neck.

"I called the cops on Greg, but those idiots nabbed James instead. Then everyone ran, and that was when you left." She leans forward. "And I saw Mimi leaving with you."

I can't feel my hands; my entire body is ice cold. *She didn't*, I want to say. But the words don't form.

"I saw the two of you leave together. You were the last person with her, Tanvi. *You*. No one's seen her since. So, what did you do to her?"

"Grace?" An employee sticks her head out of the door. "They need you inside."

"Coming," Grace mutters, gives me a narrowed look, then hurries through the door.

My heartbeats turn heavy, pounding, echoing in my ears. The parking lot, the dumpster, the café, all of it fades, and then the sidewalk is under my feet, the smell of coffee replaced by sweat, stale perfume, exhaust from the traffic, and the crush of people.

And the faint tinge of smoke from burning candle wax. Bringing with it a gathering dread, inky and cloying, turning my limbs heavy.

Grace must've told the cops what she saw.

No one's going to believe me now. Not Mr. Lee, not Krista, not Auntie.

Auntie . . .

Oh, God, I'll lose her. She'll be alone.

Someone jostles my arm and I stumble.

"Are you okay?" An older guy with straggly graying hair peers at me.

He has kind eyes like Mr. Lee, the type of eyes that say they're willing to listen to your problems. I wish I could tell him I'm not okay, that I desperately need some advice. But I must've nodded, because he smiles and walks on.

You left with Mimi, Grace said. *What did you do to her?*

Did I do anything to her? I couldn't have. But then how did I get bruised? How did I get the bump on my head?

Why the hell can't I remember?

Is it because I don't want to?

Think!

Mimi was wearing her black scarf that night, but I found it in her room the next morning, sticky and wet with the same mud splattered on my clothes.

How did her scarf end up in her room?

Because I brought it home.

The realization feels like a thunderclap to my chest.

There was something in my hand that night. I remember it now.

A piece of cloth. Silky, soft.

Mimi's scarf.

I was running. My shoes felt soggy and squished as I ran. The ground felt hard, uneven. I was stumbling; my breath came shallow and fast.

And I could feel . . . terror.

A terrible, bone-shattering terror.

I suck in a breath, and the memory shatters like fragile glass. The mental fog returns, like a black curtain at the end of a play. But the terror remains, slithering around my heart, leaving ice in its trail.

My hands sting. I look down and find them clenched so hard, the nails dig into the palms. I stare at the bloodless crescents gouged in the skin but instead see Mimi's scarf clutched in my hand.

How did her scarf end up in my hand? What was I running from?

What happened to Mimi?

God, I'm scared to remember.

Scared to return to that fog and find the truth.

CHAPTER 18

ALL I HAVE is a handful of memory fragments. The fragments form pieces of a puzzle, but each time I add a puzzle piece, the picture being revealed becomes more terrifying.

Now I know I was at the tavern with Mimi. I brought Mimi's scarf home. My mind blocked both these truths from me.

The words buzz in my head like flies around a carcass.

I pedal mindlessly, my feet directing me through ingrained paths until I reach my block and turn the corner. And see Beth's blue Porsche parked at my gate.

Just what I need for this awful day to descend right to hell.

Inside, Beth sits next to Auntie on the couch, her arm around Auntie's shoulders. The vase on the coffee table is full of fresh white lilies.

Again.

She's murmuring something to Auntie, who's leaning into her. Beth's head snaps around. Her eyes lock on me, and a glint appears in them. "Hi, Tanvi."

Then Auntie looks up, and a familiar grief and fear wraps around my heart. She's wasting away by the minute, her face sunken and skin sagging. It's like she's aged years in the past two weeks. I hurry to her side. "Auntie."

Beth's arm tightens around Auntie's shoulders. "Mrs. Taylor told me she wasn't aware of the vigil I organized for Mimi. I found that strange since I distinctly remember telling you about it and asking you to let her know as well."

My jaw drops, and I stare at her, unable to believe she'd outright lie like that. "You did nothing of the sort."

"Oh, I did. After lab when you were walking out. I told you the time and everything. You were in a rush and maybe it didn't register? Either that, or you've developed a habit of *forgetting* things lately."

She's watching me, her pupils dilating like she's trying to take in every bit of my reaction.

I rub suddenly chilled arms. Was she at the tavern, too, and saw me there? But didn't Abby say she saw Beth in her house after being kicked out of her car? Beth couldn't have been in two places at once.

Then I notice the disappointment clouding Auntie's tired eyes and feel sick to my stomach. "You should've told me, honey," she says. "I would've liked to attend."

Her words are soft and uttered in an exhausted tone, but they sting like salt on a wound. Auntie's never been disappointed in me before. I made sure to always live up to her expectations, initially because I couldn't risk losing the only home I had left and later because Auntie never expected too much. She only knew to love with her whole heart.

And now Beth's driven a wedge between us.

Is she right? Do I deserve this for overlooking Mimi? For putting so much pressure on her and not being the sister she needed?

The corner of Beth's lips curl in a mocking smile, and the grief twisting around my heart is suddenly edged with fury. The anger is so intense and white-hot, I take two steps away from her to stop myself from dragging her to the door and throwing her out.

I can't snap, not now, not when I need to stay as calm as possible.

I can't afford to allow anyone to know I'm capable of violence.

Auntie sighs, then stands. "I think I'll take a nap."

I'm about to reach for her arm, but Beth beats me to it. "Here, Mrs. Taylor, let me help you." She helps Auntie to her bedroom, and at the door she looks over her shoulder at me, and the glint in her eyes sharpens.

I watch them disappear into the room with an impotent rage.

She reappears a couple of minutes later.

"How dare you lie like that? You never told me about the vigil."

She shrugs. "But you knew about it, didn't you? You could've told your aunt on your own. So why didn't you?" Her brows raise. "Did you *forget* to tell her?"

That same odd inflection, like she's not talking about this anymore, but something totally different.

A chill runs down my spine. On the day Mimi vanished, Beth said something about my meds messing with my brain after I told her I didn't know where Mimi was. She must've just been her usual obnoxious self toward me then.

But this feels different. This feels . . . intentional, especially the way she's studying me, looking for my reaction. I want to ask her to spell out exactly what she means but am terrified to. What if she repeats what Grace said? That I knew what happened to Mimi.

Instead, I go with an offensive tactic. "I didn't *forget* to tell her, Beth, because there was nothing to tell. You're a liar and a bully and—"

"Bullshit. Do you know all the things Mimi's told me about you? How you made life hell for her?"

"Mimi . . . loved me." I hate that my voice shakes in front of this girl, that my limbs are trembling, and I can't do a thing to stop the tremors. "You manipulated Mimi, you changed her, made her into a different person."

"Is that how you comfort yourself? Pretending Mimi didn't reject you?"

She did. But . . . "You twisted her mind."

"You are unbelievable. Let me spell this out for you. She. Hated. You." Her tone is as cold as her eyes. "She was scared to go to sleep at night because she thought you'd kill her mom and her while they were sleeping. Do you understand what that means? Do you understand that type of fear?"

Yes. When I crouched in the corner in my bedroom after Auntie brought me here and watched the shut door, eyes peeled, waiting for that creak and the widening slit of darkness. Waiting for my mom to appear and kill me, too.

"You made Mimi's life hell. She wanted to be rid of you."

My face twitches, an extension of the tremors racking my body. Could Beth be right? Could it be that Mimi had always feared me? That she wasn't the one Beth changed?

That it was me who changed instead?

Lyla said I had a twisted gene.

If Beth hadn't intervened in my life, would I have become my mom?

Would I have followed Mimi out into the night?

Would I have . . . hurt her?

My body is a solid block of ice, and I can't feel my fingers or toes.

Don't go there, don't go there, don't go there!

"Do you know dull people make the best killers?" Beth says. "Because no one ever suspects them. They're so drab and insignificant, invisible, really, and so you don't pay them any attention." Her lips thin into a tight angry line, then she reaches into her purse and brings out a small, leather-wrapped diary.

It's the one she showed me earlier. Mimi's journal.

"Read this so you'll know what you did to Mimi. So you'll finally know the truth."

Did you show it to the cops? I want to ask her. Did she give them the motive they're looking for?

But I keep my lips sealed because I'm terrified of the answer. Again.

Her footsteps recede, followed by the door thudding shut and an engine starting, and then silence falls.

A silence filled with dread.

If I open this book, I'll know the answers. She'll tell me in her own words.

Do I want to know?

Do I have a choice?

The leather feels coarse under my trembling fingers. I open the cover and find lines of Mimi's characteristic cursive handwriting and looped letters.

I've never kept a journal before; these things are such a drag. It's so much easier to talk things through instead of writing it down. But Beth said writing it down will be cathartic. We learned about catharsis in drama last week. I get it now. It's odd how I never realized I had all this ugly, gooey mess inside me ever since Tanvi came home and it took Beth just a few hours to discover it. This mess that kept growing over the years into this rock of anger and resentment I couldn't shake. And so I'm writing it all down and hoping that I'll be able to get rid of it that way. Because there's no way Mom will allow me to get rid of Tanvi herself. Though sometimes I'm tempted to . . . Anyway, here goes. catharsis time!

Every word feels like a slash of a knife. My skin is in agony. I force myself to keep reading.

I was so excited when she first came to Orin. It broke my heart to see how sad she was. I wanted nothing more than to make her smile. I hated that other kids bullied her. Mom asked me to be her big sister and that was what I was. I kept the bullies away and protected her. But I did it because I wanted to. Because she mattered to me so much. Because it broke my heart every time she cried.

The paper rustles as I turn the page.

But then it became all about her. Mom was only concerned about her. We'd come home from school and Mom would immediately attend to her without asking how I was doing. She stopped making my favorite foods. It was always whatever Tanvi wanted to eat. It hurt, not gonna lie, but what hurt the most was when Mom kept shushing me anytime I tried bringing up Dad. She didn't want me talking about Dad because she didn't want Tanvi to be reminded of her father. And that hurt. It hurt that Tanvi had all these beautiful memories about her father, about how cool he was and how much he loved her. But I had none. No memories. Nothing except what Mom told me. I think I started focusing more and more on track because she had told me he was an athlete, too. At least I had something I inherited from him. And when I ran, I thought of him. My daddy.

Then she forgot his birthday. I couldn't believe it when I woke up and there was nothing, no balloons or decorations or cake like usual. But just the week before I'd organized an entire outing to celebrate Tanvi's father's birthday.

It was like Mom forgot Dad. And I couldn't help wondering when she'll forget me, too.

Beth gets what it's like to have no memories of your father—and hers is alive! He's just never around. Beth understands what it's like to be forgotten.

Tears drip from my face, but they do nothing to relieve the awful weight pressing on my chest. Oh my God, Mimi. I had no idea she was hurting so much. I had no clue that the cousin who never lost her smile around me, who hugged me every time I cried, whose very presence was my armor, my protection, was bleeding inside herself.

I'm so sorry, sis, I want to say. But to whom? Who do I apologize to now?

Beth's right. Tanvi's starting to look more and more like her mom. Watching me with those same dark eyes with that weird look. Tanvi says she misses me and loves me, but I can't take that risk. What if she's inherited her mom's psycho gene? What if she flips like her mom did and comes after Mom and me? Beth thinks I need to do something now and she's right. Mom will never allow me to kick Tanvi out. I'll need to make her leave somehow and make it so that she'll never be able to return to my home and my mother ever again. But how?

She thought I'd hurt her and Auntie. She feared me so much that she wanted me out.

I have the proof right here.

But it's not sinking in. The words float around me while my mind shuts down.

On the last page is a sketch of a face with a crooked nose, a mouth filled with fangs, and narrow, malignant eyes. The word Tanvi is written next to it. And a poem scrawled across the paper.

Watch out for the killer in your home.
She's out to take everything you own.
She'll crawl out at night and cut off your head.
First your mom's and then your own.

A sharp sting cuts into my finger. The edge of the thick parchment paper has sliced the tip of my right ring finger. A swollen line of red forms, staining the paper. Creeping toward the words.

Did Mimi write this poem? The handwriting is different from her looping one. But does it matter? She thought I was becoming my mom.

She thought I was becoming a monster.

The woman swaying inside a flaming circle of candles, thick curls of smoke rising to the ceiling, chanting in a guttural, unrecognizable voice.

The stone-faced woman sitting behind the steering wheel as she drove off with Dad, leaving me with my babysitter.

But that was not all she was. I also remember the woman before that. My mom. Who told me bedtime stories from Indian epics, stories of heroes, of gods, of people who looked like me. The mom who made it a point to cook food I liked but also insisted I eat my veggies, who laughed with me and fussed over me.

Who was smart, intelligent, creative, level-headed, and empathetic to a fault.

I need to understand what made her change. What made her hurt Daddy.

Because that's the only way I'll understand why I hurt Mimi.

If I hurt Mimi.

CHAPTER 19

ON MY BED is a pile of the stuff I dug out from under the junk in the closet. The family photo of Daddy, Mom, and me, and the letters Mom sent Auntie. The letters Auntie wanted me to read.

The papers are stuck together from being stuffed in my closet for so long. I lift out the first one, the paper crackling when I smooth out the creases.

June 1st.

A heavy lump forms in my throat. She wrote this a week after we reached Kerala, the coastal state in India where my parents were from. Daddy planned the trip for Mom, who was grieving after a miscarriage. He thought a change of scene would help.

I don't know about this trip. Ramesh thinks it'll make me feel better. He keeps raving about the natural beauty outside our cabin, about the green hillsides and the river, but all I feel is the emptiness inside me, the life that's now gone. He says I should get up out of bed and walk outside so I can smell the fragrance in the air. As if that will heal everything. But he doesn't understand how I feel. How everything hurts. How tired I feel even opening my eyes . . .

Tanvi hovers close, checking in on me to make sure I'm okay. Just this morning she came up to me, her eyes wide and anxious, and when I smiled her face lit up and she hugged me. She loves me with her whole heart, Indira, and I know she misses me, and I must remember never to hurt her again.

My fingers tremble.

Was I aware of her grief? I was eight. All I remember is she was quieter than usual after she lost the baby and would often be sleeping when I returned home from school. Or she'd be sitting still like a statue, her face blank, staring into nothing.

I open the next letter. It's from June 6th.

I joined Ramesh and Tanvi on an outing for the first time. I had to force myself to get out of bed and it was hard to get dressed and eat my breakfast when I just wanted them to leave me alone. I only went for Tanvi's sake. Ramesh wants me to join them for another trip tomorrow. He's arranged for us to go to this village. It's deep inside the forest and they don't usually invite outsiders, but our hotel manager knows someone who lives there. We're going to see a tribal ceremony.

The ceremony.

We went in a mountain Jeep up a twisted road until there was no more road. Then we trekked across waterfalls and gorges and arrived at a small cluster of thatched huts surrounding a temple in a clearing. On the walls of the temple were thousands of lit oil lamps making it feel like the building was on fire, and inside was the deity, the goddess Kali. The goddess who warded off evil spirits. I knew that already because we had a picture of the goddess in our prayer room at home.

Daddy lifted me on his shoulders so I could see above the crowd. A man in ceremonial attire danced around a large fire while a few people chanted. I remember the sounds, the hiss of the fire, the crackling from wood logs, the constant hum of chanting, and the drums that rose above everything else. The sounds echoed my excited, happy heartbeat. It was pure joy I felt at that time.

I wasn't paying attention to Mom. I assumed she was just as fascinated as I was.

June 8th

The ceremony was stunning, sister. The chants were so powerful. For a whole evening, I was able to forget the constant grief inside me, the loss, the emptiness. For the first time in a long time, I felt alive. I felt like I could breathe again. Like I'd woken up from a coma. It might sound strange, but I want to learn those chants. I don't want to be lost again. That emptiness that drags me down is an awful feeling. The chants will keep it at bay. If I can learn them, then I can forget the loss.

My chest hurts. I trace the last sentence, the indentations made in the paper, and imagine her sitting here while she's writing, imagine the happiness she was finally able to feel after being depressed and lost.

So, what happened after that? That joy from the ceremony should've transitioned into healing and closure—but why did it take her down a dark path? I lift the next page, then hesitate, the hurt in my chest deepening because I know I'm going to find out soon.

June 20th

I wish I had never returned to Michigan. I can't find anyone to teach me the chants. I talked to the priest at the temple, and he looked at me like I had lost my mind. "Those chants are too powerful for you. You need years of study and penance to learn them," he said. When I insisted and told him I'll find a teacher myself, he still didn't budge, saying that I was making a mistake and I'll get hurt because anyone who'd agree wouldn't be an authentic guru. That priest also had the nerve to tell me that I wasn't in the "right frame of mind" to learn chants and that I should first seek medical help and start on a "path of healing." But he is wrong because none of the meds or the therapy or the shrinks could help me before.

Please understand, sis. During the ceremony, I didn't feel any pain. All I felt was joy and power. I want to feel like that again and the only way is by learning those chants myself. So I can say them anytime I feel down. I will find someone who can teach me. A healer who can know my pain.

I remember her face as she scrolled through the computer, the light from the monitor reflected on her slack face. She was searching for a healer and must've found someone because then the packages arrived, containing those thick black candles. I watched from behind the bedroom door as she lit them in a circle. Then she'd stand inside it and chant as the flames cast flickering shadows across her swaying figure.

I didn't feel the excitement or happiness I felt at the tribal ceremony. That was pure joy, but this was different. This scared me.

I read through the next several letters, seeing in real time her handwriting getting more scattered, her words pulsating with an odd energy even from the dry, aged paper. She seemed happier—more energetic—but her words were all about her rituals, how they elevated her and made her forget her pain. How this guy she found on the internet, this person she called her healer, was the only person who understood her—and showed her how everyone else, including her family, were persecuting her.

I open the last letter.

> *Don't you dare advise me, sister. I am not hurting Ramesh or Janvi with my rituals. All I'm looking for is a few minutes of happiness where I can forget this constant pain. Is that wrong? And how dare you and Ramesh say my healer is a fraud? He may not be part of any temple or religion, but why does that matter? Have you read through his website? He has helped millions of believers like me. Because of him, I feel alive again, I feel powerful. He made me so much more than I am. He's my savior. Say what you want, but I'll never stop believing in him.*

Mom's letter slips out of my nerveless fingers.

In my desperate need to forget Mom, I've never even thought of this fraud who duped her. I don't even know his name. Because I was so determined to have nothing to do with Mom, to never forgive her.

And even after reading her letters, the memory I just cannot shake is of her standing by the car, stone-faced, as she asked Daddy for the keys so she could drive.

She planned to kill him; the decision was hers. It was premeditated, like the news articles said, and I can't forgive her for that.

I don't know if I ever will.

And it hurts.

It hurts that I still can't find the mom who wrapped me in warm hugs, who acted out her bedtime stories to make me laugh, who loved me so much, she told me once *my heart goes mushy with joy every time I see you, sweetheart.*

I still can't find her in these letters.

I smooth the pages, tracing the words, the letters shuddering at points where her hand shook. She was in a really dark place when she wrote this, but eight-year-old me didn't know it then and couldn't help her.

When Daddy told her to stop her rituals, she turned on him.

Did Mimi's betrayal—when she took Mom's candles to Beth and orchestrated my meltdown—flip a switch inside me, too?

Was it me standing stone-faced watching Mimi leave with Grace?

Did it make me take the shortcut to the tavern and watch them through the glass pane?

What did I do after that?

Did it make me hate Mimi so much I killed her?

CHAPTER 20

KRISTA SAYS SOMETHING, but her words fade into the commotion from the crowded hall. We're next to my locker, part of the rush of people exiting after school's done.

Her lips move, but the only words I hear are the ones from Mimi's diary. They've been circling in my brain on a constant loop.

Mom will never allow me to kick Tanvi out. I'll need to make her leave somehow and make it so that she'll never be able to return to my home and my mother ever again.

But she's the one who ended up gone.

She's the one who may be dead.

The next several minutes pass in a blur—Krista hugging me, something about calling me after practice, the rush of bodies stampeding down the front steps, people shouldering past me, my sneakers damp on grass wet from an afternoon rain—and it's when I'm unlocking my bike to return home that a notification pops up on my phone.

I'd set up notifications for when Melissa posts a new video—she seems to have the latest information—and sure enough, there's one. She titled it *#MimiTaylor part 3.*

But this one's about me.

"Hey everyone, Melissa here, welcome to my newest recap. So, have you heard of the saying fox in the henhouse? I have it on the best authority that there was a fox in Mimi's house. I'm not naming names, but suffice it to say that this fox has a dark past. I heard this fox knows what may have happened to Mimi but isn't saying anything. Now, why would they do that? Why would they hide the truth? Is it because this fox had been harboring an ulterior agenda all along? If so, it breaks my heart. Mimi didn't deserve to have her kindness repaid with betrayal and ingratitude. But what if it's worse? Is this fox involved in what happened to Mimi? Could it be a case of murder in the henhouse? Stay with me, friends, for the next edition of Melissa's recap where I'll have all the deets."

My mouth's dry as dust. I look around at the steady stream of people exiting the school building to the parking lot, with some heading to the road and waiting for rides. Many of them are on their phones, but no one seems to be looking in my direction.

They will soon, though, once they catch on.

I spin my bike around. My vision blurry with the desperate need to get out, I streak across the parking lot and onto the road, ignoring angry honks and shouts.

I've got to do something before they start closing in on me. But what? How do I prove my innocence when I'm not sure myself? When my stupid brain still won't let me see what happened after I reached the tavern.

Vehicles whizz past and it's not until I nearly face-plant into a white pickup truck that'd stopped suddenly in front of me that I realize I'm going in the wrong direction away from home. The car next to me honks, then swerves past the truck, the blond driver flipping off the pickup truck before racing away.

The driver of the truck leans out. "Fuck you," he yells.

It's James.

He takes a sharp right into a hardware store parking lot. I watch him get out, slam the door, and stride into the store.

He has an alibi for when Mimi vanished, but he knows more than he's letting on about her disappearance.

With James occupied, this'll be a good time for me to search his place and see if I can find something tangible.

If he's involved somehow, if he's hiding something, I *must* find out.

IT TAKES ME close to an hour to make it past the traffic and finally the distance to Tinder Avenue, largely because my bike tire sprung a leak and needed some urgent TLC.

By the time I reach James's place, the clouds have moved, hiding the sun and casting deep shadows across the front of the building. Every so often the wind moans as it weaves through the branches of the sprawling oak and lifts the shingles on the roof.

The front lot is empty; James's white pickup is missing. I exhale, glad he didn't beat me here, then stick my can of pepper spray back in my pocket and scurry across the road. My heart pounds so loud, it drowns the rustling from branches swaying overhead and the crunch of my sneakers on the dirt.

I try the front door, find it locked, then press my face to the cold glass panel on the door, allowing my vision to adjust to the darkness until vague shapes appear out of the gloom: shelves along the walls and long tables scattered around. The place seems deserted.

I hurry around to the back of the building, where a dirt alley separates it from a sprawling, overgrown field of wildflowers. Light from a flickering bulb on the shop wall falls on the ajar back door. I edge closer to it and listen for any sounds over my thudding heartbeats. Nothing.

The cold metal of the door feels slick under my clammy palm. I push it an inch, then another. The hinge squeaks.

I flinch, my heart slamming hard in my chest.

But except for me hyperventilating, the place is silent.

I squeeze through the opening and find myself in a narrow

hallway about six feet wide. Boxes and several odds and ends are stacked along the walls. I maneuver around them and into the shop proper.

With fading sunlight barely making it through the grimy glass pane on the front door, gloom fills the shop, turning the shelves of junk into shadows. I tiptoe across the floor, an ear out for approaching vehicles, for James returning.

A shiver runs down my spine. I stop dead.

There's someone else in the room.

I'm not sure how I know; maybe it's the faint whisper of breaths over mine, or the weird sensation of eyes laser focused on me.

Then I see a shadow with a shape at odds with the others. It's not the sharp or rounded shadows created by the stuff on the shelves. It's a long, lean shape with bony limbs.

A moving living shadow created by someone hiding behind the shelf across from me.

Someone looking straight at me.

The shadow moves, and now a long stick appears in its arms.

I strain through the gloom to see better.

It's not a stick.

Light gleams dully off the metal surface of something held by the hidden person.

"No!" James's shout bursts through the silence.

I jerk back, spinning to face the direction his voice came from.

He bursts through from the back and races toward the person. They crash down on the floor. He shouts again. "Tanvi, run!"

Wait, what? I stare at the struggling figures on the floor. He's trying to pry something out of the other person's hand. I can see it better now.

Oh my God. The gun.

My knees go weak.

"Run, for God's sake!"

The terror in his voice sends every nerve ending in my body into overdrive while my mind goes totally blank. I race to the back door, careening past the boxes, sending one thudding against the wall; then I'm outside in the alley behind the shop.

My bike is parked in the front. I race around the side of the building and am almost to the front when the door slams open.

I drop to the ground, then scuttle to the cover of the wall to crouch in the shadows.

Footsteps crunch on the gravel inches from me. Someone's standing just beyond the corner of the building. If they step back half a step, they'll see me. I hug my knees, shaking with an effort to muffle my shuddering breaths. Still unable to believe I could've gotten shot.

"She's a liar." The voice is low, too low, snatched away by the wind.

Who the hell is that?

"It's your fault." James's voice rises. "You fucked up, and now you're blaming everyone else. I'm done hiding with you."

There's a long pause, broken by the moaning from the wind, then the crunch of shoes on dirt again.

"Wait," James says. "I'll drop you off."

Erratic footsteps, out of sync, recede into the distance. I crawl to the corner and peer around it. James walks ahead of a shorter, slimmer figure in black tights and a gray hoodie. They disappear into a thicket, then an engine sputters and roars. James must've left his bike there, which is why I didn't see it.

The engine fades away, leaving me out with the breeze and my panting breaths.

The person with James tried to kill me. Who the hell was it? A guest who thought I was a burglar breaking in?

But he could've just told them to stop. Why'd he get so frantic and struggle to hold them down?

It almost felt like he was certain they'd shoot me if given the chance.

CHAPTER 21

IT'S PAST SIX-THIRTY by the time I make it back home. Orange and dark blue crisscross the sky with the last rays of evening sun falling across the front porch—and the door, which stands cracked open.

That's weird. Auntie and Mr. Lee aren't back yet. I would've gotten a call if they returned and found me gone. Auntie's car is in the garage, but Mr. Lee picks her up and takes her for her appointments. And yeah, Auntie's coat is missing from the coatrack next to the door.

Did someone break in? But the lock isn't busted and the wood around it is unscratched. Whoever opened this door used a key.

Shit. I hurry to the gate and out onto the road, then call Mr. Lee.

"What's up, kiddo?"

"Is Auntie with you?"

"No. I'm on my way to pick her up. Why?"

"Don't tell her; I don't want her worrying, but I found the door open when I came home, and I'm positive I locked it before leaving. And the weird thing is the lock and door are intact, like they had a key to get in."

There's a pause, then he says, his voice tight. "Don't hang up. I'm calling the cops."

I pace the front yard, listening to the call and response. A minute later, a cop car comes screaming up, red and blue flashing, and two cops jump out.

Just like when I found Mimi's clothes on Gaston Beach.

A wave of dizziness hit me, and I reach for the gate, hanging on to the railing to stop the world from tilting.

"Kiddo," Mr. Lee says, "I'm going to stay on the phone until they make sure everything's okay."

"Thanks." Maybe he caught my trembling breaths.

"Miss, are you okay?" The words come from a face wavering above me. An older Black cop, his eyes concerned.

"Y-yes."

"Okay. Stay here. My partner and I are going to go inside." He tilts his head toward his partner, a petite woman, who then takes off for the back of the house while he slips to the front and, gun drawn, nudges the door open with a shoulder before vanishing inside.

A couple of minutes later, the female cop emerges. "There's no one inside and no signs of any disturbance." She side-eyes me, her expression skeptical. "Are you sure you locked the door when you left, honey?"

"Yes," I say stiffly. She clearly thinks I'm lying about the break-in.

"Hey, Claudia." The male cop says from the front door. He leans in and whispers something to the woman, whose skepticism changes in an instant to rounded eyes.

She turns to me. "Why don't you come in and make sure everything's intact, Ms. Nair?"

So they know me. Obviously. This's a small town.

Have they seen Melissa's latest video, too, blaming me?

Don't think of that.

They wait in the living room while I check Auntie's room first, inspecting the safe where she keeps her gold jewelry and cash, and then the rest of the house. Nothing seems to be gone.

I tell the cops as much.

The Black cop nods at the phone in my hand. "Is that your aunt?"

I shake my head. "Mr. Lee. He's—"

"I know David." He takes the phone. "Hey man, Shane here." A pause, then, "Yeah, we'll tell the lieutenant what happened and come by later to talk to Mrs. Taylor. But, yes, the key is an issue." After giving the phone back to me, he nods again and hurries out, followed by Claudia.

I stiffen. Mimi's phone and house key were the only things missing when the contents of her purse were returned to us. I thought the cops believed they were washed away. "Mr. Lee, do they think someone took the key from her purse but left her debit card and cash behind? Why would they do that?"

"Not sure. Things aren't adding up. Stay with Krista until I can get there and change the locks."

"Okay." To leave cash behind, but take a key? That someone couldn't be a random person. They took the key for a reason.

"And one more thing. The lieutenant called me an hour ago. And I wouldn't read too much into this, kiddo." He inhales deep, like he's steeling himself. "A waitress at a diner in Gaston said she spotted Mimi the morning after she left home."

My heart slams against my sternum. "*What*?"

"Yeah. She was traveling and didn't know Mimi was reported missing. But when she returned home yesterday, she heard about Mimi's clothes being found on Gaston Beach and recognized the photo. That was when she called Orin PD. But this may not mean much."

It does. Mimi was alive the morning after.

This waitress *saw* Mimi in Gaston the next morning.

This meant I couldn't have hurt Mimi.

Oh my God. I clap my hand to my mouth, muffling my relieved sobs so Mr. Lee won't hear. I've got to talk to this waitress. "Who is she? Where does she work?"

"Her name's Mary Greer. It's Gaston Diner right off the beach."

"Does Auntie know?"

"Yes, I told her." He sighs. "And this has made her more certain that Mimi is fine and will be returning home anytime now."

I want to ask him why she'd think that, but Auntie answers my question herself when she rushes in an hour later and hugs me tight.

"It's Mimi, honey. I know it!" Auntie's face is wreathed in a smile, the first I've seen since Mimi left. "She used her key and came in."

Then why didn't she stay and wait for us? Or contact us somehow? Why be sneaky about it? And why leave her clothes on the beach . . .

But I don't want that smile to dim, and so I hug her back and say nothing.

Mr. Lee returns with a locksmith, but Auntie won't let us change the lock. After some persuasion, she finally agrees, but only after he promises to leave an extra key under the carpet. "I don't want to lock my daughter out," she says with tears in her eyes.

Mr. Lee gives me a look of frustration and grief, and I know exactly what he's thinking. She's setting herself up for another crushing disappointment, and once she's able to think it through and realizes it couldn't have been Mimi, she'll break down again.

But I don't have the heart to steal her hope, and neither does Mr. Lee. So the locks are changed, and a spare key is left under the carpet.

Once Auntie finally falls asleep, I search through the house again for anything the person could've taken. But nothing seems gone.

But the dread that'd locked in since I found the door open refuses to leave. Whoever broke in wasn't a thief. They entered with some other intention in mind.

I'm missing something.

I HEAD OUT to Gaston Saturday morning. The diner turns out to be a tiny one-story building in the corner of a strip mall across from Gaston Beach.

A couple of fluorescent bulbs wash white light over rows of tables with faded vinyl covers and a tiled floor pock-marked with stains. The sign on the glass door says CLOSED, but a thin man in an oversized flannel shirt and faded jeans strolls around, pulling chairs off tables and straightening them.

I tap on the glass. The guy glances at me, points at the closed sign, and continues wiping down a table.

I tap again.

A scowl crosses his face. He throws the rag down, stalks to the door, and unlocks it. "We're not open yet."

"Sorry. I wanted to talk to Ms. Mary Greer. It's very important." Easy with the desperation, play it cool.

"Mama!" he shouts. "There's someone here wanting to talk to you."

A woman with an apron around her waist walks out of the back of the room. Gray hair escapes her cap in straggly strands.

"This girl here wants to ask you something." He turns away to walk back to the tables.

I catch the door before it shuts on my toes. "Ms. Greer?"

She wipes her hands on a towel and eyes me. "Yes? How can I help you?"

I swallow hard. "I'm here about the teen from Orin, the one you talked to." She frowns. "The runaway."

Her face clears. "Ah, yes, that poor kid."

"She's my cousin. I was sort of hoping I could ask you something."

Her eyes widen. "Oh, you poor dear. Of course, of course." She holds the door open and reaches for my elbow. "Come on in." After dusting a chair with her apron, she says, "Here, sit. Did you come all the way from Orin?"

I nod.

"Are you hungry? How about some coffee? I'll get you something to eat. How does pancakes sound?"

The hard knot in my stomach loosens. She's so sweet. She doesn't know me, my history. I smile back. "Coffee is good. Nothing else, though."

She lifts her head and hollers. "Bert!"

The guy who's standing a couple of feet behind her and staring at me says, "I heard ya." He makes a beeline for the coffee while she squeezes into the booth opposite me.

"How are you doing, honey? I feel so awful for you and that kid's mama. My kids are all grown, you know. But I can feel her pain." She presses a hand to her chest.

Bert places a steaming cup of black coffee in front of me, along with a small pitcher of milk and a sugar dispenser. He then reaches for a chair.

Mary lifts a brow. "There's dishes needing cleaning in the kitchen."

His face falls. "But Mama—"

"No." She points a finger to the back of the room. "This kid here needs some privacy."

After he drags himself away, she pours milk into my cup and reaches for the sugar, adding two packets in and then stirring the coffee. "Your cousin's name was Mimi?"

"Yeah." I reach for the coffee cup, then realize my hands are trembling and hide them under the table. "You said you saw her here?"

"Yes." Her eyes lift to something past my shoulder. "I noticed her as soon as she came in. A pretty young thing in that red dress. She wasn't from around here; I know all our usual customers, you know. She stood at the door and looked around, like she was searching for someone. I showed her to a seat and got her some coffee. And we started to talking. It seemed to me like she wanted it off her chest. This boyfriend her mama didn't approve of and how she was so happy to be able to finally be with him."

My breath catches. "Be with him? Here in Gaston?"

"Yes. That was why she came here. He was going to join her here." Her eyes fill, and she pats them with her apron. "I didn't know she was in trouble. If I had, I'd have done something. Insisted she call home."

Was that what Mimi was trying to tell me so urgently when she rushed back from Beth's party? That she planned to run away with James? But then why wouldn't he tell me that when I asked him? Why say he didn't know? "Did she tell you when she was going to meet him?" James was arrested Thursday night; he said he wasn't released until Saturday.

"No. But she did say he had to take care of something urgent, which was why he couldn't come with her."

Being in jail would be reason enough. "What time was this? When you talked to her?"

"Hmm, around seven in the morning."

I may have forgotten the events of the night before, but I know for a fact I was at home at that time. Mimi was alive and well and talking to this waitress when I was waking up and discovering she was gone. Which meant there was no way in hell that I hurt her.

Beth is wrong, and so is Grace. And Lyla. There must be another explanation for my memory fragments, for my bruises—but I didn't cause my cousin to vanish. I wrap my hands around the coffee cup, its warmth easing the chill inside me.

"She sat there." Ms. Greer angles her chin toward a table next to the kitchen door. "I gave her coffee and could only talk to her for a few minutes, what with the customers needing attending to. When I returned to take her order, she was gone. Walked out."

"Did you see her after that?"

She shakes her head. "The next day, Bert and I went out of town, my niece's wedding in Atlanta. I just returned yesterday, and that was when I heard." Mary wipes her eyes again. "About the poor girl's clothes being found on the beach. I think she went there to wait for her boyfriend, and someone found her there alone. It's not a safe place after sunset; there are all sorts of people there, drug deals happening. She was at the wrong place at the wrong time."

But that would make it a crime of opportunity. It wouldn't explain the money left untouched in Mimi's purse and the missing key. It wouldn't explain my bruises and my missing memory.

Through the large window next to me, I can see the long sandy strip of beach with the wide blue expanse of water beyond. It's barely daylight, and the beach's already starting to get busy, with cars parked along the curb and people either walking or jogging down the sand.

"You haven't had your coffee yet, honey." Ms. Greer's concerned voice breaks through my thoughts. "Shall I get you a fresh cup?"

"No, thank you." Seeing how worried she looks, I force my lips to curve. "And thank you for taking the time to talk."

"Sure, anytime." She covers my hands with hers. "I'm sorry for everything you're going through. You must miss her terribly."

Tears threaten to fall. I can't stop them, and I don't want to cry in front of her. So I slip my hands out from under hers and stand. "Thank . . . you."

Once outside, I head over to the bike stand across the beach. The rocky area where I saw her dress and purse is no longer cordoned off with yellow tape, like it was the last time I was here. Instead, a group of preteens swarm all over it, laughing and yelling as they chase each other around. A little boy about ten years old stands next to the large boulder marking the spot where I stood, where I looked down and saw the ragged fragment of cloth.

The agony splits my chest like someone stabbed me with a red-hot knife. I wish I could reverse time; I wish I hadn't climbed up those rocks, hadn't seen what I saw.

I unlock my bike and am about to throw my leg over when a face appears in the mirror. It's a blur of wavy black hair and a sudden flash of dark eyes, and then it's gone.

Mimi?

My heart slams against my ribs. I spin around.

The road behind me is busy with cars pulling in to park at the curb and beachgoers spilling out. A group of giggling girls my age rush across the road, intent on beating one another to the sand first.

But there's no Mimi. It was just my stupid imagination.

CHAPTER 22

BIKING AN HOUR on a winding mostly uphill road can make every muscle in your legs hurt. I find that out firsthand by the time I make it to downtown Orin and Krista's Peace & Love store. After locking my bike, I wait for the blood to return to my screaming muscles, then open the door to the swell of slow jazz and the familiar scent of vanilla and jasmine.

It always feels like I'm returning home when I come here.

Krista stands with her back to me, arranging crystal beads in a cabinet. Her hair color's changed since school yesterday, the black tips now dyed purple. Warmth spreads through every cell in my body. Outside the door, the world might be dark and forbidding, but here is safety and peace. And my best friend. "Hey."

She turns. "Hey you." But instead of her usual grin, she eyes me with a worried expression. "You okay?"

I nod. "There's some stuff I want to tell you."

"If it's about Melissa—she's such a jerk, saying that coded stuff about a *fox* and shit. Anything for the views." Angry spots of red crown her cheekbones. "I've already told her to shut it down. I don't care how many followers she's got, but she's a conniving asshole who's taken advantage of—"

"Hey, hey." Her face is getting redder and redder. I side hug her. "Forget Melissa." I can afford to now since I know—after what the waitress told me—that I didn't hurt Mimi.

"Okay, fine." She huffs, then slips her arm through mine. "Let's get some tea and calm down."

I settle into the bean chair in the kitchenette, then grab her hand before she can fill the kettle. "No, sit down for a bit." Once she sits cross-legged facing me, I take a deep breath and tell her about everything I read in Mimi's journal and about Mom's letters, and how I thought I'd hurt my cousin.

Her eyes widen, shock turning them a dark green. But it's not disgust or contempt darkening them; it's solid grief and sympathy. "Oh God, Tanvi." She throws her arms around me and hugs me tight. "Girl, why didn't you tell me? I could've talked you out of that shit, convinced you there was no way in hell you'd hurt Mimi. Tanvi, you'd cut your own arms off before hurting a hair on Mimi's head. You're not a killer; you'll never be one."

Suddenly, I'm crying and dripping snot all over the place. Krista grabs a tissue box, and between the two of us, we empty it out as I tell her how bad I felt that it took me this long to read Mom's letters to Auntie. "If I read them earlier, I would've known how broken she was after the miscarriage and how that mentally affected her. She craved an escape, some relief. And that was what the rituals gave her."

"Now you forgive her? Your mom?"

I open my mouth, then shut it. She wasn't the same mom I knew when she drove that car and deliberately crashed it, but forgiving her? Every time I think of forgiveness, I feel again the loss, the fact that she killed Daddy. Forgiveness means acceptance, and I can't do that. "I understand her. Somewhat."

"That'll do for now." She jumps to her feet. "Time for some jasmine tea."

Minutes later, over a couple of steaming cups, I tell her the rest, ending with my meeting with the waitress at Gaston and what I figured out about Mimi's purse and the missing house key.

Krista gasps. "Holy shit."

"I'm going to look through the house again. There's got to be a reason someone took the key from Mimi's purse."

"Yeah. What about the lieutenant? Have you told him?"

"I think he already knows. Mr. Lee told him about the door being unlocked and how nothing valuable had gone missing from the house. He must've deduced the person who took the key wasn't a random stranger looking to burgle the place—"

"But was someone who knew Mimi," Krista finishes with a frown.

Probably the same person who killed her. A chill runs down my spine, and we stare at each other, the horror darkening her eyes echoing mine.

The waitress told me Mimi went to Gaston to wait for James. Did he go to Gaston after he was released from jail that weekend to look for her? If he did and didn't find her there, why didn't he tell the cops?

He knows something about what happened to Mimi, I'm positive about that, and so does whoever I overheard him talking to. I keep circling back to Grace, but there's also that person in his store. The one who tried to shoot me, I remember with a chill. Despite our broken relationship, I don't think that's Grace.

After placing the empty cup on the counter, I stand. The feeling that I've missed something there won't let me go. "I'm going to check through the house again."

Krista hugs me tight. "Keep me updated. Know that I'm in your corner. Always."

IT'S AFTER I finish ransacking the entire two floors of the house—and finding nothing gone—that I realize there's one place I haven't checked. The attic.

A wooden ladder on the second-floor landing leads to the tiny room above my bedroom. The only times I'd been up there were in middle school when Grace, Mimi, and I used to play hide-and-seek. At that time, I had no idea that Mimi had stolen two of Mom's candles during one of our visits home and hidden them in the attic. I didn't know until she brought me home from Beth's house, puking and exhausted, and then returned the candles to the attic.

Don't tell Mom what I did, okay? It was just a stupid prank.

A prank where she and Beth lit the candles my mother used for her rituals so they could trigger my nightmares.

Judging from the fine layer of dust covering the steps of the ladder from when I dusted it a week ago, no one's been up there since. Except . . . faint footprints are visible in the dust climbing up, and the latch on the trapdoor above is undone, the hook hanging loose. It was latched when I looked last week.

Someone went up there in the last few days. Auntie?

I hurry up and open the trapdoor, easing it back, then enter the small room, crinkling my nose at the immediate musty stink. The only place you can stand up straight is along one wall, with the sloping ceiling almost meeting the floor at the other end. Large cardboard boxes are crammed into every place possible and colored a universal gray from dust. Nothing looks disturbed from the last time I was here in middle school, except for footprints that fork away from the trapdoor and toward one of the boxes and a yellow cloth bag that lies behind it.

Mimi took two thick black candles out of that bag when we were at Beth's. After we came home, I remember her rushing up the ladder with the bag and coming back down without it.

My hands tremble as I open the bag. A candle lies at the bottom, its wick charred. But the other one is missing. Someone's taken it.

It wasn't Auntie who made those footprints in the last few days, who entered this room and walked right up to this bag. It was the person who broke in.

But why steal a random candle?

Because it wasn't random to them. It meant something. They must've known its significance . . . to me.

My heart flutters in my throat like a trapped bird. A wave of dizziness hits, and I realize I'm spiraling into a panic attack.

I can't go to the lieutenant yet. I need to think this through and figure out who it could be. And why they'd risk breaking in for one of Mom's candles.

The only place I can think straight without panicking, the only place I feel safe anymore, is the waterfall. The place I used to go to in the past to get away from my nightmares and keep the panic attacks at bay.

I hurry down the road, my shoes sloshing in puddles of water as I near the woods, and the fear clamped around my heart loosens. Then I'm among the trees, the familiar sounds of leaves rustling and birds chirps, the smell of earth and damp vegetation surrounding me.

I scramble down the trail. The spring's gurgling gets louder, turning into rumbling. By the time I reach the bottom of the rocky slope, it sounds like elephants thundering through the woods.

I'd never heard the waterfall this loud before. Or seen it this vast.

Tons of frothing, swirling water erupt from the rock face, crashing onto the rocks below and sending spray several feet in the air. The force of the water has dislodged a few rocks and sent them hurtling downstream, where they're blocking the lower end of the stream. The bank closer to me has lost a huge boulder, exposing slimy green algae.

Among the green mess is something glittering in the sunlight.

It's a bracelet, trapped in one of the dislodged rocks. A thin string of gold with a heart-shaped clasp.

When I pick it up, the stones in the clasp catch the light, gleaming like fire.

It's Mimi's. Auntie bought it for her when she graduated middle school.

I brush my thumb over the string, the pressure in my throat escalating until I can't bear it. Mimi loved it and would wear it all the time, but I believe the last time I saw it on her wrist was before she went to Beth's birthday party. That was when she started wearing the beaded friendship bracelet Beth gave her.

Did she chuck the gold bracelet into the water? Would she do something so mean to Auntie?

I sigh, then drop the bracelet in my pocket and climb the rock outcrop toward the ledge. Once I'm on the top, I lie down on my back. It should hurt to stare up at the sun blazing above, the white ball of fire should fry my eyes. But I'm numb, the bracelet another reminder that I lost Mimi twice.

But I came here to think. To figure out who used Mimi's key to enter my house. Why they took one of Mom's candles.

It must be someone who knows my past, knows about the candles.

Beth knows for sure; she'd witnessed my meltdown.

Grace does, too, though that was on me. I told her about it three years into our friendship. And she knew every inch of this house from all the times she stayed over. She'd been in the attic, too.

Lyla knows something. She said I have a "twisted gene" and ought to be locked up so everyone else would be safe.

James? Mimi could've easily told him like she told Beth.

Why would any of them take the candle, though? The only purpose I can think of would be to try and get back at me. Because of something I did.

Or because they want to cover up something *they* did.

Like Lyla and Greg. They followed Mimi from Beth's party that night, and from the mess they made of Abby's car, they could've used it to take Mimi to Gaston. But the waitress saw Mimi alive and well the next morning. So, that would rule them out . . .

I exhale, trying to ease the turmoil lodged in my chest.

What about Beth? She obviously thinks I made Mimi's life hell and wants me to pay for that. But she thought of Mimi as her sister. Mimi cut Grace and me out of her life for Beth's sake, which was exactly what Beth wanted. Why would Beth hurt her?

That thought leads me to Grace. She knew about the candles; she knew where they were kept in the attic. And she knows what happened to Mimi. She said she saw me leaving the tavern with Mimi and that I was the last person who saw Mimi. But how do I know that's the truth? She could easily have lied to protect herself. Her lack of surprise when I showed her the threatening note sent to Mimi. She has reason to hate Mimi—and me for not standing with her.

And then there's James. Grace obviously cared for him from the way she tried to stop the cops from arresting him at the tavern. He could easily have been talking to her on the phone conversation I overheard at his shop. And he chased after me with a gun though he swore afterward that he didn't know it was me.

And now there's this unknown person at his place. Who tried to shoot me.

One of them knows the truth about what happened to Mimi, and they don't want that truth exposed. They want me to believe I'm like my mother and capable of murder. They want me to believe I hurt Mimi.

And I *did* believe it because of my injuries and the flashes of memory. Until the waitress came forward.

The sunlight dims. A shadow hovers over me, silhouetted by gold. A figure filled with sun spots. The shadow leans down.

For a second, I think it's another memory appearing through the fog in my mind. Was I . . . here the night Mimi vanished?

A rustle, then another, then a swish of something heavy being swung.

A sudden pain erupts on the side of my head. Agony stabs through my skull.

I open my mouth to scream, but a hard shove to my back sends me sliding across the rock surface slick with spray and toward the waterfall.

I grab for something to break my slide; my nails claw unyielding stone, and then I tumble off the edge of the ledge and into the water.

I'm falling, drowning in sheets of water crashing on me.

I lash out blindly, feeling for the ledge, anything to keep me from hurtling onto the rocks below. My fingers brush something solid through the water.

A rope. An old climbing rope left behind by someone I'll be forever grateful to.

I grab at it and cling on, dangling over the edge, my heart thundering. Water sucks at my feet, pulling me down like quicksand. I force myself not to look down.

Keeping a death hold on the rope, its rough strands cutting into my skin, I climb, hand over hand, trying not to throw up. My feet finally find stone. I pull myself over and sprawl on the ledge.

Blurry lines swim above me, crisscrossing lines that won't stay still. A wave of nausea rises. I roll over and puke, lying there retching, unable to stop my head from pounding, unable to look up. Though I know I must. Before I'm attacked again.

I force my head up. The ground heaves and I grit my teeth against another wave of nausea.

The gray edges of my vision part. The blurry lines steady into brownish-green vines and creepers, with sunlight filtering through them.

The ledge is deserted. My attacker is gone.

But something thuds below. A person races away from the waterfall and down the trail toward the trees. A slim figure in black tights and a gray hoodie.

It's the same person who was at James's place. Who tried to shoot me.

A low branch catches the cloth of the hood and yanks it back enough for me to see a thick strand of black wavy hair. Then they're gone, vanishing into the trees.

I stare after them, my mouth dry.

Now I know who's the threat. It's this girl James knows, and they're not getting away this time.

CHAPTER 23

THE DOOR TO James's store is wide open. The parking lot is empty except for several cardboard boxes piled up next to the door, but there's someone moving around inside; I see them walking past the door every few seconds.

I creep closer, not wanting to make the same mistake I made earlier in case someone's waiting in there with a gun, and peer around the doorway.

James has his back to me and is wrapping tape around a large cardboard box. From the rows of empty shelves and tables and a strong musty smell in the air, it looks he's packing the place up.

He finishes with the box and carries it to a handtruck. I catch a glimpse of his profile. His skin is stretched tight over his cheekbones, and his eyes are bloodshot, like he hasn't slept in ages. He drops the box on the handtruck with a clank, then pushes it to the back of the store, the squeaking from the wheels amplified by the silence.

I'm about to follow him when his white pickup truck appears down the road.

The vehicle slows down to a stop. The dusty windshield obscures the features of the driver hunched behind the wheel, but I can sense them watching me.

The hair at the back of my neck rises.

I step across the parking lot and approach the truck. I need to see that driver. See if it's the person who pushed me into the waterfall.

The engine revs. Once, then again. And then the truck charges forward, tires spitting gravel. Heading down the road toward the parking lot.

Heading straight for me.

Blood turns to ice in my veins.

The truck barrels down. It's close enough for me to feel the heat blasting from its engine.

Move! my mind screams. But I can't. My body isn't responding, my muscles frozen.

A sudden shove from my left flings me to the shoulder. I hit the ground hard, the breath knocked out of me.

"Hey!" James yells. He's standing in the middle of the road, in front of the truck. Standing facing it, arms out.

My heart somersaults into my throat. God, he's going to get run over.

The truck weaves to the left. He follows suit, staying in its path.

"James, stop!" Is he trying to get killed?

The vehicle shudders. The stink of burnt rubber fills the air. About three yards away from him, the truck veers, tires crunching dirt. It takes a sharp U-turn, the movement bringing the driver's side window closer to me.

Gray hoodie, a glimpse of black hair, thick wavy unruly strands obscuring their features, then they're gone. The vehicle speeds down the narrow road and disappears, leaving a trail of stinky exhaust.

I scramble to my feet. "Who was it? Who *was* it?"

James's eyes are huge with horror as he stares after the truck.

"James!" I grab his arm and try to turn him to face me.

But he yanks his arm away. "Get the hell out of here, you hear me? She already tried to kill you once. Why the hell did you come back here?"

"Because I want to know." My heart thunders so loud, it

drowns out my words. "I'm sick of running away. This time you're going to tell me who that was and why you're hiding her."

He pushes his hand through his straggly blond hair. "Because I had to. I needed . . ." He swallows. "Mimi needed it."

I freeze. "Mimi? You're hiding this girl for Mimi's sake? That makes no sense."

His arms drop to his sides, hanging limp, and he studies the ground with a frown. Whatever he's thinking of is affecting him deeply because the color drains from his face, leaving it pasty white.

"James?"

He looks up at me then. "You're right. It made sense to me before, but not anymore." He turns and strides to the corner of the parking lot and pulls the tarp off his bike. Then he throws a leg over and starts the engine.

"Wait." I race after him. "You can't go. Not without telling me the truth."

"The truth's not going to save your life. I need to stop what I started."

What he started . . . My throat closes. "Did you hurt Mimi?" My voice is rising until it becomes a scream. "Are you the reason my cousin is dead?"

He clenches the handlebars, then swings the bike away from me and takes off down the road.

By the time I reach downtown, searching for James's truck on every road and side street along the way, it's approaching dusk. Shades of orange tinge the horizon, and goosebumps mushroom down my arms from the evening chill. I wish I'd thought of bringing a sweater, but I'm not returning home without confronting that girl.

It takes close to an hour to search the parking lots of every store until finally I reach Orin Café. The closed sign is turned on and the lights inside the glass-fronted building are muted, but I can see Grace inside vacuuming the floor. In the wash of the soft lights, with her black hair down and framing her face, she could be easily mistaken for Mimi.

She looks up, locks eyes with me. Then in one swift move, she shuts the vacuum off and strides to the door, pushing it open. "Are you stalking me, Tanvi?"

Just like you did Mimi. But that thought is followed by an immediate rush of shame that nearly bowls me over. Grace had reason to be upset with Mimi. By framing her, Mimi turned her into a thief, which ended up costing her everything. "I'm sorry for what Mimi did to you. I didn't know until now."

Her glare flickers, then hardens again. "Somehow I doubt that."

"I didn't. I swear. Not until Abby told me. But I should have stood by your side anyway."

Her expression changes, the scowl switching to something unreadable. "Against Mimi?"

"Yes. She hated me anyway, so it wasn't like she could hate . . . me any more." My voice catches in my throat.

She opens her mouth, then hesitates, like she's debating what to say. "You were supposed to be my friend, Tanvi."

"I know," I say, lowering my head. If I'd stood by Grace, we could've helped each other. Remained friends without turning to bitterness and anger. And vengeance.

"I saw how much you loved each other." The words seem torn from Grace. "What happened between the two of you?"

Why's she asking me this? "You know it was Beth—"

"I'm talking about you. Did you hate her?"

My mouth dries. I stare at her, at the expression which is all too readable now. Like she's judged me and found me guilty. "I never hated my cousin. Even when she betrayed me to Beth." Grace's eyes widen, but I plow on. "I don't care what you believe, but it wasn't me who hurt Mimi. You said you saw Mimi and I leave the tavern together and that I was the last person with Mimi. But you lied. She was spotted in Gaston the next morning by a waitress."

"What?"

My reaction exactly when Mr. Lee told me.

She whips out her phone and types something, then scrolls down the screen. When she looks up, her eyes appear hollowed. "Mary Greer. The waitress who saw Mimi."

"It's in the news?"

Instead of replying, she says, "Why didn't she tell me?"

"Sorry?" What'd she mean by that?

"I'm just so done with this shit." Her voice is suddenly ragged and filled with emotion. "I can't trust anyone anymore." She steps back and the door locks with a click.

"Hey, wait." I reach for the door handle, then freeze, spotting James's white pickup truck in the parking lot next door.

He's in the passenger seat and someone stands outside, their back to me, but the gray hoodie and black tights are easily recognizable.

I race toward the brick wall separating the two businesses.

James looks up and his eyes widen. He says something and the girl stiffens. She starts to turn around—my heart stops, my breathing quits, I can finally see her face—but then she jumps into the truck and slams the door. The truck peels away with a screech of tires and races for the exit, narrowly missing a car turning into the lot and causing that panicked driver to swerve onto the divider.

I start running for my bike, then stop when my phone pings.

The message lighting up the screen is from a number as familiar to me as my own.

It's from Mimi.

I know you saw me & there's no sense in hiding anymore.

So hello, cousin. It's me. back from the dead. I didn't want to do this, I thought I could get rid of you another way. But then you tried to kill me. You hit me with a log and left me for dead. I know what will happen if I return home. Mom will believe you over me. And one day you'll hurt her, too. The only way to get rid of you is to put you away forever. So that way Mom will be safe. Even if I can never return home again.

Confess.

MIMI IS ALIVE.

My breath feels like fire in my throat. I can't feel my feet on the bike pedals. Everything around me, the traffic, the pedestrians, has faded into a blur, and I'm in an echo chamber with the same three words repeating.

Mimi is alive.

It drills into my head, pounding, pounding.

Mimi is alive.

I'm shaking, sobbing, my heart swelling until it feels like it's about to explode.

My cousin is safe, she's okay. God, I haven't lost her.

But I did lose her.

The realization hits like a gut punch.

You hit me with a log and left me for dead.

The gut punch becomes an iron fist closing around my heart. I attacked her, which explains my bruises and the bump on my head. Why her muddy scarf ended up with me.

Confess. Leave and never return. Just like she wrote in her journal.

I tried to kill her.

The pressure in my throat is agonizing, a rock expanding, tearing through.

She faked her death after I attacked her. Because she knew I'd try again.

She's willing to forsake her home and her family to save Auntie from me.

She won't need to.

I'll call the lieutenant and confess.

I'll lock myself away before I ever hurt my family again.

My fingers are numb, and they keep missing the letters. But finally, I hit send on my reply.

I will confess but please come home, Mimi. I will leave this house forever. I promise.

Dots appear, then her reply pops up.

Meet me at Orin Tool Works in thirty minutes. I want to hear you say it for myself.

CHAPTER 24

A LONELY STREETLIGHT at the factory entrance sheds pale white light on the vines draping over the factory gate. A track of trampled weeds leads to the front door. The weeds squelch under my shoes, and then I'm on the patio. The door creaks when I push it open.

The smell hits me first—a dank, musty stink, and then I'm in a sea of deep, overwhelming gloom.

The beam from my phone flashlight falls on distant walls, a sloping ceiling, and a floor hidden under layers of dried vegetation and dirt. I'm in a large room. "Mimi?"

The word echoes around me, then fades into silence.

I continue farther in, trying to separate the sounds of my footsteps and my ragged breaths from anything extraneous.

Then I hear it. A faint swish, followed by a soft thud, like a door closing somewhere to my left. "Mimi? Are you there?"

Leaves crunch, but it's not from my footsteps.

"Mimi?" I swing the phone flashlight around, seeking the source of the sounds. "It's Tanvi. You—" My foot hits something on the floor and I stagger, dropping my phone. It slides across the floor and the flashlight switches off.

Sudden darkness falls like a thick curtain.

My heart thunders.

Then the crunching sounds return. Footsteps.

"Mimi?" I feel around me on the floor for my phone, scattering leaves. "It's Tanvi."

No response.

Why's she not answering?

"Please." The word catches on a sob in my throat. "I just want to see you. I'll confess, I promise. I'll go to the cops and tell them I attacked you. I couldn't remember—"

A sudden inhale. What I said surprised her.

I must explain, and fast. "I don't remember anything of what happened that night. If I remembered, I would've confessed a long time ago. I'm sorry . . ." I sob. "I'm sorry for not realizing how much you were hurting. I didn't mean to be so oblivious, so selfish."

My pulse hammers against my neck as I try to make out shapes, her shape, in the dark. Then I notice the darkness lightening to my right. A gap in what looked like wooden boards laid across a window.

The gap widens. It's not a window. It's a door slowly being opened. Not the one I came through. This one seems to lead farther into the factory.

"Mimi, wait." I edge forward, toward the door, sliding my feet so I won't trip again, straining to listen for her steps, but all I hear is my own heart going a million miles an hour.

I reach the doorway and step past it. A sudden chill sends goosebumps racing up my arms, like someone opened a window and let an icy draft in.

A brilliant ray of light falls on my face. Pain explodes behind my eyes, and I squeeze them shut, instinctively throwing my hands up as a shield.

The heat from the beam fades, and I cautiously open my eyes.

The beam is now focused on something on the floor.

A circle of stones arranged in a circle. Surrounding a thick black candle.

The candle wick is unlit; there's no smoke in the room.

But gray wisps surround me. They thicken into a dense fog.

There's someone lying beside the candle. A man. Arms splayed. Shirt drenched in red and sticky with a pool of red slowly widening around him.

It's Daddy.

And there's a knife sticking out of his abdomen.

I need to take the knife out. I need to save him.

But Mom blocks my way. The flames from the candles reflect off her transfixed expression. Her voice rises in the air as she chants.

Fear twists like a writhing snake in my gut. It leaches into my veins and into my bones. I can't let her kill Daddy again.

I'm next to him. My hand reaches for the hilt of the knife. The wooden edge digs into my palm. I yank it out and the blade gives with a wet sucking sound. "Daddy," I say. "Wake up."

But his eyes remain vacant.

Hazel eyes staring in death at the ceiling. Below blood-streaked blond hair. A face once strikingly handsome now gaunt and pale.

It's not my dad. Daddy died eight years ago. He was cremated, his ashes scattered.

My fingers go numb. I let go and the knife falls to the ground with a clatter. I stumble back.

My bones go liquid.

The edges of my vision curl in, like charred paper. I see the floor approaching at a rapid pace. I'm falling, and there's nothing I can do to stop it.

James is dead.

Everything goes black.

CHAPTER 25

MY EYELIDS FEEL glued to my face. I can't open them fully. Through the lashes, I see a white sheet covering me. I'm lying on a bed, also white. The walls around me are white, too.

Is this what the afterlife's supposed to look like? Like a hospital room?

Someone's arm lies next to me. The skin's dark brown and—I trace it up—is connected to my shoulder. It must be mine. A tube runs from my wrist to a plastic bag full of clear liquid on a pole. Next to it is a table with a basin and a stethoscope.

There's someone moving around beside my bed. A blond woman in scrubs. Auntie used to wear scrubs when she worked as a nurse. The woman's saying something, though my limited field of vison, barred by my lashes, doesn't show me anyone else.

"She hasn't come around yet," she says. "But her vitals are all stable. The MRI of her brain was normal. No bleeding or acute signs of damage, luckily."

MRI. Vitals. Not dead. I'm in a hospital.

"The doctors think it's dehydration and maybe the shock . . ."

The candle. The body lying on the floor.

My insides vibrate like a strummed violin string.

The woman moves away and vanishes.

No, where did she go? I try prying my eyes open and pushing off the bed, but I'm frozen, my muscles flaccid.

I hear a door open. No, don't leave.

I need to stop her. Ask her.

Please.

Urgent whispers surround me. There's someone else in the room. Familiar voices.

"You can't be serious. She's in no condition to give a statement."

Mr. Lee. He's here. My heart soars. I try shouting his name. But the sound dies in my throat.

Why the hell can't I speak or move?

"I'm sorry, Mr. Lee, but you heard the nurse. She's okay."

Lieutenant Williams. I'd recognize that voice anywhere. The last time I spoke to him was when he interrogated me at the deli. He asked me so many questions, but the real question he wanted an answer to was whether I killed Mimi.

I know now that I didn't because she's alive.

But I tried to kill her. I hit her with a log and left her for dead. How could I do that?

"Lieutenant, you can't . . ." Mr. Lee's voice fades into a murmur.

Can't what? Why's the lieutenant here now? A painful knot forms in the pit of my stomach, a foreboding. Because I know the answer.

James.

"We have a dead body and an active criminal investigation." The lieutenant's tone sharpens. "Ms. Nair was found next to the body."

No, no.

Sobs build up inside my chest, but my eyes remain dry and gritty. Even my tear ducts seem paralyzed.

"She's a person of interest in James Surrey's murder." He continues, "We're examining the blood on her clothes to see if it's James's, seeing she didn't have any injuries herself."

They took my clothes. They're examining them because they suspect I murdered James. I need to tell them I didn't.

My throat spasms with the effort to speak, but my jaw seems glued shut, too.

I'm not a killer!

But I hurt Mimi. I wanted to kill her.

Did I want to kill James, too?

Oh God, what did I do?

"If you're going to question her, I'm calling Mrs. Neely." Mr. Lee's tone is short.

"Fine." The lieutenant's is even shorter. "Call me when she's here."

Diane Neely, Krista's mom. She's a lawyer. Mr. Lee thinks I need a lawyer. Why would he think that unless he knows I'm in trouble?

You're supposed to be totally truthful with your lawyer. But I don't know how I can do that when I don't know the truth myself.

I must've dozed off or passed out again. A low murmur of voices reaches me first, followed by the sensation of light behind my shut eyelids. I open them; they don't seem glued together anymore.

The lieutenant stands at the window talking to Krista's mom, their voices too low for me to decipher. The lieutenant seems to be doing most of the talking while Mrs. Neely, a slim woman in a white pantsuit with her braids in a topknot, studies him, her dark eyes steady and calm.

Mr. Lee stands a few feet away from me, watching the wall-mounted TV, which is on mute. Michelle Bitt, the news reporter who was at the vigil Beth did for Mimi, is on the screen, her lips moving soundlessly.

The caption below reads, *A body discovered inside a factory in Old Orin has been identified as that of James Surrey, a lifelong Orin resident. He was found with a single stab wound to the chest. The investigation is ongoing.*

Next to the caption is James's photo, probably from his driver's license. Hazel eyes defiant, chin lifted, like he's challenging the photographer.

Poor James. He didn't deserve to be left splayed on a cold floor like that.

Vacant eyes with the life drained out of them staring blindly at the ceiling.

That horrible sucking sound when I pulled the knife out.

I clench my teeth, but a moan escapes.

Mr. Lee glances over his shoulder, his round face drawn with new lines of weariness and despair. Then they soften as he smiles and hurries to me. "Tanvi, kiddo, you're awake."

My chest hurts with terrible agony, knowing that I caused those lines on his face; I caused him to look like he's aged ten years. "Mr. Lee . . ." My voice is scratchy, and it hurts to croak the word out.

He grasps my hands between his, then pats my head, his eyes filling. "It's okay, you're okay. That's all that matters."

Then the lieutenant appears at his side. "Hi, Ms. Nair, I apologize for disturbing you when I'm sure you want to rest. But I have to ask you some questions."

"She's still weak," Mr. Lee says. "Can't this wait until she's discharged tomorrow?"

"No, it cannot, I'm sorry."

A warm hand falls on my shoulder. I look up into Mrs. Neely's kind eyes. "You'll be okay, honey. You don't have to answer anything you don't want to. I'm right here."

The lieutenant pulls up a chair. "Okay, let's start at the beginning. What made you go inside Orin Tool Works? The factory has been shut down for months."

Mimi. She wanted to meet me there so she could hear firsthand my intent to confess to hurting her.

But James was there, too. And he was dead already.

Wasn't he?

I remember grasping the knife and yanking it out.

Or did I push it in?

"Ms. Nair?"

Mom's candle was next to James. It was unlit, but when I first walked in, it felt like the room was full of smoke.

And that it was Daddy lying dead.

I walked toward my father; I reached for the knife. "The knife . . ."

The lieutenant leans forward. "Yes, Ms. Nair? What about the knife?"

I incline my head toward the TV caption. "It was in his abdomen, not his chest."

Mr. Lee's eyes widen at the same time as the lieutenant gives a satisfied grunt. "Where did you get the knife from?"

I shake my head, then wish I hadn't when agony explodes in my skull. "Not mine."

The lieutenant frowns. "But—"

"You heard her, Lieutenant." Mrs. Neely's voice is sharp. "She said the knife wasn't hers."

The cop keeps his gaze locked on me and doesn't spare her a glance. "Did you find the knife inside the factory then?"

Mrs. Neely makes an exasperated sound and turns to face him. "Peter."

Yeah, the knife was inside the factory, but was that what fell out of my hand and clattered on the floor? I remember something clattering, the sound echoed in that room.

No, it was my phone. I need it, it has the text from Mimi asking me to meet her at the factory. I force my dry cracked lips to move. "My phone . . . it fell inside."

"We didn't find any phones inside." The cop's tone remains even, but a spark of impatience appears in his eyes. "Ms. Nair, you still haven't told me why you went inside an abandoned factory. Did you go there to meet James? What happened after you went inside?"

After I went inside . . . The smoke, Daddy lying on the floor. No, that was an illusion.

Triggered by the candle.

I didn't bring the candle in there. It went missing from my house.

Taken by the person who entered using a key. Who knew the bag with the candles was stashed in the attic.

Because she stashed it there.

She knew the significance of the candle, how it'd trigger my nightmares, my panic attacks.

"Ms. Nair, it'll be a lot easier if you tell me the truth now. Once we prove that knife was taken from your house—"

"You mean *if*," Mrs. Neely snaps. "And that still wouldn't prove a thing, Peter."

"It shows premeditation," he snaps back.

"That's conjecture. You don't have any evidence to prove Tanvi held that knife."

"Not unless we find her fingerprints on the hilt."

Which he will find because I held the hilt when I yanked it out.

Fatigue washes through me, leaving my body limp.

Mrs. Neely looks at me, her dark eyes grave and concerned, then turns to the cop. "She's not answering any more questions, so I think we're done here."

He sighs, then stands. "Okay, but be prepared to produce her at the station when required."

My stomach churns nauseatingly as I meet his watchful gaze before he walks out.

CHAPTER 26

BY THE NEXT morning after a final run of testing, I'm discharged from the hospital and home, folded on the living room sofa. The cops will formally interview me according to Mrs. Neely, but she's fighting for time. She'll be coming by later today for an interview so she can get all the facts before preparing her case.

But I still don't know the facts. Yesterday, the lieutenant said, *Start at the beginning.*

But the beginning wasn't when I walked into the factory or even when I received the message asking me to go there. It was when I decided to try and kill Mimi. When her betrayal triggered a darkness inside me—one I thought I inherited from my mother—which made me follow my cousin into the night, hit her with a log, and leave her for dead.

I need to understand my actions before I can meet with my counsel. And for *that*, I need to understand my mother's actions. Not just forgive her, but fully understand her.

As a kid, I knew that she was hurting after losing the baby. She'd stopped being my mom; the light went out of her eyes, and she'd often remain still, lost in her world. Daddy would take her for a gazillion appointments and give her pills every day, but she never improved. After she killed my dad, I decided I would never forgive her. Or understand her.

But now I do.

It takes a short search of the internet to find a series of articles on mental illnesses after miscarriage. Miscarriage can trigger depression, anxiety, PTSD, and even peripartum depression or psychosis. I read through each, page after page, my agony escalating by the time I'm done. My mom had so many of the symptoms the articles mentioned. The sense of alienation, the mood swings, the way she withdrew from Daddy and me, her irritability and paranoia, the wild accusations against Daddy and Auntie. The way she believed that guy on the internet was the only one she could trust.

Hours later, after the text has blurred and my head is aching, it finally makes sense. While she was witnessing the tribal ceremony, she was able to forget the pain. I'm not sure how, but maybe the chanting and spiritual energy suppressed her symptoms for that short while. Believing that the chants were what helped her, she began seeking a spiritual healer. She turned to the internet where she found the "healer" who sold her a bunch of candles and some rituals. Who knows what else he told her. And when Daddy told her to stop the rituals, he became her enemy.

Mom's mental state was such that she was susceptible to manipulation by this fraud. Whatever "teachings" he had online must've been geared to specifically target people like my mother, who were desperate for some peace of mind and happiness.

He manipulated Mom to make a quick buck.

Another search through the internet and I find other stories of fake healers and cult leaders who have ruined lives by such manipulations.

My hands are clenched so hard, my fingers turn numb. I blamed Mom all this while when it was this fraud who killed my parents. If he hadn't preyed on my mom, things might have been different. She and Daddy might still be alive.

I jump off the chair and pace the room, unable to sit still as it all begins to make sense.

I made a mistake. Mimi's betrayal of me to Beth wasn't the beginning after all.

It all started when I landed in Orin. I suffered from such significant anxiety and panic attacks, and Auntie was desperate to help me. I wonder if there was some guilt involved because she couldn't help her sister. Auntie's focus on me made Mimi feel overlooked. To the point she was scared Auntie would forget her.

Beth saw her pain and manipulated it just like this "healer" manipulated Mom. Beth turned Mimi's resentment to fear. Fear of me, the daughter of a killer.

Beth told me you're a psycho, just like your crazy mom. She told me you'll try and kill me or my mom one day. Stay away from us!

But that did turn out to be true, didn't it? I did try to kill Mimi.

I uncurl my fingers and study the deep crescents formed on my palms by my nails. These hands wielded a weapon and hurt my cousin so badly, she nearly died.

So maybe Beth wasn't distorting Mimi's thoughts; maybe she was just telling the truth.

A sudden squeak from the front door makes me jump. It came from the mail slot hinge downstairs.

An envelope is on the floor. Inside is a note from Abby. *Hey, Tanvi, tried texting and calling you. I had some photos of Mimi from spirit week and thought you'd want them in her memory. You can cut Beth and Grace out if you want.*

The cops haven't found my phone yet. So far, apparently, they've managed to keep my name out of the news about James's murder.

Abby left me a handful of five-by-seven Polaroids of Beth and Mimi. They're in spirit week costumes of matching tie-dye shirts and shorts and wearing wigs of shoulder-length green hair. In one of the photos, Grace stands slightly behind them, wearing the same green wig and tie-dye shirt, her face tight with anger.

Looking at them, I'm struck again by the similarities between Mimi and Beth. Mimi inherited Uncle Dan's skin coloring, and it's the same shade as Beth's tanned skin. They also share the same aquiline nose and high cheekbones. But their eye colors are distinct, one a dark brown and the other blue like the sky above them.

Then my gaze falls on the thin gold bracelet on Mimi's wrist. It's the same one that I found at Orin Springs.

Was Mimi wearing the bracelet the night she vanished?

The memory appears through the fog in my brain.

Mimi in her red dress silhouetted against the wash of light from the scooter. She turns to wave to me. One slim arm raised in a wave, the other with the gold bracelet circling her wrist reaching for Grace's shoulder.

The memory is so clear, it feels like a movie reel stuck in limbo.

So, Mimi was wearing the bracelet when she left for the tavern with Grace.

But how did it land in the waterfall?

My heart begins a rapid drumbeat.

I need to get to the waterfall. Find out if there's anything else there I missed.

Since I don't have my phone, I leave a note for Auntie on the coffee table.

Heading out to my favorite place in the world. Want to think things through.

THOUGH IT'S MIDMORNING, the air feels heavy and dark, and the breeze carries a prickly chill that raises goose bumps along my skin. At the edge of the woods, the watery sunlight dims further, with the rays barely penetrating the heavy canopy of branches overhead.

A twig snaps behind me.

I freeze, my breath snagging in my throat.

Then leaves crunch, the sound steady and just a few feet away.

I remain still, not daring to move a muscle.

The sounds continue, but now they seem to be moving away from me.

I wait until the sounds fade away, then thread my way through the trees. Within minutes, the gurgling sounds of the springs replace the rustling of the leaves, and the undergrowth changes to stone. I've reached the bottom of the rock outcrop leading to the waterfall.

There's someone on the outcrop. A person in black leggings and a dark brown hoodie kneels at the edge of the springs and seems to be searching among the rocks. They're looking for something.

The bracelet?

I take a step forward and my shoe scrapes on the stone.

The person freezes. Then they lift their head.

I duck behind a thick clump of bushes and hold my breath. Trying to hear over my thundering heartbeats. But all I hear is water crashing down on the rocks.

After a couple of beats, I sneak a peek. They've disappeared. Then I hear a scrape and muffled grunts come from behind the rocks. They must be climbing up to the ledge above the waterfall.

I edge toward the stream. My sneakers slip on the slick surface of the slope, but I catch my balance and scamper for the rocky ledge. Flattening myself against its hard surface, I wait for sounds, a movement, something that'll show me where they are.

But I hear nothing.

Gripping the ridges along the rocks, I haul myself up, feeling for finger and toeholds. The rough, flinty surface cuts into my skin. My fingertips are raw by the time I reach the top of the rocky ledge and throw a knee over.

Nothing moves in the overgrowth and the bushes that extend up to the lip of the ledge.

Where did they go?

I tread around the creepers and reach the tip of the rocky ledge.

Water falls in a steady sheet onto protruding rocks below before the stream bubbles and froths into a crevice to disappear underground. This part of the ledge, overhanging the waterfall, is slick from years of spray. Remembering the last time I was pushed off, I step back from the edge.

A sudden swish sounds from behind me. A blur in the corner of my vision.

I start to turn just as something hard slams into my back.

My breath bursts out in a gasp. My feet slip. I tumble off the ledge and down, toward the rocks waiting below.

No, no! I lash out with my arms, grabbing blindly for the rope that was there before. My desperate fingers only clutch water, seeking the familiar feel of rough strands.

There's nothing.

I'm hurtling toward the rocks below.

Thunder fills my ears, my mind. I squeeze my eyes shut, bracing for the hit. For my body to slam against the rocks.

Something brushes my face. Instinctively, I grab it, breaking my fall.

It's the tip of the climbing rope. Someone cut through it, leaving only a short length behind.

I cling onto the wildly lashing strands with all my strength. My shoulders are on fire, my arms numb and disconnected.

The waterfall crashes down on me in a deluge. Then I'm behind it, rolling and tumbling through space. My shins scrape on stone, and my shoulder slams something hard.

I sprawl—onto a carpet of weeds and sand.

A loud roar fills my ears.

I am alive. Hurt and bloody, but alive.

The water forms a wall in front of me. By some miracle, I managed to land behind it instead of being crushed on the rocks. I've never been back here before.

Shudders rack my body. Someone cut through the climbing rope.

I'm in a shallow cave behind the waterfall, if you can even call it a cave. Granite and packed earth form the roof and walls, barely three feet high, with the waterfall in front, shielding it from view. A stench of rotting vegetation fills the place.

The hair rises along the back of my neck. No, I have been here before. I know this cave. I remember this place. Vomit pushes into my throat.

There's something stuck in a crack above the water line. Something that projects out of the greenish-black slime coating the walls. My hand shakes as I reach for it and draw out a tattered and stained red shoe.

Mimi's favorite heels. The shoes matched her red dress.

She was wearing them the night she left. I saw them when I followed her out of the house.

The stench is stronger at the back of the cave, the fumes overwhelming. Coming from the deep bed of leaves and twigs pushed against the back wall by the water.

Browned, yellowed foliage, patterned with chunks of dirt and small stones. And longer black fibers clotted with mud.

Black fibers attached to something white and swollen.

A scalp. Bloated, peeling skin disappearing under its blanket of rotting vegetation.

I scream. The sound erupts from my mouth, shattering my eardrums.

I throw myself backward, back through the waterfall, scampering, falling over the rocks. My skin rips, but I keep going. Away, as far as I can. Gasping, retching, as the memory floods back.

I know now what happened that day.

I know what had happened to Mimi.

And for the first time since Mimi disappeared, I wish I didn't remember.

CHAPTER 27

Before

MIMI'S AT THE front door, silhouetted against the rain outside. "T, I messed up bad," she says, looking up at where I'm standing at the top of the stairs. "I didn't know, not until Beth got high and told me everything tonight. But I'm going to fix it now."

"Mimi, wait!" I fly downstairs and outside. Raindrops drum on the road and wind gusts whip my hair out of its ponytail. "What did Beth tell you?"

"That she hadn't deleted the video though she'd promised me she did. She's going to show everyone tomorrow—"

"She won't." I tell her about the threat Krista left in her voice mail about suing her if she did since I'm a minor.

"She'll find a way. We need that video *gone*." She presses a trembling hand to her mouth. "I'm so awful for what I did to you. I didn't realize, not until I saw you panic, and Beth *promised* me . . ."

The betrayal is etched on her face. I throw my arms open, and she runs into them. "Oh my God, I love you so much."

A headlight appears down the road, its beam wavering in the rain.

"I got to go now, T. I've got to get to Orin Tavern. Lyla and Greg almost ran James and me off the road on our way here, and now James's gone and challenged Greg to a fight at the tavern."

The headlight steadies and Grace appears out of the night, pulling up to the gate on her scooter.

"You're going with *Grace*?"

I don't know if the dampness on Mimi's face is from the rain or her tears. "Beth lied about Grace, too. She put my laptop in Grace's backpack and made me believe my best friend . . ." She sniffs. "And she had the nerve to laugh when she told me that, like I'd be fine with it!"

Mimi's red shoes are spattered with mud, but she doesn't seem to care as she rushes across the slushy yard to Grace. They talk, heads angled toward each other. Grace's grin is wobbly and finally, she hugs Mimi. Their voices waver in and out, but I hear Grace say, "You ready?"

Mimi climbs on the scooter, the bracelet on her wrist glittering in the headlight. "Once we stop the guys from killing each other, we'll go to Beth's." She smiles at me, her expression a sure, fierce beacon in the dark. "No one's gonna bully you ever again, T. I promise."

Once the scooter's taillight vanishes into the rain, I take off running for the woods and the shortcut to the tavern. I lost her once. I can't lose her again. I have to make sure this is real.

The scuffle's already broken out by the time I reach the tavern. Greg and James roll on the ground, punching and kicking each other. Grace and Mimi try to separate them. Then the crowd swarms in and hide Mimi and Grace from sight.

A siren blares, cutting through the night, and red and blue lights light up the road. Then the tavern door bursts open, and people shove me aside, racing for their vehicles parked at the curb.

Mimi breaks through the crowd and runs toward me. "What the hell are you doing here, Tanvi? Get out. Go home."

"But what about you?"

"I have to make sure James is okay. Then I'm going to Beth's."

"Mimi . . ."

"I'll be okay. And I'll make her delete that video." She

glances at the approaching cop car. "Go, now! Mom will kill me if anything happens to you." She hurries into the tavern.

The flickering red and blue lights reflect off the wet pavement and the drizzle is blinding. And it's not until I round a curve in the road and the lights fade that I sense—from the hair rising on the back of my neck—that someone's following me.

But the road behind me is deserted. Darkness fills the abandoned shops on either side. Ahead, the factory gate stands open from when I came through on my way to the tavern.

I slip through the gate and hurry down past the knee-high weeds, glancing over my shoulder every few seconds, unable to shake the feeling of being followed. But the only thing moving is the wind moaning through the weeds like a creature in distress.

Then the gate behind me creaks. Like someone's walked through it.

I swing around. Bulldozers and other construction equipment form hulking shadows, still and silent in the night. But through them I see another shadow. A figure standing a few yards away.

"Mimi? Is that you?" Maybe she's making sure that I'm returning home like she asked me to.

The person scoffs. "What are you, a baby that needs Mimi to tag along wherever you go?"

It's the same voice she used when she mocked me for my panic attack after she lit Mom's candles. I clench my jaw. "What do you want, Beth?"

She walks forward, her scowl visible in light cast by the solitary lamp above the factory's side wall. She looks worse than she did at the party. Mascara streaks her blotchy face and her mouth twitches uncontrollably. "What do *I* want? I want you gone! You're nothing but garbage, filth—"

"But Mimi doesn't think so. Not anymore." A feeling of

satisfaction rushes through me when I see her go still. "Yeah, she told me everything. How you told her you hadn't deleted the video though you promised her you would. And how you framed Grace. How could you do that? You made Grace's life hell."

"Who cares? She's insignificant, just like you."

"Not to Mimi. She's back with us now that you showed her exactly who you are. A mean, spiteful, vindictive person under everything."

Her facial twitching increases, and I wonder if it's the effect of whatever drug she's on.

"Karma can be a bitch." I turn away, heading across the yard to the wire fence in the back.

"Hey!" she yells. "We're finishing this now."

"Finishing what . . ." Then words shrivel and die on my tongue.

She's yanked something off a rusted excavator—a long metal rod—and is advancing on me.

"What the hell are you trying to do?"

"Trying?" She hits the windshield of a dilapidated truck, and the glass shatters. "I'm going to end you, bitch."

I want to laugh at her pathetic ploy—but her expression's changed from a fiery rage to something colder, more calculated. I freeze.

"I'm going to do Mimi a favor." She swings the rod again, slicing a creeper in two, the wet squelching sound forcing a whimper from my locked throat.

My muscles turn to stone. My feet root to the damp ground.

"People like you don't deserve to live." Another swing of her arm, and metal rattles. "You're going to be squished like the pest you are."

Her strides get longer. Then her feet become a blur. The distance between us is shrinking.

Oh my God. *Run!*

The wire netting of the fence catches on my bare arms, tracking fire across my skin, and then I'm through and racing for the woods.

"Only *I* deserve to be with Mimi," Beth yells. "Your stupid meltdown messed everything up. She'll see." Her voice bounces on the tree trunks whipping past me.

The light from the factory fades and night closes in. The rain's increased, sheeting through the branches and clogging my vision. My sneakers slip on the slick grass. I stagger, grabbing for a shrub, and look over my shoulder.

Light flickers through the undergrowth behind me, throwing her figure into silhouette. She's using her phone flashlight to find her way.

My phone. I can call for help. I reach into my pocket and find it empty.

Her thudding footsteps break through the rain and my panting breaths. "Mimi wanted me to apologize to you. Can you fucking believe that?" Her voice is closer. She's catching up.

My heart beats out of my chest. I risk another glance.

She rounds a tree just yards away. Light reflects off the dull metal rod clutched in her hand. "Well, no apologies, psycho, because you're gonna die today."

A wave of dizziness hits me. I'm hyperventilating. I can't pass out. Not now.

I need to get home and lock myself in.

My legs are numb and heavy. I can barely drag them along.

It's not until the sound of rumbling water reaches me that I realize I missed the fork branching off the path to my house.

I turn to backtrack and she's there at the fork. A gleam lights her narrowed eyes. She knows she's cut me off.

The ground changes from packed earth and foliage to hard rock. I'm on the slope leading to the waterfall and the ledge above it. Using the crevice in the rocks as foot and handholds, I climb up and throw a leg over the top of the ledge. The stone digs into my skin as I flatten myself and crawl to the bushes in the middle.

A clatter of metal hitting rock comes from below. Then I hear panting breaths and scrabbling sounds.

She's climbing up. I'll be trapped if I stay up here. There are footholds on the other side of the ledge. It's closer to the waterfall and therefore slicker, but if I can get down that way, I can make it back to the path leading home.

I jump to my feet just as she appears, dragging herself over the edge and onto the ledge. Her hands are empty. She had to lose her weapon to free her hands.

I back away, pushing through the undergrowth. Twigs crunch under my shoes.

She straightens and blinks the rain out of her eyes. Her gaze locks on me. "You got no place to run now."

But she doesn't know this place like I do. Gripping the brush to keep my balance on the slushy ground, I angle for the edge where the footholds are located.

"Beth, stop."

Mimi's voice cuts through.

My heart leaps to my mouth.

She's on the slope, racing up the rocks, surefooted as ever. "Don't you dare touch her."

"Go away, Mimi." Beth snaps. "This doesn't concern you."

"What the hell?" Sounds of clambering, and Mimi appears, having scaled the ledge in half the time I took. She looks at me. "I saw her following you. You're okay?"

I nod, the lump in my throat stopping my words. Mimi's here; she came to protect me.

Mimi faces Beth, her hands clenched. "What do you mean doesn't concern me? Of course, Tanvi does!"

"What about me?" Beth's chin trembles, then her face collapses into rage. "You said you'll be my sister! You know I have no one, with my mom abandoning me and my dad not even caring if I live or die."

"You hurt people, Beth. What you did to Tanvi with that candle—"

"Seriously? You were there, too. I remember you laughing."

"It was a mistake, something I'll pay for the rest of my life. You made me fear my own cousin." She reaches for my hand. "Please don't hate me, T."

"Never," I say through sobs. And that was the truth.

"What's this? A fucking family reunion?" Beth spits the words out at Mimi. "I made you popular. If it weren't for me, you'd be a nobody. Everything you have is because of me!"

"Yeah? Like trying to force me to snort that poison?"

"You kidding me? Your boyfriend's a drug dealer. You're lucky I let you keep him!"

"He grows *weed*." Mimi takes a deep breath. "You're *poison*, Beth. You made me believe that shit about Tanvi. It was only when I saw her reaction with the candles that I remembered she feared her mom, too. When I took those candles, I brought that horror back upon her." Tears flow down her face, and she grips my hand harder. "I won't do that to Tanvi again, and I won't let you, either."

Beth stares at her. "So, what do you want me to do?"

"Apologize to Tanvi. And delete that video."

Beth's expression turns venomous, a snarl twists her lips. "You're delusional if you think I'm going to apologize to anyone. Or delete that damn video. Tomorrow, everyone's gonna know about your psycho cousin. They're going to be all over her—"

"Then I'll tell everyone you threatened us. We'll make *your* life hell—together. You can't bully all of us, Beth."

"You won't dare."

"Oh, I will."

Beth pushes Mimi hard, sending her stumbling into the shrubs. A branch snags her bracelet and rips it clean off her wrist.

"Hey!" I scream and shove Beth away from Mimi. "Leave her alone!"

Beth glares at me. Then she lifts her hand and slams her palm into my chest.

My feet slip on the slick surface. I grab for a bush, but my momentum is too strong. The ledge disappears from under me and I'm in the waterfall.

Tumbling down, sputtering, water filling my nose, my mouth. My lungs are on fire.

My head slams into something hard. My vision goes dark, and the world spins around me in dizzy, nauseating waves. I can't move. My head feels like it's blown up to thrice its size. My limbs are sluggish and disconnected.

I close my eyes, welcoming the inky, dense, jelly-like darkness that descends on me, and start to drift off to sleep.

Shouts ring out from above. "Oh my God! Tanvi?"

The fear in my cousin's voice jerks me awake.

"Are you okay? Tanvi!"

I want to respond, but my brain can't form the words. I'm not in the waterfall anymore. My eyelids weigh a ton. It takes all my strength to force them open.

I'm lying on leaves and sand and half a foot of water. Behind the waterfall?

"Hang in there, Tanvi!" Mimi shouts. "I'm calling 911."

"You can't tell the cops!" Beth's voice is shrill.

"Back off, Beth. Beth, no!" Mimi screams.

Then she stops screaming.

Forcing back the darkness, I drag myself to the mouth of

the cave. The water around me is changing color, turning pink. Mimi's scarf, the one she was wearing, drifts through the falls into the cave. I reach for it. She won't want to lose it.

Through the curtain of water, I see my cousin sprawled on the rocks.

Her hair trailing in black strands behind her, her body still. The water slowly turning red around her.

"Mimi." I whisper. Flinching under the bruising, the water stinging into my back, I crawl over and reach for her, shaking her shoulder. "Get up. We need to go."

"Fuck, fuck." Beth curses from the ledge above.

I glance up. She's staring right at me.

She's going to come for me now. I need to get out, get help. Gritting my teeth against the pain, I scramble down the stream, clutching Mimi's scarf, throwing myself over the bank and in a dead run toward the trees.

My vision goes in and out. Through a haze, I watch Beth grab Mimi and disappear behind the falls.

Get help. I take off in a drunken, stumbling run down the trail. I can't feel my body or the ground. My world becomes the terrible pain in the back of my head. I need to focus, stay on my feet, keep pushing forward.

The tunnel keeps closing in. The darkness returns, slimy tentacles invading my brain.

I grip Mimi's scarf tight and repeat the mantra. *Get help.*

My house appears in the gloom.

Get in.

I stumble past the gate, through the front door.

Get to the phone.

Call 911.

The night descends again. This time so heavy, it crushes me. Everything goes dark.

CHAPTER 28

MIMI DIED FOR me.

She died because she saw Beth following me. She came racing after us to protect me.

And I forgot.

I curl up on the rocks, the jagged edges digging into my hip. My throat burns from vomit as I retch again and again.

The sound of splashing breaks through the pounding in my ears. The person in the hoodie approaches me. Thick waves of black hair spill past their shoulders and frame the lower part of a tanned face, a pointy chin, with the rest shadowed. Then they raise their hand and flip the hood off.

Brown eyes under arched brows and a thin nose, framed by waist-length dark hair.

"Beth . . ." My voice is hoarse.

She stops. Her gaze snaps to the cave and back to me. "So, you found her. Good. I was getting sick of this." Her fingers curl under the hairline and she tugs the black wig off. Her blond hair spills out. A quick flick of her wrist and the contacts come off, and Beth's blue eyes lock on mine. "Hi there."

Sweat crystallizes to icy dust on my skin. "You killed her." The words stick like shards of glass in my throat. "You put her in the cave."

"I had to." She squats on the ground and lets her feet trail in the swirling water. "I had to hide her before you returned with help. But then you didn't. I went by your house, and it was dark, no movement, no cops, so I used the key in Mimi's purse and went in, and there you were, fast asleep in your bed. I thought you were dead. Hoped."

I forgot about Mimi. I went to sleep and forgot my cousin.

"I didn't know what was wrong with you, but what the hell. That's when I had this brilliant idea—wear the red dress I'd bought for Twin Day and pretend to be Mimi, make sure someone saw me in Gaston, and then dump the dress and Mimi's purse on the beach to make it like some rando killed her there. Then I came back to hide her." She inclines her head toward the waterfall, her wild eyes glowing with malice. "But I couldn't move the body; it got stuck under the rocks in that fucking cave. I figured it was only a matter of time before you called the cops. Imagine my surprise when you acted like Mimi ran away."

I never knew grief could hurt like this. It feels like a physical pain, shriveling my skin, eating into my bones until they shatter.

"It was like you remembered nothing, and that was when I realized you really did remember nothing. Could I get any luckier?" She laughs. "But I had to get rid of you before you started remembering. Mimi told me how often you'd visit this place. So I waited for you to turn up, and you did. Twice. Only this time I made sure to cut the rope, couldn't have it saving your life again." Her brows raise. "But you're like a cat with fucking nine lives. You never die."

But Mimi's dead, and it's all my fault. If I hadn't fallen asleep, if I had somehow fought it and called 911, they would've saved Mimi. My heart splits and cracks, the agony unbearable, shuddering through my body. "You . . . killed James, too."

She shrugs. "I had to. I told him not to go to the cops or they'd nab him. I mean, the boyfriend's always the killer, right? And he needed cash for his dad, which gave me an excuse to swing by often. I could've shot you that day and told the cops

I thought you were a burglar. But that's when he started suspecting me. The asshole was going to go to the cops. So, I had
Mimi return to life and lure you to the factory." The corner of
her lips lifts in a smirk. "A perfect frame-up, if I say so myself."

Beth knew how I felt about my mom; she drummed the
idea into my mind that I was a psycho, a killer. When she sent
that text from Mimi's phone, I believed it. I believed I tried to
kill my cousin and deserved to be locked up forever.

Oh God, I even thought I could've killed James. I retch
again, saliva dribbling from my mouth.

She lifts something out of her hoodie pocket. It's Mimi's
phone with its bejeweled case and her house key with its dove-
shaped tag. "I won't need these anymore." She flings both into
the stream where they land with a plop and then sink into the
slime-covered rocks, then turns to me with a smile. "I'm keeping your phone, though, just for a bit until I can type in your
suicide message. Because you're not going to be talking anymore." She mock-shivers. "It's good to get all this off my chest.
I've been dying to tell someone. Dying, ha. Isn't that clever?"

Mimi lying in that awful cave all by herself. I left her there.
Oh God, my sweet cousin.

James splayed out on the floor of his shop, the knife buried
in his body.

"It's all your fault. You're a freak. No one wanted to be
around you, not even Mimi."

My tongue feels heavy, but I force the words out. "Mimi
loved me."

"Yeah?" She shrugs. "She's dead now, isn't she? She's not
going to come swooping down to rescue you anymore. And
once they find your body next to Mimi's, they'll know you
couldn't take the guilt. A killer just like your mom. Case closed."

No, I can't let her win.

Mimi loved me all along. She was going to stop Beth.

That's what she had to tell me that night. She protected me to the end.

I've lost my cousin. Auntie lost her daughter.

And it's Beth's fault. She twisted Mimi's mind like the con man twisted Mom's. She made Mimi believe I'd kill her and Auntie. And when Mimi realized the truth and tried to stop Beth, Beth killed her.

But this time, I'm not forgetting. This time, I'll make sure Beth pays.

My heartbeat becomes a heavy pounding in my ears. Fire licks through my muscles, turning them to iron.

Through the spray from the waterfall, I watch her as she sits not more than three feet from me. The track leading to my house is behind her. To get to it, I'll have to either cross the stream or go around the ledge.

Because I'm not going to get trapped up on that ledge again.

She plans to drown me or push me onto the rocks, and I'm not going to let her.

She killed once—twice—and she'll do it again.

I start inching backward, my fingers slipping on the slimy rocks.

She jumps into the stream. "Time to wrap this up."

I leap toward the opposite bank. My sneakers slip on the slick rocks, and I fall, sending water spraying all around.

Using the rocks as stepping stones, she makes her way toward me. Her gaze is fixed on me, her feet steady.

My heart thunders. I turn and scramble for the rocks away from her. My fingernails split on the slick, hard surfaces. I ignore the pain and keep clawing. Past the eddying currents sucking at my feet.

The splashing sounds behind me get louder.

I throw myself toward the opposite bank. Across swirling water and sharp-tipped stones.

My right shoulder hits the frozen ground. I tuck and roll.

Clutching whatever I can—trailing weeds, twigs, earth—I crawl up the bank. My palms sting; my elbows feel like they could come out of their sockets.

She's almost to the bank.

I scramble across the rocky slope and toward the trees.

A thud sounds behind me, followed by a grunt.

I pump my legs faster, leaping over tree roots, Beth's harsh breathing behind me spurring me on.

Then the sounds suddenly cut off, replaced by my pounding heartbeat. I look over my shoulder. The trail lies empty behind me.

I turn back.

She emerges through the trees a few feet in front of me, a knife clutched in her gloved hand. "Why do you always complicate things? I was hoping you'd just drown yourself. But now . . . I can't let you get away this time."

Ice slithers through my veins. I must get out of here.

Her arm lifts in a deadly upswing. The knife flashes.

I leap for cover behind the tree next to me and fall, crashing through the undergrowth. The creepers and bushes fold over me. Staying deep in the cover, I crawl away from the trail.

"Fuck!" she yells. Footsteps hurry toward me.

I hold my breath and listen. Her steps get closer. And closer. Now!

I slide through the thick foliage and swing my right leg with all my strength toward where I'd heard her last.

The sole of my shoe strikes something solid.

Beth gasps and staggers back.

The next instant, I am on my feet and lifting my leg again, intending to go for the knife hand.

But she ducks and comes at me. The blade glints in the sunlight.

She slices down.

Instinctively, I reach out, grabbing her wrist.

She bears down, the tip of the knife inches from my eyes, clawing at my face with her free hand.

My hand tremors; my grip on her wrist weakens. The knife descends another inch.

I can't let her kill me. If I die out here, people will believe Beth's story. Auntie will think I took her daughter from her. I destroyed her family.

I won't let that happen.

Using a Tae Kwon Do self-defense technique, I wrest Beth's clawing fingers from my face and twist her knife hand back until the knuckles brush the back of her wrist.

She screams. The knife falls out of her grip.

I smash my right fist into her face. She stumbles and falls back. I follow, swinging my leg into her chest, then follow with another roundhouse kick to the back of her knees.

She sinks to the ground, clutching her wrist, her face pale.

Over our panting breaths, the distant wail of a police siren rapidly builds to a crescendo.

Her eyes widen. She shoots to her feet, spinning toward the trail. I tackle her and we crash into the undergrowth.

Car doors slam and boots rush up the trail. I hear the lieutenant call my name.

Relief floods my veins. "Here," I shout.

Beth bucks and tries to roll to throw me off, her rigid fingers reaching back to scratch at my arms, my face. I pin her down with my knees and hang on.

THE NEXT HALF hour passes in a blur of uniforms and loud voices and Beth shouting at them to arrest me, too.

They've left me in a room in the station while they wait on Mr. Lee to come in with Auntie. The table I'm sitting at is faded and scratched, stained with heat circles from numerous coffee cups like the one in front of me. I haven't taken a sip; I'm using it to warm my numb hands. Though I doubt the rapidly cooling coffee will help a bit since the numbness is all through my body and I'm shivering.

It wasn't my hands that killed Mimi. She loved me. She died protecting me.

And Beth will pay for this. I'll make sure of it.

I take a deep breath.

It's over now.

Voices sound in the corridor, and through the blinds in the window, I see Mr. Lee with his arm around Auntie. Her face is haggard, eyes sunken and glazed. And that's when it hits me.

How do I tell Auntie that Mimi is never coming home?

CHAPTER 29

IT'S BEEN THREE weeks since I found Mimi, and I haven't slept a wink. Every time I close my eyes, I see the cave. The same image.

I can't sit still. I keep moving, keep busy so the thoughts ricocheting in my brain don't take over. My eyelids feel heavy and leaden, my skull is stuffed with cotton balls, and I want desperately to fall unconscious again.

I told Dr. Ajay everything when I resumed therapy last week. He made it clear that we have a long path ahead. I know it'll be harder to forgive myself for allowing her to feel over-looked and neglected, for allowing Beth to prey on her and manipulate her.

But mostly for forgetting what happened to her.

My psychologist asked me to start by celebrating Mimi's life and by helping Auntie do the same. The first two weeks were hectic, with various pujas and ceremonies for Mimi all facilitated by the temple in Detroit. She was cremated in the same crematorium my parents were.

Auntie knows now that Mimi is never coming home, but as Dr. Ajay said, give it time. Just be there for her.

I plan to.

There's no possible way for me to repay Mimi's debt. I'll always remember how she hugged me in the end, how she said she loved me.

My cousin Mimi.

• • •

"HEY." GRACE RUSHES around the counter as soon as I enter Orin Café and throws her arms around me. "How're you doing?"

I hug her back. With my memory returning, I remember how relieved and happy she looked when they reunited. Grace thought she'd got her friend and her life back, but it was all taken away that night. She lost Mimi twice, just like I did. I tighten my arms around her. "Doing. And you?"

Her smile falters, and the cloud appears, hiding behind that smile. "The same." She leads me to a table in a corner. "How'd it go with the lieutenant?"

I sit down opposite her. "Krista's mom thinks they have enough to link Beth to James's murder."

"And Mimi's?"

"They're working on it. Because she was in that cave for so long, some of the evidence . . . deteriorated." I clench my hands tight until my fingers turn numb. "I forgot Mimi, Grace. How could I do that?" How do I deal with the guilt of leaving Mimi alone in a lonely cave? Beth might have killed my cousin, but I forgot her. I let Beth walk free until now. Until she killed James. He died because of me, too.

Grace's expression softens. "It's not your fault. Beth planned it well."

She did. She chose Gaston, a predominantly white town where they hardly see other ethnicities, and she chose a friendly motherly waitress and spun a story about a boyfriend whom the family didn't approve of. The perfect way to gain sympathy and attention. The red dress she dumped on the beach was an exact replica of Mimi's, which she'd bought for Twin Day but not worn yet.

"She kept James from going to the cops by telling him they'd suspect him first." I pick at my nails, ignoring the stinging from the bloody cuticles. Remembering the phone call I'd overheard at his shop and how Beth was in the shop with a gun when I entered the second time. She stuck close to him by giving him money for his dad's treatment so she'd know his every move. "He must've started suspecting her when she tried to shoot me even after he identified me by name."

Grace visibly shudders. "That girl is pure evil."

"I played right into her hands." She knew the waterfall was my favorite spot and I'd visit it sooner or later. All she had to do was cut the climbing rope so it couldn't save me again and then wait for me to show up. And I did without any memory she'd killed Mimi there. The bitterness in my throat makes me want to gag. "She got me convinced that I tried to kill Mimi and deserved to be locked up. I even started believing I killed James, though logically I knew I couldn't have."

"A master manipulator." Grace sighs. "It's my fault, too, for not telling you everything. But I knew you'd followed us to the tavern and couldn't believe you told the cops Mimi left when you were sleeping. And then you started acting like we were enemies again, even though Mimi told you Beth framed me. So, I started wondering . . . if you hurt her, if it was *your* plan all along." She grips my hands. "I'm so sorry."

"How would you know? You knew about the photo. You thought I hated Mimi and wanted her gone. And I thought it was you. Beth convinced me you wrote that threatening note I found among Mimi's things."

"She must've planted it. That bitch." Grace exhales, her eyes filming with tears. "You know what's really crazy? Once the fight at the tavern broke up, I couldn't find Mimi, and so I went to Beth's house looking for her. Beth was there, in drenched clothes, huddled in a corner, shivering. I thought she fell in her pool." She swallows. "Fuck, Tanvi, if only I knew."

The sickened feeling gripping my heart is mirrored in her eyes. Beth returned to her house after killing Mimi, and Grace saw her.

A tear slips down her cheek. "Oh, fuck. I miss her so terribly, Tanvi."

I do, too. I wish I could reverse time to when we were outside our house before Mimi left for the tavern. I wish I could've told her not to leave.

She'd transformed back into the Mimi I knew: my big sister, my protector, my shield against the bullies out there. And she died because of that.

I release one of my hands from Grace's and reach out to the empty chair next to us, and Grace does the same. And we sit there in silence, imagining Mimi holding onto our hands and completing our circle.

LATER THAT NIGHT, I light the lamp in the prayer room. Auntie hasn't stepped inside this room since we finished the religious ceremonies for Mimi. The Bhagavad Gita has remained unopened since then.

It's like she has nothing left to pray for.

After my prayers, I take the Gita and the prayer beads to the living room.

Auntie sits on the couch, gazing at the Bollywood song sequence on the TV. Her face is totally blank, her spine tense. She's lost somewhere else, not in the dance playing on the screen.

I sit next to her, place the Gita on the table before her, then snuggle closer. Wrapping an arm around her waist, placing my head on her stiff shoulder.

Dr. Ajay said: *Remind her of your presence. Remind her of the living. Be there for her, with her. Show her life is worth living.*

He told me it'll take time. Months. Years. She'll never get

over losing Mimi. But the wound will heal. She'll learn to cope, to survive.

"I love you, Auntie."

She shifts, then lifts her hand and pats my head. The movement is slow, sluggish, but my heart swells, and I hug her tighter.

EPILOGUE

SUNLIGHT GLINTS OFF the blanket of untouched snow covering the park. Fall is long gone, and we've slipped fully into winter, with about a foot of the white fluffy stuff falling last night to cover this nature park an hour's drive from Orin. This was my parents' favorite hangout, a sprawling area of rolling meadows and winding trails. Krista brought me here, and she remained in the car with Grace—at my insistence, since I wanted to be alone—while I headed into the park.

It's been four months since I found Mimi's body. I've taken a leave of absence from school, which means I may not graduate on time. But I don't care. Not about colleges, not about grades. Nothing except Beth paying for what she did. They denied her bail, saying she was a flight risk. Which means she gets to rot in jail until her trial comes up in another four weeks.

But I'm here for a reason. I'm here to do something I should've done a long time ago. When Auntie came here with my parents' ashes eight years ago, she asked me to join her in scattering the ashes. But I didn't join her. I couldn't accept Daddy was gone, and I didn't want to do anything that would give Mom peace.

But now it's different. I not only understand her, I forgive her. The con man was a predator who convinced her that her family was her enemy, that her husband was evil. Who pushed her away from getting help and support when she needed it.

The trail I'm on meanders past a shallow pool. My parents

would sit on the nearby bench and watch the ducks while I ran around the flower beds and played in the dirt.

I take out our family photo from my purse and place it on the bench. Then I sit down next to it and stare at the frozen water, my breath forming tiny cotton wisps in the air.

In my pocket is the letter Dr. Ajay sent me yesterday.

Hi, Tanvi.

I'm glad you were willing to talk to me about your mother. There is an update. I have written a link below. The con man who manipulated your mom had done the same to other people. He has been arrested. I know this is too late to help your mother, but I hope this will give you some comfort and ultimately peace of mind to know that he won't be hurting anyone again.

Please also know, as I've stressed before, that this person was a fraud. He twisted her mind. There is not enough research on post-partum effects, including psychosis, when it comes to those who have experienced miscarriages, but know that he manipulated her while she was suffering mentally. I hope you understand that.

As for your questions regarding Kerala, I do think another visit will do you good. It is a very beautiful place. I have been there several times myself. Go with your aunt, Tanvi. Take a relaxing stroll through its green fields, visit the waterfalls, and go on a boat ride. Imbibe its culture. After all, it's a part of you. It's your land, too.

It's time for closure, and I know you can do it.

Anyway, I'll be seeing you soon and am available anytime you want to talk.

Sincerely,
Ajay

Underneath the name, he has written out a website. So they tracked down that fraud. I want them to try him for murder.

The question is, will I be able to handle visiting Kerala again and remembering the last time I'd been there was with Mom and Dad?

But that's what life is about—making amends and moving on. Making amends to Mimi by getting her justice. And making amends to my dad for surviving while he died, and to my mom for blaming her for something she had no control over. By remembering her as the whole person she was.

It's time for me to move on, too. I have my aunt and she has me, and together, we'll plan a visit to Kerala. And we'll take Mimi's ashes with us.

ACKNOWLEDGMENTS

When Mimi Went Missing would not have been possible without the help of numerous people along its long journey from the first draft to the final version.

To my agent, Zabé Ellor, who believed in this story right from the start and insisted that it'd find a home, even when I was doubting it myself. You remained solid all through its numerous revisions, always proclaiming its worth.

To my editor, Alexa Wejko, I owe you so much I can't even describe in words. This story would be nothing without you. You found the thread in my complex, jumbled plot and coaxed sense and direction into it. Now every time I edit a story, I'll have your advice and wisdom in mind.

A huge thank-you to everyone in the Soho Teen team, including Erica Loberg, Rachel Kowal, and everyone else who has been solidly behind this book. Thank you for all your (often unseen) hard work.

One of the best features of this book is the amazing cover; it blew my mind when I saw it for the first time. It wouldn't have been possible without the exceptional skills of cover artist Colin Verdi and the cover design by Janine Agro.

To CrimeReads, thank you so much for hosting my cover reveal, and *Teen Vogue* for giving me my first editorial review.

I owe so much to my mentor and Pushcart Prize–nominated writer, Dana Mele. Dana, your editing and mentoring skills were what finally gave this story a shot, and I owe you an eternal thank-you.

To DVpit and Beth Phelan, thank you for everything you've done to give visibility to marginalized authors. Without you, I doubt my pitch would have surfaced enough to be noticed.

My first critique group was Critique Circle and I found invaluable support there, especially from Kieran Fanning, Eamon Ó Cléirigh, and Kathryn Estrada, all exceptional writers who went above and beyond to help polish my writing.

I'm also hugely grateful to Justine Larbalestier for mentoring me in the Writing Margins mentorship.

Finishing an entire book would not be possible without beta readers and this book would not have been possible without several amazing writers who gave their time and expertise unflinchingly to critique and support: Tanaz Bhathena, Kelly deVos, Kimberly Johnson, Megan Verhalen, Britney Brouwer, Nicole Wolverton, Sarah Emery, Kathleen Allen, Reena Deen, Maggie Soares, Michelle Hazen, Katerina Baker, to name just a few. I owe you all—and anyone I may have missed here (please forgive me if I did)—my wholehearted gratitude.

I found Crime Writers of Color and the amazing Kellye Garrett more recently and found an amazing bedrock of support for marginalized crime writers who often get sidelined in the mainstream.

And on that note, this book would get nowhere without the librarians and educators who fight to keep multicultural books accessible to kids. My heart swells with gratitude when I think of all the work you do to broaden the minds of young people, remove barriers, and promote tolerance and peace. I love you all and thank you as a parent and a BIPOC author.

Finally, to my husband, Suresh; my daughter, Aishwarya; and my son, Govind, thank you for being the amazing people you are—creative, kind, empathetic, and courageous—and for supporting me throughout my journey, writing and otherwise. The same goes for my brother and sister and extended family. Thank you from the bottom of my heart.